A WARTIME REUNION AT GOODWILL HOUSE

FENELLA J. MILLER

Boldwood

First published in Great Britain in 2023 by Boldwood Books Ltd.

Copyright © Fenella J. Miller, 2023

Cover Design by Colin Thomas

Cover Photography: Colin Thomas & Alamy

Every effort has been made to obtain the necessary permissions with reference to copyright material, both illustrative and quoted. We apologise for any omissions in this respect and will be pleased to make the appropriate acknowledgements in any future edition.

A CIP catalogue record for this book is available from the British Library.

Paperback ISBN 978-1-80162-865-5

Large Print ISBN 978-1-80162-864-8

Hardback ISBN 978-1-80162-863-1

Ebook ISBN 978-1-80162-867-9

Kindle ISBN 978-1-80162-866-2

Audio CD ISBN 978-1-80162-858-7

MP3 CD ISBN 978-1-80162-859-4

Digital audio download ISBN 978-1-80162-862-4

Boldwood Books Ltd
23 Bowerdean Street
London SW6 3TN
www.boldwoodbooks.com

For my daughter, Annabel, out of sight but never out of mind.

1

SEPTEMBER 1940

Joanna, Lady Harcourt, was becoming inured to the constant drone of bombers coming across the Kent coast from France and they no longer seemed as threatening. London and other cities were being bombed most days, but since last month, nothing significant had dropped on Ramsgate and nothing at all on the village.

The last telephone call she'd had with Sarah, her daughter, had told her that she'd just completed her exams for her first year as a medical student at the Royal Free Hospital in London. Therefore, she was entitled to a week free from her studies.

Sarah was the youngest student and, if the results were anything to go by, one of the brightest too. Joanna was proud to be the mother of such an intelligent and determined young lady.

Joanna was hopeful that the planned joint birthday party for her adopted children, Joe and Liza, and her daughter Sarah could go ahead as planned at the end of the month. The twins would be fifteen and Sarah would be eighteen.

Joe and Liza had arrived at the beginning of the year, barely able to read and write, but now, with the help of the tutor she'd employed to come every morning, they were both going to pass their school certificate easily next year.

She listened as the sirens wailed in the village, interrupting her thoughts, and indicating that yet another wave of Luftwaffe was on its way. Manston, the RAF base next door, remained out of action after the pounding it had taken three weeks ago. Ramsgate had also been severely damaged, and she'd never forget the devastation she and her fellow WI and WVS ladies had witnessed when they'd gone down to the town to offer what help they could.

'Ma, that's the siren. Are we going down to the summerhouse or ignoring it?' Joe asked as he appeared from the library, where he was completing the work set that morning by his tutor.

'They've not dropped any bombs in this neighbourhood since the raid last month so I'm going to ignore it. Your grandmother refuses to come with us, so one of us would have to stay with her anyway.'

'Liza and I are happy to carry on and disregard it like we did last time.' Joe gestured towards the far end of the house, where the noise from the builders could be heard over the persistent moan of the air-raid siren. 'It's going to be a lot quieter when those builders have gone. Do you know when that will be, Ma?'

'They've still a bit to clear and then there's the brickwork to do on the end wall so the house is weatherproof.'

They were standing in the grand hall and she was trying to ignore what seemed to be the noise of an approaching German plane.

'Bloody hell, Ma, I reckon it's heading straight for us. We need to get down to the cellar.'

Joe's East End ancestry always reappeared when he was stressed but Joanna's reply was drowned out by the roar of a plane directly overhead. She was frozen to the spot, staring out of the window, praying a bomb wasn't going to drop on the house.

Her son was now standing next to her and she put her arm round him, as much for her comfort as for his.

No bombs dropped but the Junkers plunged nose first into the recently harvested potato field. She watched, round eyed, holding her breath, as it skidded through the field on its belly, waiting for the explosion.

'Blimey, that was a close one.'

'Joanna, there's a German bomber in the potato field,' her mother-in-law called out cheerfully.

'Stay away from the window, Elizabeth, it could blow up,' Joanna replied as she raced into the drawing room. Her mother-in-law had ignored her instructions and was in the process of walking out onto the terrace.

'Good heavens, there are two German pilots scrambling out. I do hope they don't come here.'

'Quickly, inside and lock the doors. Joe, make sure all the others are locked and the windows are shut.'

Her son rushed off and she bundled her mother-in-law back into the house. She prayed the two men in the field hadn't noticed the activity on the terrace. She wasn't sure if these Germans would be armed but thought it likely.

'We'll be safer in the kitchen with Lazzy. The dog won't let anybody in.'

Jean, the housekeeper, had heard the crash and met them, flour smudges on her face.

'Please take care of Elizabeth, Jean, I'm going to ring the base. It's possible they still have somebody there who could come and arrest these men.'

'What we need is the LDV – or the Home Guard, as they're now called – it's their job to arrest the enemy,' Jean said.

'I've no idea how to get in touch with them, but I do have a telephone number for the base, so I'll ring them.'

She wasn't sure if there would be anybody left to answer the telephone as the base had been so badly bombed last month, but to her surprise, it was picked up almost immediately.

'Lady Harcourt of Goodwill House speaking. I don't know if you can help me, but a German plane has just crashed in the field in front of my house. I'm not sure how many were inside the plane, but I saw two men jumping out.'

'Stay out of sight, my lady. We're on our way. We knew it had crashed close by.'

Whoever had been speaking didn't identify himself, but that wasn't important. What was, was the fact that there must be sufficient men remaining on the base to come and apprehend these Germans.

Joanna almost tripped over her feet when she stepped into the kitchen because it was unexpectedly dark in there. The blackouts had been drawn but no lights switched on. Everybody was gathered around the table, chatting and drinking tea as if it was perfectly normal to be hiding from armed German pilots. They had Lazzy and he would warn them if there were intruders, so there really wasn't anything to worry about, was there?

Corporal Bob Andrews dropped the telephone receiver on the table, not bothering to restore it to the cradle. The car was waiting for him. The driver was Jimmy Mills, the other two men were Chalky White and Arthur Smith – like him, they were ground crew, mechanics who were trained to maintain and repair Spitfires and Hurricanes. They'd remained on the base after most of the personnel had been evacuated, in order to patch up as many of the damaged kites as they could.

Two Hurricanes had shot down the Junkers when it had been heading for Goodwill House and he'd fully expected it to crash on top of the house. There were bombs on board, the bastards hadn't had time to drop them, and it was a miracle the plane hadn't exploded on impact. Small wonder at least half the crew had got out as fast as possible.

'It went down in the field behind Goodwill House – that was Lady Harcourt on the phone. She saw two men get out but didn't mention seeing any more.'

'Blimey, Corp,' Chalky said, 'I hope you warned her the whole bally thing could blow up. Two Germans are the least of her worries.'

'I didn't have time.' He gripped the dangling strap above the door as the driver, Jim, put his foot down and screeched around the corner into the main road that led to the house. 'Lady Harcourt said the Junkers had pranged in the potato field.'

They'd just turned into the drive when the car seemed to take off, the air was punched from his lungs, part of the windscreen exploded and then the vehicle was upside down in a ditch.

Bob was covered in glass and everything hurt but when he flexed his limbs, he was pretty sure nothing was broken. His back was pressed against the roof, his feet jammed under the dashboard.

'Chalky, are you okay?'

'Tickety-boo, apart from cuts and bruises.'

'Arthur, anything broken?'

'Not me neck, thank god. I don't like the look of Jimmy.'

Bob didn't either. This was why he'd left his enquiry about the health of the driver to the last. Jim was in a crumpled heap, his head resting on the steering wheel and ominously still. There was no pulse. The poor bloke had gone for a Burton. Poor sod – what a bloody rotten way to die.

'He's dead, but we're not and we need to get out smartish,' Bob said. He could smell petrol but the liquid dripping onto his boots was water from the radiator. The petrol must be coming into the rear of the car. If he was correct, then they could be engulfed in flames at any moment.

'Bugger if I know how we're going to do that, Corp, the doors are jammed shut and we're wedged in this bleeding ditch,' Arthur replied.

Bob didn't want to move too quickly in case the car slipped even further down. After bracing his feet on the seat, he attempted to brush the fragments of glass from his shoulders and face.

It was obvious they couldn't kick their way out through what had once been the floor of the car, therefore they'd have to wriggle out through the semi-shattered windscreen.

'Do what you can to cover your faces; I'm going to kick the rest of the windscreen out. When I've done that, I'll go first, and then, Arthur, you'll have to help Chalky and I'll grab him from outside.'

The pungent aroma of fuel was filling the car so neither of them argued. If Bob got these two out safely, then they could have a go at removing Jim's body. But nobody was going to risk their life to do that.

It took one heavy kick to clear the remainder of the glass. He then manoeuvred himself, using his hands and arms, into a position that allowed him to go feet first through the opening.

He was halfway out when he was grabbed under the arms. 'Out you come, it's not safe in that car.'

With the girl's help, he was on the edge of the ditch in seconds. He didn't stop to thank her but leaned in to grab hold of Chalky's arms as he emerged head first.

'Arthur's right behind me, Corp. We've both been doused with petrol. I won't be having a smoke until I can get my jacket off.'

'Remove it now. That's an order. A stray spark from the burning kite could land on you.' Bob didn't need to elaborate. He glanced over his shoulder, expecting to see his female rescuer, but there was no sign of her. He frowned – she'd probably made the right decision. Hanging around the crashed car or the German bomber was a very bad idea.

Arthur scrambled out and, just as he did so, there was a further explosion – not as significant as the first but enough to knock them all to the ground.

'Let's scarper sharpish, Corp, it won't matter to poor old Jim.'

The three of them took off at the double and reached the relative safety of the barns and outbuildings at the rear of the big house without further mishap. Chalky was jacketless but Arthur hadn't had time to take his off and did so now.

'There's a well over there, I'll tip a bucket of water over it,' he said with his usual cheerful grin.

'I'll wet my handkerchief and try and clean some of this gore from my face. You two need to do the same,' Bob said. 'We'll frighten the residents if they see us dripping blood everywhere.'

The water in the bucket was red by the time he and his comrades had cleaned up.

'You might need stitches in a couple of those cuts on your head, Corp,' Chalky said helpfully.

'Maybe Lady Harcourt has a first-aid box and a few plasters. That'll do until I can see a medic.' Their conversation was interrupted by the arrival of the dog he'd heard barking when they'd arrived.

It was a huge shaggy grey beast that looked as if it had a lot of wolf hound in its ancestry. Thank god it was friendly.

'Hello, mate, sorry for the intrusion, we come in peace.' The dog danced around him and then paused long enough for him to stroke his massive head.

He followed the animal to the back door and thumped on it

with his fist. It was answered immediately by an attractive woman, who didn't seem at all put out at their sudden and disreputable appearance. She stood aside and smiled.

'I'm so sorry, gentlemen, I should never have asked you to come. It just didn't occur to me that you might be blown up.'

'How much damage has there been to your house, my lady?'

'I haven't let anybody go and investigate. I imagine from the noise earlier that most of the windows have been blown in at the front. We were safe in the kitchen.'

'I lost one man, thought it better to leave him in the car. I should stay inside, ma'am, and let us have a dekko around the property.'

'There were builders working at the far end, I'm in the process of having the fire-damaged Victorian wing demolished. I fear they might not have survived the blast. I think it highly unlikely there are still any Germans around for you to arrest.'

* * *

Land girl, Daphne Taylor, had borrowed a bicycle and cycled to Stodham to get some stamps and see if Raven's general stores, where Goodwill House was registered, had got any biscuits. Mr Pickering, her boss at Fiddler's Farm, had allowed her and her friends to leave early now the threshing was finished. Their next job would be harvesting the late crop of potatoes and he said the team of Shire horses needed a couple of days' rest before they started that.

She was pedalling merrily along the road that led to Goodwill House, delighted that she had two packets of custard creams in the basket, when the siren started to howl in the village. She was about halfway between the village and home so decided to take the bicycle into the nearest field and shelter under the hedge. It was unlikely even the most enthusiastic German fighter would bother to machine-gun her.

Daphne watched from beneath her leafy hideout with admiration as the RAF fighters attacked the wave of Luftwaffe planes. Two Hurricanes were on the tail of a Junkers, and she couldn't keep back a cheer as the German bomber began to trail smoke and head for the ground.

The cheer turned to a gasp of shock. The plane might come down on top of Goodwill House, where she and the other land girls were billeted. She held her breath, her fingernails digging into her palms, as she watched the stricken plane fly barely fifty feet over the roof. Then, from the sound of it, the bomber crash landed in the potato field that had once been the park that had surrounded the house.

The all-clear hadn't sounded, so she remained in the shadow of the hedge, watching the brave boys in blue turn back the Luftwaffe, who were intent on destroying London and other cities. Whilst she was waiting, she heard a car go past at speed and thought it might be something to do with the crash.

Curiosity got the better of her common sense and she pushed her bicycle around the hedge, through the gap and out into the road. She'd barely travelled a few yards when there was a massive explosion which almost knocked her over.

Without a thought to her own safety, Daphne pedalled flat out for Goodwill House. She almost tipped over the handlebars when she skidded around the corner into the drive. Although the crashed bomber was in the middle of the field, it was close enough for her to smell the fire and she was well aware that if the wind changed, the house could be in direct danger.

Then she noticed an upturned car in the ditch that ran along the left-hand side of the drive. Daphne was beside the vehicle in seconds and dropped her bike and leaned out to grab the arms of a man clambering out through the windscreen.

The man was dripping blood from several cuts on his head. Her mouth snapped shut and she bit her tongue. It wasn't the injuries that had shocked her. She recognised him – it was her missing fiancé.

Since Bob had broken their engagement three weeks before their wedding, she'd tried not think about him, to get on with her life. When she'd discovered he was based at Manston, two miles from Goodwill House, she'd half-hoped, half-dreaded that one day they'd meet again.

She grabbed her bike and pedalled furiously towards the house. After dumping it against the barn, she burst into the boot room. Once the door was safely closed, she leaned against it, trying to catch her breath, and wondering why she'd fled when she'd just found the man she'd been looking for since January.

Lazzy, Lady Harcourt's dog, arrived at her side and whined for attention. 'I'm all right, silly boy, just had a bit of a shock.'

Joe appeared from the kitchen. 'I thought I'd locked all the doors. You're lucky you weren't blown up.'

'I got a bit of a scare, and an RAF car got blown upside down. I think the men that survived will be coming here. Are Sal and Charlie in the shelter in the basement?'

'I don't know. It all happened so quickly.'

'I'm going to check.' Daphne was through the door that led down to the rabbit warren of cellars that ran underneath Goodwill House and was heading for the shelter before the boy could question her further.

'Thank goodness, Daphne, we thought you might have been caught in the raid,' Charlie said from the safety of the converted cellar.

'A German plane, a Junkers bomber, crash landed in the middle of the potato field and then blew up. Did you feel the explosion down here?'

'Blimey, what a turn-up for the books,' Sal said. 'Good thing we ain't up there.' Her cheerful smile slipped. 'Are them Harcourts all right?'

'I only saw Joe, and he was fine; I'm sure the others were, or he'd have said something.'

Daphne collapsed onto one of the chairs that edged the large table that ran down the centre of the room. 'I need a drink of some sort – water will do if there's no tea. Then, when I've caught my breath, I'll tell you what happened.'

Sal made a fresh pot of tea, boiling the kettle on the Primus stove. Daphne sipped it gratefully, trying to make sense of what she'd done and more importantly why she'd done it.

She told them exactly what had happened and who she'd seen.

'The bloke you've been looking for? Your ex-fiancé? Why didn't you stay and speak to him?' Sal asked.

'I don't know. It was such a shock to see him so unexpectedly that I just ran away.'

'Surely he recognised you? With your flaming red hair, even a glimpse would be enough to identify you,' Charlie said.

'He didn't look round, I pulled him out from behind. There's something I didn't tell you about him. The reason we became friends was that we were the only redheads in the street – folk used to say that we looked more like brother and sister than a courting couple. He's got exactly the same colour hair and green eyes like mine. My dad was never keen on us being engaged and, for some reason, neither was his mum. My older brother has dark hair but I'm the image of my dad's mum.'

Her friends looked at her in astonishment. Then Charlie shook her head and blurted out. 'You said your fiancé vanished the week before your wedding – do you think he might have discovered that you were in fact related and that's why he ran away?'

———————

2

Joanna had surprised herself by being so blasé about the death of quite possibly more than one man. The fact that two of them were the enemy, and only in her potato field because they'd come to bomb and kill civilians, made no difference. They were still humans and deserved a modicum of respect.

The RAF chap didn't seem at all shocked by her blunt speaking. Blood was dripping down his face and his startlingly red hair reminded Joanna of Daphne, one of the land girls staying with them at Goodwill House.

'We need to attend to your injuries, and those of your two men. If you'd care to come into the kitchen, my housekeeper's a qualified first-aider.'

'Yes, good idea, thank you. They look worse than they are, they're just superficial cuts.'

'Judging from the amount of blood, I rather think that you're underestimating the severity of your injuries.'

The blackout curtains were now drawn and the kitchen was back to normal. Jean must have heard her speaking to the men as she already had the first-aid box out and had three chairs set out for her patients.

Liza was enveloped in a large wraparound apron, obviously determined to help. She was attending the St John's weekly meetings and had taken several exams last month. She wanted to be a nurse when she was old enough. That would make two medical professionals in the family – Sarah had another three or four years of hard study to complete before she qualified as a doctor.

If Joanna's younger daughter did decide to train as a nurse, then she could register when she was seventeen, which would mean that both girls would qualify at roughly the same time.

'I'll leave you in the capable hands of my daughter and housekeeper, gentlemen, I'm going to inspect the damage to my windows and then I must see if the builders have been injured.'

'It's not safe to go to the front of the house, my lady, there have only been three explosions, which means there's one more bomb yet to detonate.'

'Thank you for the warning. You know who I am, but you've yet to identify yourself.'

'Corporal Robert Andrews, my lady, we're one of half a dozen teams of ground crew doing our best to patch up the damaged kites so they can be flown somewhere safer.'

With some reluctance, the young man sat down and let Jean begin her ministrations. The other two were less damaged and Liza was cleaning them up and would no doubt apply dressings where necessary.

Joanna exited through the boot room door, walked across the large courtyard and through the gate that led into what was once the separate garden for the Victorian wing. The door was a little stiff but with a vigorous push it opened, and she hurried across the neglected garden.

The four builders were obviously unharmed, as she could see them quite clearly across the rubble and they were about to clamber into their lorry.

'My lady, that was a close thing,' the builder shouted. If there was one thing she really didn't like, it was raising her voice, but she had no option.

'I came to see if you and your team are all right.'

'All tickety-boo, we were just finishing for the day when the siren went off. We saw that German bugger coming our way so scarpered and hid in the coal cellar.'

'Very sensible. I've been told there's a fourth unexploded bomb that could go off at any time.'

'The plane's burning, I think if it was going to go off, it would have done so by now. We're off home, we won't return until it's safe.'

He hopped into the cab of the lorry and the driver engaged the gears; the vehicle left at speed. She didn't blame them – the sooner they were out of range of a possible explosion, the better. Look what had happened to the unfortunate Corporal Andrews and his men.

The air was hot, the smell of the burning bomber most unpleasant. She didn't want to look too closely, as she feared she'd see the dismembered remains of the Germans who'd been trying to get to safety.

On her return, the kitchen was empty apart from Liza and Jean. 'Have the men gone to look at the damage?'

'I'm not sure, Joanna, but they certainly went to the front of the house. The corporal asked permission to use the telephone, so I expect he's ringing whichever authority needs to know.'

* * *

Bob thanked the housekeeper for patching him up and went in search of the telephone, which he'd been told was in the hall. He'd expected something impressive, for this was a stately home, after all, but he wasn't prepared for the size of the space he walked into.

'Gordon Bennett! You could get a hundred noisy erks in here and still have room to dance,' he said as he looked around. 'Watch your feet, both of you, we don't want to be tramping broken glass everywhere.'

Chalky had negotiated the shards and was peering into a room with double doors. 'I don't reckon there's a window left whole on this side of the house. It's going to be hard to find the glass to repair them.'

'Keep away from them – if that other bomb goes off, the blast might well send glass splinters flying across the room.'

It was probably unnecessary to state the obvious, but as the NCO, it was his responsibility to ensure that his men didn't make foolish mistakes. He'd already lost Jim and he didn't want to lose anyone else.

He made his way into the huge hall, where the telephone was on a side table which probably cost more than he earned in a year. He picked up the receiver and dialled zero for the operator.

'Corporal Andrews from Manston. I need the bomb squad and the Home Guard at Goodwill House. I don't know the people who can organise this but I'm hoping you do.'

'I do, Corporal, and will send your message immediately. Is anybody hurt? We heard the explosions from here.'

He wasn't exactly sure where 'here' was and didn't have the time to enquire. After a brief conversation he replaced the handset in the cradle and headed for the magnificent staircase that wound its way up one wall. He wanted to check how many of the bedrooms were now unusable.

The all-clear hadn't sounded yet and he could still hear dogfights overhead, but he thought they were safe enough despite being so close to the base. As he'd expected, the rooms that faced the crashed bomber had no glass in the windows and three bedrooms had also lost the frames. His boots crunched in glass that had scattered everywhere.

This main part of the building had a Georgian feel and from the furnishings and so on, he thought this must be where the family slept. He retraced his steps onto the gallery and walked to the other side and then investigated the rooms that must be used by the land girls.

Here, only the bedroom at the front of the house was out of action, the other six were habitable. The last one was obviously unoccupied, so it wouldn't be too hard for the ones from the front room to relocate. Be safer at the back anyway. The bomb squad could well tell Lady Harcourt and the others to evacuate the premises.

Bob paused to stare out at the still burning wreck, puzzled that the last bomb hadn't detonated. Belatedly it occurred to him that maybe one bomb had, in fact, been dropped somewhere before the kite had been shot down. He took the stairs at the double and snatched up the receiver for a second time.

The number for Fighter Command at Bentley Priory was one he knew, and the operator connected him. He explained the reason for his call and the girl who'd answered went off to make enquiries.

'Corporal Andrews, the Junkers that was shot down at your location dropped one bomb on the outskirts of Dover.'

'Thank you, that's all I want to know.'

There was no longer any necessity for the bomb squad to come and he was relieved that the operator was able to connect him in time to prevent a wasted journey. The Home Guard were still required, as they would have to post men at the site to prevent inquisitive schoolboys trying to filch pieces of the plane for their collections of war memorabilia.

He walked across to the front door and was surprised it opened smoothly, in fact, was impressed that it hadn't been blown from its hinges. They'd made things to last back in the day.

His next task was to check if there were any remains of the German pilots that needed to be collected and given a decent burial. Nobody could have survived a blast of that magnitude.

With no transport, they would have to walk back to the base, which was over two miles by road. There were still about a hundred blokes on the base scattered about doing various jobs and maybe one of them could be persuaded to come and get them. There were teams attempting to patch up the runway so that it could be used for emergency landings, but that was an impossible job. Bob doubted Manston would ever be fully operational again. There were four other bases in Kent and incoming and outgoing kites would have to use them for emergency landings, refuelling and rearming, and so on.

He made his way to the edge of the somewhat flattened flower garden and then checked the field. There was no sign of any remains, no flapping pieces of grey uniform, or dismembered bodies – in fact, if Lady Harcourt had been correct and she had actually seen two of the crew climb out of the plane, then they'd obviously and miraculously survived the blast.

The Germans would have sidearms and Bob suddenly realised he was potentially a sitting duck standing where he was. He turned and, trying to look casual, glanced around the extensive garden, hoping to see where these missing men could be hiding.

There was a summerhouse a couple of hundred yards away – the roof just visible through overhanging foliage of some sort. They could well be sheltering in there until they thought it safe to... safe to do what? They were in enemy territory and the chances of them making it to the coast and stealing a boat were nil. Surely, if any of them had survived, they would surrender and could then spend the rest of the war relatively comfortable in a POW camp somewhere.

Once inside, he was about to bolt the door but changed his mind. Doing this would be futile as the Germans could come in through any of the shattered windows if they so wished. Bob realised that he could hardly abandon the ladies so had to put aside any thought of returning to base at the moment.

Chalky and Arthur were waiting for him. He didn't need to say what he'd surmised as, from their faces, they'd worked it out for themselves.

'Those buggers are hiding up somewhere, ain't they, Corp?'

'I think it's quite likely that they're in the summerhouse. Let's hope they stay there until the Home Guard turn up. I hope these blokes are armed – I've heard that some of the platoons have just one rifle between them.'

'Do you think her ladyship has a gun room?' Chalky asked.

'Can either of you hit a barn door? I certainly can't. I could knock either of them out if I got the chance. I know we all had basic training when we signed on, but I didn't enjoy it and wasn't any good at it.'

Arthur shook his head. 'I can point the bloody thing, pull the trigger, but I ain't sure I'd hit anything even at close range. Sarge said I was a danger to meself and anyone else within half a mile of me when I was an erk.'

'What about you, Chalky?'

'I've shot the odd rabbit but that's about all.'

'Then that's better than nothing. Let's go and ask Lady Harcourt. They must have a shotgun, at least; these sorts of people like to shoot things.'

* * *

Daphne gripped her mug hard and stared at Charlie in horror after grasping the possible significance of she and Bob looking so alike and their parents living so close to each other.

'I don't see how we could be related. But our parents certainly didn't want us to get married...' Her voice petered out as she registered what she was saying. 'My parents don't get on. I never knew why. Maybe this was because Dad had an affair with Bob's mum before I was born.'

'Did he always live in your street?' Charlie asked.

'I'm not sure. Bob's three years older than me. I seem to remember that they moved in when I was just starting school.'

'Then it ain't likely they was involved. Your fella's ma wouldn't move near the bloke she's had a baby by, would she?' Sal said.

The more Daphne thought about this, the more likely the horrible, upsetting answer was that she and Bob were actually brother and sister. This would explain the fact that their proposed wedding hadn't been popular with any of the parents.

'I don't know why we're sitting around down here when you can go and ask the man himself. He's probably still upstairs. He no longer has a car so can't leave unless he goes on foot.'

'It's all very well for you to suggest I confront him, Charlie, but I've not spoken to him for over a year. I wouldn't know what to say.'

'Was you having it off?'

For a moment, Daphne didn't understand what Sal was asking, but then she blushed. 'Of course we weren't. How could you suggest such a thing?' No sooner had she spoken than she regretted her words, as Sal had been quite open about having lived with someone without the benefit of marriage.

'I'm sorry, that was tactless.'

Sal grinned. 'Don't worry about it, I ain't bothered. Where I come from, people aren't so fussed – well, me ma was – but most people ain't worried if you drop your knickers for your boyfriend.'

Charlie was shocked by this comment. 'Please, Sal, let's not talk about that sort of thing. I'm not passing judgement on you, but Daphne and I think differently about such things.'

'No offence taken. I made me bed and had to lie in it. I ain't going to let any other bloke take liberties with me.'

'Good for you,' Charlie said. 'Now, Daphne, shall we venture upstairs and see what's going on?'

'You go, I'm going to stay down here until I'm quite sure Bob and the other two have gone. I'm just not ready to talk to him, especially after what you said. I really don't want to believe that my father might have been unfaithful.'

'Blimey, we're jumping the gun a bit. It's more likely to be coincidence and your bloke just got cold feet and did a runner.'

'That's what I've always thought. We'd been sweethearts since we left school, friends before that, but I never really understood why he did what he did.'

'Then why don't you ask him? You won't get a better opportunity than this to be reunited with your lost fiancé.'

Daphne shook her head. 'I'm staying down here, but you go ahead. Tell me when the coast's clear.'

Her friends left her in the shelter. The Lord Harcourt who'd died at Dunkirk had had this converted from a cellar under the house last year. It was a lot better than an Anderson shelter, but Daphne didn't like it underground. It had been okay when there were others with her, but being alone wasn't nice.

She picked up a discarded book and tried to immerse herself in it. It wasn't working and the walls and ceiling began to press in on her, her heart was thudding uncomfortably, she was finding it difficult to breathe.

There was no option but to follow Charlie and Sal and risk

coming face to face with Bob, and at the moment, she just didn't want to do that. Then she remembered that the door at the end of the shelter opened into a long, dark, narrow passageway that had been built years ago for the Catholic priests to come to the house during the Puritan years. She was fairly sure that this eventually came up somewhere a fair distance from the house.

If she went out that way, then she'd avoid an unwanted meeting and also be in the fresh air. She'd hidden under trees and in ditches several times during the past few weeks to avoid being strafed by German fighter planes. She'd be perfectly safe and might well be able to watch the house and see the RAF chaps leave.

There was a torch on the shelf for emergencies and Daphne considered that this was one. She unbolted the door and then hesitated. There was nobody in the shelter to lock it after her and this meant that somebody could come into Goodwill House unnoticed. Exactly who this somebody might be, she wasn't sure, but it seemed wrong to use the passageway if she couldn't leave the house secure.

She dithered for a few moments before coming to a decision. She would wait in the fresh air until she was sure it was safe to go back and then return the way she'd come. Nobody could go into the house if she was guarding the secret entrance.

As soon as she stepped through the door and onto the steep, stone steps, she regretted her choice but was determined to avoid Bob even if it meant suffocating in the dank, dark tunnel ahead of her.

She left the door open, the light on. If it shone behind her, then maybe she could grit her teeth and hurry to the far end without collapsing in a shivering heap. She took several deep breaths, reminded herself why she was doing this, and set off at a jog. It seemed to take an hour to get to the end but was probably only a few minutes. She hadn't realised how severe her claustrophobia was until now.

Daphne removed the cap that limited the beam of the torch so it was on full beam and could see, a few yards ahead of her, stone steps and a timber door. She threw herself at it and scrabbled to push the bolts back so she could escape into the fresh air. The door opened smoothly and she fell out onto her face in the dirt, gulping in air like a drowning person.

It took several minutes for her to regain control and stumble to her feet. She blinked in the bright sunlight. For some reason, she'd expected it to be dark, but it didn't get dark until nearly eleven nowadays and it could only be around five or six o'clock. She brushed the soft leaf mould from the knees of her dungarees and pushed aside the thick bushes that camouflaged the hidden entrance.

She was behind the house, somewhere in the woods. She could smell the burning plane and could see smoke in the air but was too far away from Goodwill House to hear any voices. It was good to be outside but as she couldn't see the drive, she wouldn't know when Bob and his men left. Therefore, she might as well have stayed in the cellar until Charlie or Sal came to fetch her.

In her panic to get out, she'd not thought this through. One of her friends might arrive to fetch her and, finding the door to the underground tunnel unlocked, would immediately push the bolts across. Daphne was certain neither of them would even consider that she'd gone through the door herself.

There was nothing she could do but find herself a dryish spot and sit down until it was likely the RAF men had returned to Manston. One thing she did know was that she wasn't going to go back the way she'd come out, just in case, when she reached the second set of steps, the door had been locked from the inside.

It should be possible to hear the other land girls returning from their work sometime after six and that would be when she'd go back.

Was she being a bit daft trying to avoid seeing Bob when she really wanted to know why he'd all but jilted her last year? He'd broken her heart and she couldn't see that there was anything he could say that would make her forgive him.

3

Joanna escorted Elizabeth to the small sitting room at the rear of the house, the safest place for her at the moment, and once her mother-in-law was comfortable, she headed for the front of the house. It was all very well for this man, Corporal Andrews, to take command and issue orders to his men, but Goodwill House and its occupants were none of his business. This was her house – her responsibility.

She'd braced herself for a few broken windows, but what she saw was quite devastating. The hall floor was almost invisible beneath a carpet of broken glass. She remained transfixed, appalled, dismayed, not sure what she should do next. A clatter of boots coming from the drawing room made her move forward.

'Lady Harcourt,' the corporal said when he saw her, 'it's not safe here. None of the bedrooms facing the front are habitable – your boarders will be able to manage, but I'm not sure about you and your family.'

'Oh dear, that's very bad news indeed. I don't suppose it's going to be possible to get sufficient glass and timber to make the necessary repairs either. However, there are half a dozen rooms at the rear of the house that aren't being used and we can just decamp to those. I'll have to get the builders to board up the other windows until the end of this war.'

'I'm going to get my blokes to sweep this area for you – you don't want to be crunching through the glass in order to get upstairs.'

'That's very kind of you, Corporal Andrews, but not necessary. There's a staff staircase and a secondary staircase from which we can access all the rooms without walking through this mess.'

The young man with the startlingly red hair exchanged a glance with his comrades, cleared his throat and then introduced a totally different topic of conversation – one that was equally, if not more, concerning.

'At least two of the German bomber crew are loose somewhere in the neighbourhood. They will be armed and, although I doubt they'd do this, they could walk in here and hold us all hostage.'

'What a very disappointing day this is turning out to be. The rest of the girls who are living with me will be returning in the next half an hour. They've got to cycle along the drive and could be in grave danger.'

'This brings me to my second question, my lady, do you have a gun room?'

'No, but there's a locked cupboard by the butler's pantry and my son puts the shotgun away in there. To be honest, I've never looked inside and don't know what other weapons there might be.'

Joanna returned to the kitchen, where Joe and the others would be waiting. When she asked him about guns, he nodded.

'I'll get the key, Ma, and take the men. We just need to keep the Germans out until the Home Guard arrive.'

'Thank you, I'll leave you to sort this out with Corporal Andrews whilst I start organising the transfer of our belongings to the guestrooms at the back of the house. Thank goodness only one of the rooms the land girls use will have to be abandoned.'

Jean was already on her feet as well as Liza, Charlie and Sal. Daphne wasn't with them, which Joanna thought rather odd, but was far too preoccupied with what she had to do to worry about the missing girl.

* * *

Bob followed the Harcourt boy to the cupboard at the end of a long passageway.

'I only use one of the shotguns, but there are other guns in here. I've no idea if they still work as I doubt any of them have been out of the cupboard for decades.'

'Are you a good shot, son?'

'Pretty good – I keep the larder filled with rabbits, and game birds in season.'

'Then I'm afraid that you've got to be on patrol with us. I'm sure your mother told you that at least two of the bomber crew survived the explosions. A lot of the Germans that have been taken prisoner have been only too happy to spend the duration of the war in a POW camp – but some haven't been so accommodating.'

'Nazis, I expect,' Joe said. 'Bloody hell! The rest of the girls will be coming down the drive at any moment. I'm going to get out there and make sure they get here safely.'

Bob didn't argue. He wasn't quite sure how old the lad was, not much more than sixteen probably, but if he was a good shot, then he and Chalky were the best chance they had at keeping everybody safe.

Bob stepped aside and left the two who knew what they were doing to fill their pockets with ammunition and head for the front door, ignoring the glass underfoot. They could be protecting the drive far quicker going that way than if they went through the kitchen area.

'Arthur, I'm going to go out with the other two – there's another shotgun here that I can use. It's just a matter of putting in the cartridges and pointing it. Even I should be able to manage that.'

'Fair enough, Corp. As I told you, I ain't too clever with firearms and that. I'm a dab hand with a broom, though. I'll get started sweeping up and that, shall I?'

'Ask Lady Harcourt what she'd like you to do.'

'At least they ain't going to be blown up, Corp. Good job them buggers had already dropped the other bomb.'

Bob dropped a handful of cartridges in his uniform pocket, checked the barrels were empty, picked his way across the glass and followed the other two through the front door.

He was about to turn onto the drive when a flash of movement some distance away, behind the house in the woods, caught his eye. He ducked down behind the balustrade, hoping he hadn't been seen. Calling to the other two wasn't an option as it would warn the Germans that they'd been spotted.

Keeping in a crouch, he retreated and made his way back across the hall and down the passageway that led to the back of the house. He was pretty sure he couldn't be seen by anyone in that part of the woods. He would approach from the rear, hoping that his quarry would be looking towards the drive.

He didn't put any cartridges into the weapon but did push the barrel up so it connected with the grip. He carefully reversed the gun so he was holding it by the end of the barrel and could use the heavy wooden grip as a club.

As he moved forward stealthily, he could see a figure hiding in the undergrowth. He covered the last two yards at a run and burst into the clearing, already swinging his weapon, knowing he had to knock this one out before he could raise the alarm.

The grip was about to make contact when he realised that he'd almost made a fatal error. This was a girl, a land girl from her uniform, and he'd almost killed her. His heart was hammering. He was about to make an apology when the terrified young woman turned to face him.

He dropped his makeshift club. 'Jesus wept! Daphne – what in god's name are you doing here?'

Her face was the colour of paper, her beautiful green eyes wide. Then they closed and she slowly collapsed in a heap at his feet. He'd already tossed aside the gun and now dropped to his knees beside her.

He'd thought never to see the woman he loved again. It had nearly destroyed him when he'd jilted her so cruelly, but he'd had no choice after what his mother had told him.

She remained in a deep faint, despite him chafing her hands, calling her name and rubbing her face. Then she began to stir. He had her head in his lap and thought she probably wouldn't appreciate that when she came round.

He pulled off his jacket, carefully folded it, and gently pushed it beneath her head then knelt beside her. Close, but not actually touching. Her eyes flickered open and immediately turned to him.

'Bob, you terrified me. What are you doing prowling around in the woods with a gun?'

She sat up and then got smoothly to her feet, obviously no longer in need of his assistance.

'I thought you were one of the German bomber crew – there are two of them at least lurking around. More to the point, Daphne, why are you here?'

Her smile still had an electrifying effect on him. 'I was hiding from you. It was me that pulled you out of the car and I was so surprised that I ran away. Then I decided I didn't want to see you.'

'I don't blame you. But, now we have met, will you come back to the house with me, as it's really not safe out here?'

'I'll go back to the house, but not with you. You broke my heart,

Bob. Since then, it's been my dearest wish to be reunited with you one day, but now that's happened, I've realised I've moved on. I'm in the Land Army, I don't need a man in my life and even if I did, it wouldn't be you.'

'Okay, message received loud and clear.' From the noise drifting across to the woods, the expected land girls were arriving on their bicycles. 'Your friends are on the drive. Why don't you go in with them?'

She nodded. 'I'll do exactly that. It's why I was waiting. Goodbye, Bob. Take care.'

With a casual wave, she pushed through the overhanging branches and moved nimbly down to join her friends, leaving him conflicted. He'd never wanted to have to tell her why he'd abandoned her but now had no choice. They couldn't ever be together, but he would always love her.

After collecting the discarded shotgun, he followed Daphne to the drive and walked back to the house in the company of the lad and Chalky. He pushed the very brief conversation he had had with Daphne out of his mind to be considered at a later date. Personal feelings had to be ignored when he had his duty to perform.

'I didn't see any sign of them in the woods – what about you two?'

'I don't reckon they're around here any more, Corp, and if they are, they won't bother the residents of Goodwill House now they know that there are armed men guarding the place.'

Bob wasn't sure that Chalky's assessment of the situation was the right one. 'We'll stay until the Home Guard turn up and then we've got to get back to the base. Our duty's to repair the kites, not footle about here.'

'What about the car and poor Jim?'

'I'd better let the authorities know, get a medic out to look at him so they can arrange to transfer his body to the nearest morgue.'

There was the sound of a vehicle of some sort approaching the far end of the drive. Hopefully, it was the blokes from the Home Guard. The sooner he could get away from Daphne and the memories she stirred up, the better.

* * *

Daphne was shocked at the damage the exploding bombs had done to the beautiful old building. 'There's not a window left intact anywhere on the front of the house. Heaven knows what Lady Harcourt will do; she certainly won't get enough glass to repair all of them.'

The girls had dismounted from their bicycles and were staring at the damage. One of them pointed to the window of the room that Daphne shared with Charlie and Sal. 'That's your room. Good thing there's a spare bedroom on the far side of the house, as you won't be able to sleep in there any more.'

'I think we should offer to help clear up the broken glass and help the family move their belongings somewhere else. The house will look miserable with boarded-up windows, but I suppose we can be grateful the damage is superficial,' Daphne said.

'Did you know there's a body in that car halfway down the drive? Poor blighter must have been killed when the car was thrown into the ditch,' someone said sadly.

'Yes, I helped one of the RAF men get out of the car and saw him then. They were lucky not to have all been killed. I'd better warn you, girls, there could be a couple of armed Germans hanging about somewhere, so I don't suggest anybody goes for a walk.'

The bicycles were hastily wheeled into the barn and the other girls made a dash for the back door. Daphne hoped her two closest friends didn't mention Bob, as she really didn't want to be the subject of gossip. She was last in and, as she was closing the door, she thought she could hear the approach of a vehicle. With luck, this would be the expected local defence corps, which meant the RAF – and Bob – could leave.

She pushed the bolt across and turned the key, which gave her a few precious moments to process what had just happened. She'd never fainted in her life but thought that any girl might have done the same if suddenly attacked by a very large redheaded man waving a gun.

Telling him that she was no longer interested in him had felt like a good move on her part. She was pretty sure he'd believed her. If Charlie hadn't suggested that the two of them could be siblings, then she would have thrown herself into Bob's arms – but now things were different. She had to put her feelings aside, forget what he'd once meant to her, and try to ignore him. She didn't want to have her heart broken a second time.

* * *

Lady Harcourt was in the kitchen, making tea and stirring something tasty in a large saucepan. 'Good, I'm glad you're all in safely. I'm sure Daphne will have informed you of the reason for my concern.'

There was a murmur of agreement from the girls.

'Have Charlie and Sal gone upstairs to start moving our belongings, Lady Harcourt?'

'They have, Daphne, and they're waiting for you. I'm so sorry that the three of you are the only ones having to move.'

'At least we have somewhere to go, my lady. As soon as we've finished, would you like us to come and help on the other side of the house?'

'How kind of you to offer,' Joanna said. 'Jean has to remain down here to prepare everybody's evening meal and Joe's out somewhere with a shotgun.'

'I hope they find the Germans soon. I don't like the idea of some armed enemy hanging about outside.'

'Neither do I. Use the back stairs, Daphne, there's far too much glass in the hall.'

'Goodness me, we were beginning to think you were going to stay in the cellar for ever,' Charlie greeted Daphne when she came into the bedroom.

'I'm sorry, I got waylaid. I'm here now. It's a real mess, isn't it? Thank goodness most of our clothes were safe inside the closet. I don't think we can use the bedding, do you?'

'It ain't safe, that's for sure. Bits of glass everywhere. I'm bundling it up and I can take it in the garden to give it a bit of a shake, then hang it on the line. What we need is a good drop of rain – that might help remove the splinters.' Nothing fazed Sal – she was always cheerful, regardless of the circumstances.

'I'm not sure that's a good idea, Sal, you might get badly cut carrying the bedding. What we need is something large, something that hasn't been smothered with broken window. Then we can pile everything in the middle of that and take it down safely.'

Talking about housekeeping was a lot easier than talking about what had happened between her and Bob. Daphne considered these two as her best friends and they always spoke freely to each other.

'I said that once we'd sorted ourselves out, we'd help Lady Harcourt and the family move. I hope you don't mind me volunteering the pair of you.'

'Blimey, it's the least we can do. I'd expected some of the others to offer to help us but they ain't here, are they? They should be offering to help, not swilling tea in the kitchen.'

'Don't worry, Sal, we don't need anyone else. We take care of each other,' Charlie said as she dropped the last of her underwear into her expensive suitcases.

They left the ruined bedroom as it was, and Sal had heeded Daphne's warning, so the glass-covered sheets and blankets remained where they were.

Daphne managed to stay out of the way of the RAF, in particular Bob, who had remained until the Home Guard arrived in a dilapidated butcher's van. She'd watched with some amusement as a motley assortment of more or less uniformed men got out of the rear of the vehicle.

'Look, you two, the cavalry has arrived. I swear there's one old bloke who must be ninety if he's a day. There's a couple of lads who look as if they should still be at home with their mum, but the others don't look too bad.'

Her friends crunched across to join her at the window. 'At least they've got half a dozen rifles between them,' Charlie said.

'Now the boys in blue can push off to the base,' Sal said. 'I never knew there was still anybody there. I thought they'd all been evacuated and them planes was hidden somewhere where them bombers can't get them.'

'I expect they need a few people there in case a damaged plane needs to land, refuel or something,' Daphne said. 'Those Home Guard chaps look efficient enough, despite some of them being grandads, and they seem to know what they're doing. If those Germans are still here, then I'm sure they'll capture them soon enough.'

She'd still not told Charlie and Sal why she'd taken so long to come in – that was something that could wait until they'd sorted themselves out, had their supper and then taken their cocoa upstairs to their new bedroom.

They trooped down for the evening meal later than usual and the other girls had finished and were already in the ballroom enjoying their leisure time. Daphne thought that at least some of them should volunteer to help with the clear-up; although nobody was obliged to help the Harcourts, it seemed the right thing to do.

It was almost eleven o'clock by the time she had the chance to explain her encounter with Bob. The girls listened to her and were suitably shocked by her near-death experience.

'Crikey! Nearly being killed by the very person you've been pining for all these months,' Sal said.

'I thought I was over him but seeing him so unexpectedly has just brought everything back. Not the love, but the pain he caused when he vanished without any explanation.'

'Well, he knows where you are and I think it's a good thing for you to get things settled finally between you,' Charlie added.

As Daphne was dropping off to sleep, she remembered that the shelter door remained unlocked. If the Germans had seen her emerge from the tunnel, was it possible they'd come into the house that way?

She rolled out of bed, snatched up her torch, rammed her feet into her slippers and was out of the bedroom in moments. It was lucky she'd not fallen over anything, as the layout of the room was unfamiliar.

This was the first time she'd been up in the middle of the night; she paused at the end of the passageway before turning onto the gallery listening, her stomach churning unpleasantly. Not because she was scared that she might meet two armed Germans but at the thought of having to go down the long, dark passageway to lock the outside door.

Lazzy was on duty at the bottom of the back stairs and stood up to greet her. 'Good boy, you come with me, it'll be much easier for me if you do.'

The dog padded along beside her, apparently happy to have an excursion in the middle of the night. His ears were pricked, his tail wagging, which meant there was nothing amiss anywhere in the house.

'I'm going down to the shelter, Lazzy, I know you don't like it there, but I'd be very grateful if you'd come with me.' Silly to be talking to the animal but it gave her much-needed courage.

Daphne paused just long enough to switch on the lights in the shelter and pick up the large torch she'd abandoned on the central table. With this shining a narrow beam in front of her, she stumbled down the dank, narrow underground passageway to the outside door. With a sigh of relief, she slammed the bolts across and then, with the dog a few paces in front of her, returned almost at a run.

Safely inside the shelter, she closed that door and pushed those bolts across. Satisfied things were now as they should be, she put the torch back on the shelf from where she'd removed it earlier, glanced around the room to check she'd left it tidy, and then was up the stairs and back into the positively spacious flagstone corridor at the top of the cellar stairs.

There was the faintest glimmer of dawn in the sky; if she wanted to get a few more hours of much-needed sleep, then she'd better get back to bed immediately. She cut a thin slice of bread from yesterday's loaf and gave it to the dog as a reward.

Before she returned to her bedroom, she used the WC and then washed her face and hands in the bathroom, just case she'd picked up any tell-tale cobwebs. She was settling down when Sal spoke from the darkness.

'Blimey, Daphne, thought you'd gone down the bleeding plug-hole, you've been gone so long.'

'Sorry, a bit of an upset tummy. Must've been all the excitement earlier. I'm fine now. Good night.'

4

Joanna spent the next few days getting the broken windows temporarily boarded up. The builders had completed their work demolishing the burned wing and restoring the end wall and were happy to help out.

'I reckon I might get some glass for the drawing room, my lady, but not for the others,' Mr Lane told her.

'Whatever you can find will be splendid, thank you.' The broken glass was being collected to be melted down, so every last shard and splinter had been swept up and piled on old dustsheets in front of the terrace.

She was anxiously awaiting a call from the Land Army organiser, Mrs Dougherty, and feared the girls might be moved somewhere deemed safer than Goodwill House. Therefore, when the telephone jangled in the hall, she hurried to answer it herself. The house was quiet, the twins at their morning studies and Jean and the ladies from the village busy about the house.

'Goodwill House, Lady Harcourt speaking.'

'Good morning, my lady, I'm so honoured to be speaking to

you,' a complete stranger gushed. 'Mrs Dougherty has, for personal reasons, resigned and I, Cecelia Ramsbottom, have taken over her position.'

'I see, thank you for informing me.'

'It is my absolute pleasure, my lady, to be of service to you and any member of your family.'

'Excellent. Mrs Ramsbottom, the house is now weatherproof and only three of the girls had to change their bedroom. I take it there's no necessity for the girls to be relocated.' If this garrulous woman wanted to ingratiate herself, then now was her opportunity.

'No need at all, my lady. I spoke to some of your girls at Fiddler's Farm and they are very satisfied with their accommodation with you. And why wouldn't they be? I can assure you that even with broken windows, Goodwill House is far better than anywhere else they might be sent to.'

Eventually the woman paused to draw breath, allowing Joanna to stop the flow of words. 'Thank you so much, Mrs Ramsbottom. Please excuse me, I have visitors and must return to my meeting. Goodbye.'

She hastily replaced the receiver and smiled. This replacement for Mrs Dougherty might be long-winded, but she was obviously efficient, having taken the time to seek out Charlie, Sal and Daphne prior to calling.

As Joanna turned to go in search of Elizabeth, the telephone rang a second time. With some impatience, she picked it up.

'Joanna, it's Peter. I was expecting an invitation to the party next week. Have I been removed from the list?' Lord Harcourt! She'd been meaning to contact him, but it had slipped her mind.

'Peter, I'm so sorry. It's been chaos here. Let me tell you about it.'

When she'd finished, he was no longer laughing. 'God, Joanna, you can't stay there. It's far too dangerous so close to the base. I'll find you something safer.'

A faint prickle of annoyance at his reaction made her speak more sharply than his well-meaning suggestion warranted. 'No, there's no need for you be involved at all. I've handled the repairs and we're all perfectly safe. The base is no longer active and once the remaining aircraft have been repaired and can fly, it will be more or less abandoned.'

After her outburst, there was a long, worrying pause from the other end of the line. She was about to rush into an apology when he got in first.

'I'm sorry. I promised not to interfere and immediately stepped in with my two large boots. I take it the birthday party for the twins and Sarah has been postponed.'

'I'm afraid it's been cancelled. Sarah is now unable to get away as, with bombs dropping most nights on London, she's needed at the hospital. Even a second-year medical student is better than someone with no skills at all.'

'What about the twins? Don't they get a party?'

'They don't want one. If Sarah can't be here to share it, then they want to wait until things improve – if they ever do – and then reschedule the celebration.'

'Would I be intruding if I called in next time I'm in the area? I've got to visit a couple of places in Kent at the beginning of October and hoped I might see you all then.'

'Yes, please do. The main family rooms are now out of service, but we still have two spare guestrooms and I'd be happy for you to stay for a night or two.'

Again, there was a short silence, but this time she didn't recognise the reason for it.

'Thank you, I'd love to take you up on your kind offer. I hesitate to suggest this, but if, amongst my contacts, I have somebody who might be able to at least restore some of your windows, would that be acceptable?'

This was a different side to the Peter Harcourt she'd met a few times. He wasn't a man to ask permission to do anything, she believed, so he must be very keen not to offend her for some reason. He was a difficult man to like, as he had an irritating tendency to patronise her in the same way her dead husband had.

'I'd be delighted to have anybody get in touch who has access to sufficient glass to repair some of the windows. I look forward to seeing you again soon – please get your secretary to let me know exactly when to expect you. Thank you so much for your call. Goodbye, Peter.'

She replaced the receiver thoughtfully. Peter was a very senior officer in the intelligence corps of the army – was used to subterfuge – and for some reason, she felt as if she was being manipulated – as if his bonhomie wasn't genuine. Did he want something from her? There was only one thing she had that he might be interested in –herself, and she was never going to think of him in that way.

She hoped she was wrong, as she was beginning to rather like him. The noise of a squadron of fighters flying overhead towards the Channel made her think of her lost love. John would only have needed to go to an OTU – operational training unit – where fully qualified pilots learned how to fly other aircraft before being sent to join a squadron. She wasn't exactly sure how long it took but she thought after four weeks he could be part of a fighter squadron. Perhaps he had been one of the men who had just screamed overhead.

She blinked back unnecessary and unwanted tears. They'd had their brief and passionate affair and it had ended. She wished him well, would always hold a secret place in her heart for him, but doubted she'd ever see him again, and that was just how it had to be.

* * *

Bob, Arthur and Chalky worked well as a team but the absence of Jimmy affected them all. His body had been hastily ferried off to somewhere the other side of Kent to be buried in a family plot. The only way to survive this both mentally and physically, Bob decided, was to pretend everything was tickety-boo.

'That's the best we can do, boys. This Hurry can now go where it can be fully repaired.' Bob was not just ground crew, but a trained fitter – somebody qualified to complete a full engine overhaul – whereas Chalky and Arthur just kept the kites flying with minor repairs.

'There's a couple of ATA blokes in what's left of the Officers' Mess, Corp, shall I pedal over and fetch one?' Chalky asked hopefully.

'Okay, do that. Thank god for the Air Transport Auxiliary, as without those pilots ferrying damaged kites, we'd have even less flyers available to fight.'

'I heard there were girls doing it now – I suppose there ain't no reason why they shouldn't,' Arthur said as he straightened, wiping his oily hands on a filthy rag.

'Chalky's a good bloke but he doesn't really pull his weight. He's far too eager to slope off given the chance.' Bob looked at the hangar behind him. 'Four more to patch up. I wonder where we'll be sent next.'

'I reckon we'll be done in a couple of weeks. I ain't sure about the other teams, though – maybe we'll be asked to help them out.'

'No point in speculating, we've got work to do. You get the kite fuelled and I'll fetch the battery trolley.' The kites were started this way as it saved their batteries.

Bob had kept busy the last couple of days and managed to avoid

thinking about Daphne. How the hell had she ended up so close?
Was it just an unfortunate coincidence that she'd been at Goodwill
House when he'd turned up or had she somehow followed him
here?

The Home Guard captain – an old duffer from the last war –
had been only too happy to take over the search for the missing
Germans. Bob supposed they were now in a POW camp some-
where, but that was none of his concern. The two of them were
obviously not still wandering around the neighbourhood or they'd
have been spotted. There were no strangers in this neck of the
woods.

Chalky returned with the ATA pilot balanced perilously on the
back of his bicycle. The bloke had his parachute over one shoulder
and his overnight bag in the other hand. Bob grinned as they
wobbled to a halt beside the kite.

'Good luck with this one. The engine's fine but there are still
bloody great holes in the fuselage.'

'I've flown worse. I'll hop in and get off. I expect I'll be back to
collect another one tomorrow.' The pilot, a bespectacled bloke of
about fifty, handed his chute and bag to Arthur and then clam-
bered onto the wing. He then reclaimed his possessions and shoved
the chute into the tiny cockpit first, jammed his bag behind the seat
and somehow manoeuvred himself inside as well.

The engine fired first time. Arthur detached the terminals from
it and wheeled the trolley to a safe distance. The Hurry wasn't as
pretty as a Spit but was proving invaluable in the battle for the air
that was going on right now. There was no air traffic control, the
pilot was on his own. He had to decide if it was safe to take off and
also find somewhere that wasn't full of craters from the air-raid a
few weeks ago. A Hurry and a Spit could take off on grass and there
was still plenty of that down the sides of the ruined strip.

The kite taxied away and Bob watched anxiously until it was in the air and no longer his responsibility.

Chalky was in the process of propping his bicycle against the wall when he called out. 'Look, Corp, isn't that the van the Home Guard arrived in at Goodwill House the other day?'

'It certainly looks like it. I'd better get over there and see what they want.' He had a slightly better bicycle than the others, as his had brakes, but it didn't have much else to recommend it.

Captain Fullerton must've seen him pedalling across the pitted runway as he was waiting to greet him when he eventually rolled to a stop beside him.

'Corporal Andrews, jolly good show, you're the chap I came to see. We've abandoned the search for those two men and are beginning to think that maybe they were incinerated in the fire after all. When the salvage team took away the remains of the aircraft, there were no signs of any bodies, and you were certain at least two of the crew perished in the crash.'

'Lady Harcourt could have been mistaken when she said she saw two men scrambling out, but I doubt it. I think it more likely they've managed to slip through your net and are now somewhere on their way to the coast in the hope of stealing a small boat and getting back to France.'

The man's eyes bulged alarmingly, and his face turned puce. The old codger obviously wasn't used to being told that he was wrong – or maybe he was upset at the thought that his motley crew had buggered up the search.

'I'll have you know, young man, my men might not be as well trained as you, but I can assure you they know how to do their job. If two men escaped the crash, which I very much doubt, then someone is hiding them. They absolutely, definitely didn't get through our cordon.'

'Right, sir, if you say so. Was there anything else?' Not exactly polite but he'd more important things to do than hang about chatting with this old fool.

'I'm going to continue my search. We'll find the blighters. No Huns are going to escape on my watch, don't you know.'

Bob wasn't sure why Fullerton had come to the base, but what the Home Guard did wasn't his concern. He returned to the hangar and with the assistance of his remaining men pushed the next damaged kite to the front of the space where they could work more easily on it. They continued until dusk and then packed it in for the day.

'You coming to the mess tonight, Corp?' Chalky asked. There was now only one mess for other ranks and one for the few remaining officers.

'Just to get my scoff and then I'm going for a spin around the countryside. That old fool has made me think there might be two Nazis on the loose.'

'Leave it to them, it's not our job to catch them. We—'

Chalky's remaining words were drowned out by a squadron of Spits flying low; a few moments later, two flights of Hurries followed. The sirens wailed, but he and his men ignored them. There was nothing visible to bomb on Manston now, so the Luftwaffe ignored them. He wished he didn't know Daphne was so close to the base. The thought of her in danger made his stomach churn.

* * *

Daphne tried to put Bob from her mind and concentrate on doing her job. Mr Pickering, their boss, was a changed man nowadays and she rather thought she, Sal and Charlie were the luckiest team at Goodwill House.

'Mr Pickering said he's going to slaughter two of the pigs tomorrow, Sal. You'd better make sure you're working at the other end of the farm,' Daphne said on the way home that night in the pony cart.

'Ta for telling me. I've become fond of the porkers, but they ain't pets, so it has to be done. Does he do it himself?'

'Golly, I shouldn't think so,' Charlie said as she flicked the reins to encourage Star to walk a bit faster. 'He'll get someone from the local abattoir in. That's what happened on the farm I lived on before coming here.'

'As long as he don't ask me to butcher them after, I'll be fine,' Sal said with a smile.

They passed a group of Home Guard, who looked hot and fed up, marching along the road. Seeing them made Daphne think about the meeting with Bob a few days ago and that was something she was trying not to do.

'I think those Germans that Lady Harcourt saw are still not captured,' Charlie said.

'Those men could just be on a routine patrol – after all, there's a war on.' Daphne's suggestion was ignored.

'I were down the village after work yesterday and it seems even the fat bloke on a bicycle – the local bobby – has been making enquiries,' Sal said. 'I reckon they think someone's got them Germans hiding in their back room or somethink.'

'Not all Germans are Nazis,' Charlie reminded them. 'There was a story in the *News Chronicle* the other day about German pilots eager to be captured so they don't have to fight for Hitler. I wouldn't be surprised if quite a few of those sent over here to bomb us had no alternative. We have conscription and the men involved have no choice but to serve.'

'Then I think the men would surrender as then they'd be kept as prisoners of war and not have to fight for something they didn't believe in,' Daphne said.

'That's true. But on the other hand, they might have been told that they'd be executed if they were captured. I don't suppose Hitler's too bothered about the Geneva Convention, do you?'

'What's that when it's at home?' Sal asked.

'The Geneva Convention's an agreement between all countries not to mistreat POWs, civilians and so on. A Swiss man came up with it last century, I think,' Charlie told Sal.

'So our blokes what've been shot down or taken prisoner should be looked after?'

'That's the general idea, Sal. Lady Harcourt and her WVS ladies pack parcels to send them via the Red Cross.'

Charlie was right – but then she usually was. Since she'd had her accident and spent two weeks being looked after by Dr Willoughby's housekeeper, she'd become less prickly, more relaxed. She'd told them she hoped that she and the handsome doctor might be interested in each other, but so far, Daphne had seen no real evidence of this.

'There's going to be some sort of social event at the village hall on Saturday afternoon, Charlie, will you and the doctor be attending together?' Daphne asked.

'I think I might have exaggerated the actual situation a little when I said we might be involved. I certainly am quite fond of him, but since I returned here, he's made no effort to continue the friendship. I'm beginning to think it was just my feverish imagination when I was concussed.'

Charlie reined back gently so the cart could turn smoothly into the drive and Daphne wished she'd not mentioned it. Doing so would now give both Sal and Charlie the opportunity to question her further about Bob and she'd deliberately not told them all that had happened in the woods.

Just then, three squadrons of fighters screamed overhead, making conversation impossible. Nowadays they ignored them – even the once-nervous mare just trotted on with her grey ears pricked. No doubt she was eager to get into her field and roll about on the grass.

'Blimey, them blooming sirens never stop,' Sal said.

The siren still went off at the base, even though it was no longer active. Daphne and Sal left Charlie to take care of the horse and headed indoors. They were halfway to the boot room door when the ominous sound of approaching heavy aircraft made them look up anxiously.

'Bleedin' hell – that ain't good. Down the cellar's quickest,' Sal said, and Daphne agreed. The door to the cellar was right in front of them, and as they arrived, so did the rest of the household – including old Lady Harcourt. Must be bad if the old lady had agreed to go downstairs.

With twelve land girls, the twins, the two Lady Harcourts and the housekeeper, Jean, it was a bit of a squash, but a lot better than one of the damp, miserable Anderson shelters other people had to use.

'I'm glad you got back in time, girls, I wouldn't have wanted you to be on the road with a genuine raid in process,' Lady Harcourt said.

'Charlie will be down in a tick,' Daphne replied as she pulled out a chair and sat down next to Sal.

Jean and Liza were opening various tins and boxes on the shelves and muttering. The housekeeper turned to face them. 'I'm sorry to ask this, ladies, but have any of you helped yourselves to the supplies we keep down here? There's no tea or sugar and all the tinned food has gone.'

'Nobody here would take it,' Joe said, 'and no one could get in from outside because the cellar door's always locked from the inside.'

Daphne gripped the edge of the table. Her throat constricted. It was impossible to swallow, let alone speak. She knew exactly where the supplies had gone – this was all her fault. She'd left the door open and now the Germans must be hiding somewhere in the cellars with them.

5

Bob was close to Goodwill House when the sirens went off. He was exposed on the road so turned into the drive and roared up to the house. The fighters had screamed over a few minutes before and the sound of dog fights a few miles away wasn't good. Then the ominous drone of approaching bombers told him this was going to be a real raid.

The Harcourt shelter was in the cellar, but he thought he'd be safe enough in the old summerhouse one of the land girls had pointed out to him. He hauled his motorbike onto its stand and was about to run for the garden when someone called his name.

'I say, you must be Bob. Come into the barn, you'll be safe enough in there.' The speaker was a pretty land girl with brown hair and a lovely smile. He sped across the courtyard and joined her in the cool shade of the Dutch barn.

'I'm certainly Bob. How the hell do you know my name?'

'Daphne told us about you.' The girl eyed him speculatively. 'She said you looked like her brother and that was no exaggeration.'

There was something about the way this girl was staring at him that made him think she'd somehow guessed why he'd abandoned the only woman he'd ever loved or probably ever would.

The anti-aircraft guns around Manston were still in action, the brown jobs had remained when the RAF had evacuated the base and the steady, heavy thump-thump of them firing into the sky unnerved him, making him ignore the girl's earlier remark.

'We're not protected in here. If they crash, or drop their loads, this barn will go up like a pile of matchsticks.'

'I'm well aware of that, Corporal, but I think it highly unlikely Goodwill House would be deliberately targeted. The bomber that crashed in the field the other day was just bad luck.'

'Are the others in the shelter under the house?'

'I assume so. I had to unharness the horse and decided to stay here. I don't like the cellars; they're damp and unpleasant.'

They moved to the rear of the building and sat on a couple of dilapidated deckchairs. 'Did Daphne tell you I almost killed her the other day?'

'Goodness me, did you? How did that happen?'

He explained briefly and she was silent when he'd finished. 'Did you jilt her because you found out you're closely related?'

He was shocked that this girl had guessed so easily and nodded. It was a relief to be able to talk about it with someone.

'I was adopted and so was my sister. Neither of us knew until Mum and Dad were forced to tell us the week before my wedding.'

'What happened?'

'Mum said she'd always worried that I was Daphne's brother as we looked so alike, so as the wedding approached, she got in touch with the woman who'd arranged my adoption.' He paused, stretched out his legs, closed his eyes and marshalled his thoughts before continuing. Telling this nameless girl was easier than explaining it to Daphne.

'It seems that although I'm legally adopted, I don't have the same rights as a natural child. I know it doesn't mean I can't marry, of course I can, but I'm not the person Daphne thought I was. Why would any girl want to tie herself to me knowing my background? Both me and my sister were adopted before we were a year old, and I don't recall my birth mother.'

'I take it your sister's older than you?'

'Yes, by two years. I'm surprised she didn't remember my coming, as she must have been about four when my parents adopted me.'

'But you believe that you and Daphne are half-brother and sister?' The girl wasn't shocked or at all judgemental, which helped.

'I am pretty sure that we are.' He found it too difficult to continue for a minute, and she didn't push him. When he'd recovered, he continued. 'The only explanation is that my birth mother – if that's what I should call her – had an affair with Daphne's dad. This would have been a couple of years before Daphne was born, about the time her mum was expecting her older brother.'

'I see. You loved Daphne but didn't try to find out if what you'd been told was true. I just don't understand why.'

He ignored her question and continued. 'It was just sheer bad luck that I ended up living across the street from Daphne. We both got teased about being carrot tops, ginger nuts and so on, and it was inevitable we were drawn together. We were friends before we became involved romantically.'

'What did your mother say when you started going out with her?'

'She did try to discourage me but didn't say why, so I just carried on, thinking it was nothing important – just motherly worries.'

'What exactly did she say when she told you about being adopted?'

'Mum said she couldn't find the family I came from but thought she had to tell me as she was convinced Daphne and I were siblings.' He swallowed. 'I'll never forgive either of my parents for not telling me sooner. If I'd known there was the faintest chance of us being related, then I'd never have gone out with her.'

'Did you check with her father, just to make sure?'

'Of course I didn't. I could hardly go up to him and ask if he was my dad. My mum knew for certain that he had been unfaithful, kept a fancy woman somewhere, so it all fitted.'

'Do you regret not confronting her father?'

'I do now. At the time, I was so angry with my parents, I wasn't thinking straight. I behaved badly and I'm not surprised Daphne wants nothing to do with me, even if it proves to be wrong that we're siblings.' He swallowed the lump in his throat, unable to continue for a moment. 'Also, kicking up a stink would have made things worse for Daphne and could have split up her family.'

'How terribly sad for both of you. I don't understand why you didn't tell Daphne – at least you could have been brother and sister, even if you couldn't be husband and wife. Running off without a word was cruel.'

'I know that now, but you've got to understand I'll never be able to think of her as my sister. It's better if I keep away – for both of us.'

He heaved himself to his feet, not wanting to continue the conversation. Just talking about it brought it all back and he wished with all his heart that fate hadn't brought Daphne into his life again.

'Do you want me to tell her what you've told me?'

'Yes, if you don't mind.' He wandered outside, in that moment not caring if a stray German bullet or bomb ended his life. The noise had abated somewhat and the dog fights were no longer directly overhead. He shaded his eyes and stared up.

'I'm Charlie, by the way,' the girl said. 'I forgot to introduce myself.'

'Pleased to meet you. I'm glad that Daphne's got friends like you. In case she asks, her dad didn't tell her mum about the affair, so things are still all right at home.'

'Then how did your mother know about it?'

'I've no idea, and didn't ask. With hindsight, I should have spoken to her and got more information, but the double shock had knocked me off kilter.'

'I understand. I'm curious as to why you're here when you so obviously don't want to see Daphne.'

'The Home Guard captain told me they've not managed to locate the two missing German pilots. I was just taking a spin, having a dekko in empty barns and so on. Jimmy was a good friend and he died when we came over here to look for them. I owe it to him to not let them escape.'

'Do you think they might be lurking in the grounds somewhere here?' Charlie looked around anxiously, as if half-expecting the two men to suddenly pop out from behind a hedge brandishing guns.

'I thought it was worth having a look. You've not noticed anything out of the ordinary? Missing fruit and veg, not as many eggs as usual, that sort of thing.'

'Nobody's said anything but then we're out all day working. You need to speak to Jean, the housekeeper here, or one of the twins. They'll know.'

Seeing Daphne again would be difficult, but he must put his duty first.

* * *

Joanna didn't think for one minute any of those present had taken the missing items. There was, however, a possible explanation. 'Are you quite sure that the tins were full, Jean? Remember we've been down twice recently.'

Liza shook her head so vehemently her pigtails bounced. 'No, Ma, I definitely replaced everything we'd used.'

Daphne cleared her throat. 'I know who's taken it and it's all my fault.'

By the time the poor girl had explained how she'd left the outside door unlocked, they were all looking nervously at the exit that led into the cellars.

Joe hastily closed the door and, as there was no internal lock, pushed a chair under the handle.

'Blimey, are you saying there could be a couple of Germans hiding down here with us?' Sal asked.

'I'm afraid so. I thought that because I came down and locked the door during the night, no one would have got in.'

'I think we're all overreacting. Remember, a few weeks ago, I thought there was a man trying to murder me, who'd set fire to the Victorian wing deliberately, but it just turned out to be an accident,' Joanna said.

'I don't see how missing food can be an accident, Ma,' Joe said.

'Look at Lazzy – he's flopped out on the floor with not a care in the world. Don't you think if there'd been anybody here when we came down, especially two armed German pilots, he'd have been snarling and ready to tear their throats out?'

The atmosphere in the room changed from worried to relaxed. 'Of course he would, he's the best guard dog in the world. Good boy, Lazzy, you'd tell us if there was anything unto-ward going on, wouldn't you?' Liza dropped to her knees and hugged the dog, who revelled in the extra attention he was getting.

'That's all very well, my lady, but it doesn't explain the missing items.' Jean was the only one not convinced by Joanna's reassurance. 'And another thing, the gardener said someone's been helping themselves to the soft fruit and vegetables.'

This was news to Joanna. 'I still think it unlikely a pair of Germans would wish to hide in our cellars half the time and then creep about in the garden stealing food. Lazzy would have barked at them, even if he didn't attack.'

The other girls were looking askance at poor Daphne and Joanna really couldn't blame them. If there were, in fact, any men lurking down here, then it had to be her fault. There was no way they could have got into the house apart from through the underground passage, as coming in via a broken window would have been too risky.

'There's one way we can find out, Ma, let Lazzy search,' Joe said, and she agreed with him.

'Everybody stay in here whilst the dog sees if he can sniff out any unwanted visitors.' Joanna didn't expect an argument so was somewhat surprised when Daphne disagreed.

'I'm sorry, my lady, I don't care if there are a dozen Luftwaffe hiding with your wine, I'm not staying down here. We could all go out through the underground passage and then it only needs one person to remain behind to bolt the door.' Daphne was already heading for the exit. Her face was pale, clammy, she obviously really did suffer badly from claustrophobia.

There was a murmur of assent around the table. Elizabeth was already on her feet.

'I'm going with you, Daphne, I might be decrepit but I'm sure I can manage with your assistance. I've no intention of staying here and being murdered by the Nazis.'

'Are you quite sure, Elizabeth?' Joanna said. 'It's not an easy route. Wouldn't you be better staying with Joe and me?'

'Absolutely not. I've got twelve strong girls as well as Jean and Liza to assist me if I need it.'

'Very well, if you insist. I suggest that you make your way down to the barn.'

This time, Joanna did expect there to be disagreement, for at least Jean or her daughter to protest and insist that they remained with her, but this wasn't the case. One by one, they trooped down the narrow staircase into the dark and Joe and Lazzy went with them in order to lock the outside door when they were safely out.

It was all very well appearing to be in charge, to be courageous in the face of the enemy, but now, left on her own without even the dog for company, Joanna's heart began to pound uncomfortably, her knees gave way beneath her and she collapsed on the nearest chair.

She was being silly. If there were Germans in the cellar, they'd had plenty of opportunity to harm them but hadn't done so. By the time Joe came back with the dog, she was more composed.

'Is the air-raid still in progress?'

'The all-clear hasn't gone and the ack-ack guns are still firing.' Joe touched her arm. 'The girls are staying under the trees, Ma, they'll be perfectly safe.'

'As Charlie didn't join us, I expect they'll meet up with her.' Talking about the missing girl was better than removing the chair blocking the door and starting the search.

'I'll just bolt the back door and then we'll see if Lazzy can find us some intruders.' He seemed excited at the prospect, not daunted as she was. He was a brave and intelligent boy and she thanked god he and his sister had agreed to join the family.

He carefully put the chair back under the table. He wanted things neat and she liked this in him. 'I'm going to turn the lights out, Ma, we don't want to warn them.'

Joanna nodded, her mouth dry, unable to answer. Joe plunged the room into darkness and then opened the door.

'Go on, Lazzy, find them.'

The dog didn't move but sat down next to Joe, wagging his tail, his huge head tilted to one side, as if waiting for a sensible command.

'I still can't believe there's anybody hiding down here. Look at him – he's perfectly relaxed and he wouldn't be if there was any danger.' Joanna decided to take matters into her own hands. 'You know my dog, if someone gave him a biscuit, he'd be their friend for life. He's only fierce if one of us is in danger.'

'He's followed me down here a couple of times and vanished. I should have realised why.'

She stepped out into the pitch-dark cellar and her dog moved with her. 'We know you're in here, we wish you no harm, why don't you come out and give yourselves up?'

Her voice echoed and, for a moment, she felt rather foolish and wondered why she wasn't terrified. Was she placing too much faith in the dog's assessment of these Germans? Then Lazzy rushed off and she heard him greeting the German pilots.

'We are coming out, we will willingly give ourselves up to you.' The speaker had a slight accent, but his English was perfect. 'I am Leutnant Claus Müller, my companion is Leutnant Wolfgang Schmidt.'

Joanna was relieved they didn't say 'Heil Hitler' and perform the Nazi salute. 'Put the lights on, Joe, there's no need for them to be off.'

Her son switched them on in the shelter and then went to the head of the stairs and switched on the main light. The missing men emerged, hands raised as if they expected them to be armed, with Lazzy trotting happily beside them. They were somewhat dishevelled, and unshaven, their once smart beige flying suits grubby.

They looked painfully young, perhaps around twenty, and were apparently as nervous as she was at this meeting. Both were fair-haired and blue-eyed and could be said to be typically Germanic in appearance. She sensed that they would be no immediate threat to the household. At least, she hoped so.

Joe nodded at the two of them. 'How come you speak such good English?'

Leutnant Müller replied, 'We were attending your excellent Oxford University when we were recalled to Germany and obliged to become pilots.'

'You can put your hands down, gentlemen. Why didn't you surrender?' This was something that had bothered her.

'We were told by the captain of our aircraft that we would be executed on sight. Therefore, we thought it advisable to remain hidden.'

'We don't do that sort of thing, young man, we're British and fully support the Geneva Convention. However,' she continued quickly, 'I think it might be best if you remained in the shelter until I can make arrangements for you to be collected. I have a dozen land girls living here and your unexpected appearance would probably upset some of them. They have been regularly shot at by some of your compatriots whilst working peacefully in the fields.'

'I can only offer my apologies for such behaviour. Civilians should not be deliberately attacked,' Müller replied, and Joanna agreed with him. They didn't seem hostile, but she still didn't understand why they had been hiding if they were happy to be POWs.

'I will get my son, Joe, to bring your meals. Of course, I'll tell the girls that you are here but will not be coming upstairs. Lord Harcourt, a distant member of my family, is a lieutenant colonel and I will ring him immediately. I am sure that he will know what to do in the circumstances.'

She realised she'd been speaking in a slightly stilted manner, echoing the formality of the German pilot.

They nodded simultaneously. She wondered if the one called Schmidt spoke English, as so far, he'd made no attempt to join in the conversation.

'You must remain in the shelter, not go outside, as I cannot guarantee that an overenthusiastic member of the Home Guard might not shoot you. Ramsgate was dreadfully bombed a few weeks ago; almost a hundred people died and a thousand lost their homes. It might not have been either of you, but Germans of any sort are not popular around here.'

The two exchanged a glance. 'We understand, my lady, and will do as you ask,' Müller said. He spoke rapidly in German to the other man and for some reason, this made her less confident of their good intentions. Lazzy wasn't growling at them, she decided firmly, so she would follow his lead. One thing she was certain of was that if these men intended her harm her, Lazzy would pick up on it and react accordingly.

Joe took the dog by his collar and made sure he didn't stay in the cellars. Once they were through the door at the top of the steep steps and into the boot room, he released the dog and immediately turned the key in the lock.

'Better to be safe than sorry, Ma. I'm going to race round to the outside door and block that too. They came out with their hands up, but they had guns in their holsters and didn't offer to hand those over.'

'I know, but it would have been too dangerous to try and confiscate them. They might have resisted and someone could be hurt.'

'Right, but it doesn't seem right leaving them with sidearms.'

'Lazzy can't be wrong. He's such a good judge of character.'

'He can be bribed with treats. I won't be long – I hope Lord

Harcourt can arrange for them to be collected today. I'm not happy having them downstairs.'

Joe rushed off, the dog at his heels, and Joanna hurried into the hall, gloomy now the windows were boarded up, but light enough to see. She waited impatiently for the operator to connect her to the number she'd been given by Peter for emergencies. If her son was concerned about the two men in the cellar, then maybe she was being rather naïve.

6

Daphne led the girls out of the shelter and into the welcome evening sunlight under the trees.

Jean and Liza had escorted the old lady and they'd all emerged unscathed. 'The guns might still be firing, but I can't see any German bombers or fighters. I think it's safe to go down to the barn.'

'Sounds like a plan,' someone said, and the others agreed. 'If we go in twos or threes, keeping to the shadows, then even if a lone fighter suddenly appears directly overhead, I doubt they'd see us.'

It had taken a considerable time for all of them to negotiate the narrow underground passage, but they were all safely on terra firma now. Daphne hung back, letting the others go ahead.

'Right, it's our turn now,' Daphne said to Sal as the last trio vanished through the dense undergrowth.

'Do you think there are bleeding Germans hiding in the cellars?'

'I've no idea, Sal, but they can't be dangerous or Lazzy would have tried to tear them apart.' Daphne checked the hidden door that led into the shelter was obscured by the branches and then followed her friends.

They were halfway down when Joe, Lazzy close behind, ran towards them. 'Good, I need some help. The Germans were there all right, seemed friendly enough, speak perfect English, but neither Ma nor I trust them. We need to make sure they can't get out this way.'

It took the three of them twenty minutes to be satisfied nobody could push the door open from the other side. Daphne had taken charge of the operation and even Joe hadn't objected.

'There, I defy even the most determined German to escape through that.'

'Let's go to the barn,' Sal suggested just as the all-clear sounded. 'Good, now we can go straight into the house. I'm blooming starving. Too much excitement ain't good for me digestion.'

Daphne could hear the girls laughing and chattering as they headed for the back door and increased her pace. Joe had gone ahead with the dog and Sal was humming a tune she'd heard on the wireless. 'Is that "A Nightingale Sang in Berkeley Square"?'

'Blimey, I'm surprised you recognised it. Cor, would you look at that! I love a motorbike and that's a smasher.'

Daphne's foot slipped and she fell headfirst into a patch of nettles. She'd know that bike anywhere – it was Bob's pride and joy. Sal hadn't noticed her sudden descent into the nettle patch and continued merrily on her way, leaving Daphne to scramble out. In fact, she was relieved her embarrassing tumble hadn't been witnessed by anyone.

If Bob was on the premises, then she certainly wasn't going in until he left. She could hardly skulk in the bushes, so she carefully retraced her steps, rubbing vigorously at the patches of red nettle rash liberally sprinkled on both hands and forearms. She looked around for a dock leaf and was relieved to find one. She wasn't sure how rubbing the affected parts with it would help, but she did it anyway.

'Daphne, please don't feel you've got to hide because I'm here.'

She paused in mid-flight when Bob called out to her. There was little point in hiding from him now, as he'd come out at just the wrong moment and seen her, so she might as well follow the others inside.

It was so wrong that he still made her heart beat faster, that she just wanted to run to him. If the reason he'd left was that he was her half-brother – although she didn't know the circumstances – incest wasn't just considered a mortal sin but was also a criminal offence.

He appeared to be unaccompanied. Presumably Charlie had gone in with the others and Daphne wasn't sure if she was more comfortable talking to Bob alone or with her friend standing by to offer support.

By the time she reached the courtyard in front of the Dutch barn, she'd gathered her thoughts, pushed her unwanted feelings aside and was ready to speak to him as if he was a friend and not the man she'd hoped to marry and spend the rest of her life with.

'Why are you here? I think I might have guessed why you ran away, and I understand, but I can't ever forgive you for being such a coward and not telling me in person.'

'I'm sorry, Daphne, I regret how I handled it,' Bob said. 'Please don't ask me to give you the details, I told your friend and she'll pass the information on.'

'I see. You haven't answered my question. Why would you come here when you know it's impossible for us to be near each other?'

He explained that he thought them being close wasn't a good idea. He didn't need to say any more. He must still find her attractive and she certainly felt the same way about him. She nodded. 'The Germans are in the basement, which is why we came out through the passage. I expect Lady Harcourt's dealing with it now.'

'How do you come to be at Goodwill House? I never expected to see you again and hoped you would have moved on – it's a year since I abandoned you.'

'I discovered that you'd joined the RAF and one of your mates told me you were based here. I was going to write to you but then, by some strange quirk of fate, I was billeted next door to Manston. Believe me, I now wish with all my heart that we hadn't met like this.'

She swallowed the lump in her throat. As he moved into the sun, she saw his eyes glittering with unshed tears. He was as upset as she was and, despite her anguish, this gave her some comfort.

'I'm going in now. If I don't, then I might not get any supper. Please don't come here again.' She was about to head for the house but paused. 'What exactly do you do at Manston? I thought everybody had been moved elsewhere.'

'I'm a fitter – a qualified mechanic able to repair most kites – I lead a team of three ground crew. I'll be gone in a few weeks.'

'Good. It's better that we have no further contact and that there's no possibility we could bump into each other. The situation's awful for both of us.'

It was becoming impossible to hold back her tears and she didn't want to cry in front of him. She dashed off without saying goodbye and was just closing the back door behind her when she heard the familiar roar of his motorbike as he left.

Neither Charlie nor Sal said anything as Daphne entered the house, but she received sympathetic looks from them both. She was able to push her sadness aside and immerse herself in the general excitement at there being two Luftwaffe pilots locked in the cellars. Last year, her dearest wish was to see Bob again, and now she had she wasn't sure how she felt. She'd tried to move on and forget how much she'd loved him, but seeing him had brought everything back in a rush. It would be so much simpler if the reason he'd gone had been cold feet or something like that. The possibility they were siblings was insurmountable.

She retired early, leaving the other girls to enjoy what little leisure time they had listening to the wireless, playing cards, writing letters, or just sitting about enjoying a chat. Getting nettle stings wet just made them more painful, so tonight she had a lick and a promise, not her usual head-to-toe wash, and was safely in bed before she heard her friends outside. Why were they coming at such speed? Had some other disaster occurred?

* * *

Bob returned to the base more depressed than he had been when he'd set out to clear his head. This past year, losing Daphne had become a little easier to bear, but he'd not forgotten her, still loved her, and the only positive in his life was the fact that he had been the only one to know the true reason for their separation. Only he'd had to bear this burden. But now she knew that for years they'd been having an incestuous relationship and that was tearing him apart.

Thank god they hadn't slept together – she'd wanted to wait until they were married and he'd respected her wishes. Although they'd exchanged passionate kisses, had declared their undying love for each other, at least they hadn't committed the ultimate sin. He should feel nauseated by the thought that he'd been kissing his sister but when he thought about their relationship, he couldn't believe any of it had been wrong.

He parked his bike in place, kicked it onto its stand, and in a foul mood, headed for the bar. There was no longer a NAAFI, no NAAFI vans, recreation rooms or decent accommodation. At one time, when the base had been fully active, there must have been over two thousand personnel based there, now there couldn't be more than a hundred or so.

'Here, Corp, drown your sorrows.' Chalky handed him a brimming pint. 'Did you have any luck?'

For a moment, Bob didn't know what Chalky was referring to and then remembered he'd said he was going in search of the missing Germans. 'Lady Harcourt found them hiding in her cellars. I was just passing the end of the drive when the siren went and took shelter there.'

'Right, that's good news. Don't want those bastards wandering around the countryside.' Chalky took a slurp of his beer. 'One of the teams left today. An Annie arrived and they've been posted to an operational base. I reckon this place will have no kites in a couple of weeks.'

'I'm surprised an Anson managed to land safely. I don't care where I'm sent as long as it's away from here.' He spoke more vehemently than he'd intended and Chalky squinted over his beer at him.

'I know what you mean, Corp, it's not the same without Jimmy.'

Better his mate thought his mood was caused by the death of their friend and didn't ask awkward questions. He'd not told anybody, obviously, about Daphne.

'I'm going to take this into the canteen, see if I can get some scoff before I turn in.'

'Just a minute, there's something else,' Chalky said. 'Someone from admin said that the engineers and such will be arriving in the next day or two to start rebuilding the runway.'

'They'll have to doss down in the WAAFs' accommodation – there isn't any room for them here.'

'Good point, Corp, let's hope the powers that be don't try and cram them in here. I reckon they've got to bring everything on lorries. Heavy equipment can't be flown in.'

'I don't really care; I'll just be glad to move on. Manston used to be an important operational base, it's like a ghost town now. I want to be somewhere active, working on operational kites.'

Bob took his half-drunk beer into the makeshift canteen and was pleased to be able to get a heaped plate of bangers and mash. The spotted dick and custard went down a treat too. There was one benefit of being at Manston now, the rules were less rigorously applied and nobody objected if he took beer from the bar into the mess hall.

As he was settling down for the night in the cramped billet he shared with another corporal, he changed his mind about seeing Daphne again. He wanted to sit down and talk to her about what had happened. He owed it to her to tell her everything he'd discovered; she shouldn't hear it second-hand.

He'd turned in before his roommate, so the other bed was empty. He was out of bed, dressed and ready to leave the room in minutes. He glanced at his wristwatch – it was late but not disastrously so. He was going to telephone Goodwill House and see if he could speak to Daphne. He'd go over now if she'd agree to see him.

The operator connected him immediately. 'Goodwill House, Charlie speaking. How can I help?'

'Charlie, it's Bob. Have you spoken to Daphne yet?'

'No, there's not been the opportunity and she went up to bed a minute ago.'

'I'm coming over. I want to tell her myself. I know it'll be dark soon, but I need to do this. She deserves to hear it from me. Do you think you can persuade her to meet me in the barn?'

'I'm sure I can. Good for you, Bob, she'll appreciate you coming back and explaining everything in person. How soon will you be here?'

'Ten minutes.'

He hung up and, for the second time that evening, kicked his bike into life. He roared through the gates, drove like a lunatic down the lanes and skidded up the drive, arriving in eight minutes. The sun had set; the blackbirds were singing their final songs. Soon it would be too dark to see even in the open barn. Perhaps that was for the best.

He scarcely had time to check the ancient deckchairs when Daphne came in.

'Thank you for coming back, Bob, despite what I said earlier, I think it'll help both of us if we talk this through.'

He waited until she was comfortable and then told her exactly what he'd told her friend. When he'd finished, he waited for her to comment, to express disbelief and dismay at hearing that her beloved father had been unfaithful. What she said was totally unexpected.

'Let me get this straight, Bob, you didn't actually ask my father who he'd had an affair with?'

'No, I didn't. What difference does that make?'

'Don't you see, the fact that we look so alike could still be a coincidence. I'm sure there are hundreds, if not thousands, of others with the same colouring as us and they can't all be related.' She continued, 'Isn't it just possible this could simply be a huge misunderstanding? I do understand why you didn't go and see my dad, so I'll have to ask him myself.'

For the first time in over a year, he felt a flicker of hope. 'Are you suggesting that your father's affair isn't anything to do with me?'

'I am. I'm determined to find out the exact truth. Did your mother give you any names?'

'No, and I was so angry, I didn't ask.'

'You gave up on us. If you'd told me instead of running away, then we might have found out the truth.' She stood up and stared down at him in a way that made him feel small. 'I intend to get the facts straight; I still can't believe we're related, but that doesn't mean we're going to get back together.'

'Then why bother?' He sounded bitter and felt it.

'Because I loved you, Bob, and we were happy for a long time. I need to know the truth, don't you?'

* * *

Joanna had left a message with Peter's secretary. Poor woman must work very long hours to still be in the office at eight o'clock. He would be uncontactable until the following morning. She could go to bed without worrying about his phone call. She was, however, concerned about having the Germans locked in the cellar.

Joe had taken the prisoners something to eat and she was on edge until he returned safely. 'Do they still have their guns visible?'

'They do, Ma, but seemed friendly enough and happy to have a decent meal.' He hesitated, looked a little uncomfortable, before continuing. 'They'll have to use our privy, won't they? I don't fancy emptying it when they've gone.'

'Good heavens, I'd not thought of those practicalities. I don't think any of us want to use it knowing we were sharing it with the enemy. I'll see if I can get old George to do it. If I give him a half a crown, he might be willing.'

The gardener was happy to take most of his wages in kind, so some extra cash might well be very welcome.

'I wonder if they know we've locked them in. If they'd been going outside, not using the Elsan, they'll be aware soon enough that we don't trust them.'

'As long as they can't get into the house or escape into the countryside, then that's good enough. I'm sure that Lord Harcourt will arrange to have them collected.'

'I was thinking, Ma, that I could ride down to the police house. Even though PC Sykes is useless, he'll know who to contact.'

'That's a good idea. If you leave now, you'll be back long before blackout.'

The girls were still finishing their supper and Liza would be helping Jean in the kitchen. Joanna went to find Elizabeth in the small sitting room, which was now the only place they had to sit as the drawing room was boarded up. She sighed, 1940 had been an absolutely dreadful year. Her dearest friend, Betty, had died, the Victorian wing had been set fire to and now all windows at the front of the house had been blown out. She didn't add having to part with John to the catalogue of woes.

She was smiling wryly when she walked in to join her mother-in-law. 'What are you finding so amusing, my dear? I would have thought having two German pilots incarcerated in our cellar nothing to smile about.'

'I was just running through the various disasters that have befallen this family this year and I'm not counting the war. I neglected to add the death of my husband to the list.'

'I'm not surprised. David was a cold man; he didn't deserve such a lovely young woman as you. That said, I am so pleased you agreed to marry him, as I think of you as my daughter now.'

Joanna leaned down and kissed Elizabeth on the cheek. 'Thank you; you've become very precious to me too. This year has had some high points. We now have Joe and Liza in the family, Sarah is in her second year of medical training and engaged to Angus.'

'Don't forget that we've also paid off the debts and you own the house and the estate outright,' Elizabeth said. 'Which reminds me, do you know how the prosecution of the fraudulent bank manager and solicitor is progressing? Are you likely to get back any of the monies they purloined?'

'To be honest, I'd forgotten all about that.' She could

hardly tell Elizabeth that her brief but passionate affair with John had made her forget everything – including common sense.

'I take it you didn't manage to speak to Peter Harcourt.'

'No, unfortunately he's unavailable until tomorrow morning. I left a message and I'm certain he'll get back to me as soon as he gets into his office.'

'I keep thinking that for the past few days there have been two Nazis living in the cellars unbeknownst to us. We could have been murdered in our beds, as your dog appears to have taken a liking to them.'

'I'm certain that if they'd shown any aggression to any of us, he would soon have changed his mind. At least they can't go anywhere now. They'll be safe enough where they are until the proper authorities come to arrest them.'

'I think I'm going to go up, my dear. No, I don't need your assistance tonight. You stay where you are and enjoy your coffee when it comes through. I don't suppose we'll have it for much longer.'

'True, there are only three tins left of those you brought with you from France.'

Joanna stood up and embraced her, pleased that the old lady no longer felt quite as insubstantial as she had a few months ago. She prayed the occasional bouts of confusion wouldn't get any worse and that Elizabeth would remain an active member of the family for another decade at least.

* * *

Joe returned after an unsuccessful search for the constable. 'No luck, Ma, the house was locked up and his neighbours said they'd not seen him or his wife for a week.'

'How odd – surely it's not acceptable that Stodham has been left without police protection, however inadequate that might be.'

'I suppose he might be having a week's leave. Anyway, it won't hurt to have those two here another night. I guarantee they can't get out.'

'I don't want you going down there again. They've got water and have had a decent meal tonight. It won't hurt them to do without until the authorities come.'

'I'm going to get my gun and keep it beside me just in case.'

'You'll do no such thing, young man. That gun is for shooting game and rabbits, not people, even if they are German.'

'Fair enough,' Joe said. 'I'm going to the study to finish an essay for Mr Kent then. I never thought I'd ever be writing an essay on anything – to be honest, I didn't even know what one was until I started working with my tutor.'

'Mr Kent said he's very pleased with the progress you and your sister are making. I just wish we could have had the grand birthday celebration for the two of you and Sarah that we'd planned. It will be your birthday next week – you both look so much older than fifteen.'

'We had to be independent, resilient, growing up the way we did with just our other ma in the East End. I sometimes want to swank around the streets in my posh clothes where people used to turn their noses up at us for being bastards.'

'I do dislike that word, even if it's accurate,' Joanna said. 'Both of you are members of the Harcourt family now. You never need to see those people again.'

Joe hugged her and strolled off. He was several inches taller than her now and was going to be handsome young man. He had regular features, grey eyes and hair that had once been a nondescript mouse brown, but was now slowly turning darker.

When he and Liza had arrived to work as live-in servants, he would never have used words like resilient. How they had both changed and she was so glad they'd come into her life.

She decided not to have her evening coffee as Elizabeth wasn't there to share it with her. Liza had gone to join her brother in the study and Jean was alone in the kitchen.

'I was hoping you might have thought of some sort of celebration we could hold for the twins next week,' Joanna said. 'Do you think we could arrange something similar to the one we had to celebrate their becoming part of the family?'

'I was thinking that myself. I can make a nice Victoria sandwich, scones, sandwiches and so on. If you invite their friends from church and include the girls living here, that's more than enough for a decent party.'

'Then that's what we'll do. I've got a pretty necklace for Liza and am going to give Joe my husband's watch.'

'They'll be thrilled, Joanna, with whatever you give them,' Jean said. 'What do we do if the siren goes off during the night? We can't very well go downstairs and to get to the summerhouse in the dark would be hazardous.'

'Then let's pray it doesn't go off. Good night, Jean, don't stay up too late.'

7

Daphne returned to her room, more optimistic than she'd been since Bob had abandoned her over a year ago. He'd agreed that they should investigate the circumstances but hadn't seemed as enthusiastic as she was to do so.

This was probably because she'd made it very clear that whatever the outcome, their relationship was over. She didn't know if she meant this, but better that neither of them got their hopes up.

Her friends were sitting up in bed, waiting for her to come in. 'Thank you for arranging this, Charlie. I needed to speak to him and get things sorted out in my mind.'

'You poor old thing. Must have been hard to say a final goodbye,' Charlie said sympathetically.

'Actually, it didn't go quite as I'd expected.' Daphne explained her theory and they listened avidly.

'Blimey – that's a turn-up for the books, ain't it?' Sal said. 'I reckon that's worth a look.'

'I agree, Sal. I'm going to speak to my dad and Bob's going to get the details of his adoption from his mother. If only my father and Bob's parents had been honest at the outset, all this could have been avoided. At least it explains why my parents don't get on.' She frowned. 'I've said I'll talk to my dad but I'm not sure I can. If I'm honest, I'm scared of him. He was ready to step in with a spanking when my brother and I misbehaved, even when we didn't deserve it.'

'Blimey, that's not good. Don't hold with hitting kiddies,' Sal said. 'Mind you, I got a few clips round the ears, and it didn't do me no harm.'

'Bob's mother didn't want you to marry a man she thinks is your half-brother. She did the right thing, really,' Charlie said.

'We need to find his real birth mother, but I've no idea how to do that. I'm not exactly sure how I can even start to look for this woman as I don't get any time off. None of us do.'

'What about Bob? I should think his job at the base repairing aircraft will be over fairly soon. He might be able to wangle a few days' leave then.'

'You're right, Charlie. We parted on bad terms, as you might imagine,' Daphne said. 'He ran away like a coward and that's not the sort of man I want to marry.'

Charlie looked at her strangely. 'I thought you were going to contact him as you knew he was based at Manston. I know he took the easy way out but that's what most people would do in the circumstances, isn't it?'

'But Bob wasn't *most people* to me, Charlie. He was special, different to everybody else. I do have feelings for him, but it's not the same now. Being apart from him for so long has given me time to reflect. I think I'd made him out to be something he wasn't in my mind and seeing him has opened my eyes to the truth.'

'What's that when it's at home?' Sal asked as she slid down the bed, yawning loudly.

'That I've grown up, become independent and don't need to be married to him or anyone else to be happy.' As she spoke, Daphne understood that she wanted to be in the Land Army doing her bit for the war effort and not become just a housewife and mother. Deep down, she knew she still loved him, but that didn't mean they had to be married.

'Same for me, a bloke can't hold a candle to what we've got now. Ta for sharing. Night night.' Sal settled down and was asleep instantly.

'I'll get the light, Charlie. No one can say our life's dull now, can they?'

'We've certainly had our share of excitement – let's trust the arrival of the German pilots is the last of it. I just hope this new woman, Mrs Ramsbottom, doesn't decide it's too dangerous for us here and move us somewhere else,' Charlie said.

'We're working on Lady Harcourt's farms so we have to stay here,' Daphne replied as she switched off the main light.

Daphne lay awake for a while, mulling over what she now knew. She'd told Bob that whatever the outcome of the investigation, she no longer wanted to be with him, but if she was being honest with herself, that wasn't entirely true.

* * *

The next morning, Daphne still hadn't decided what she would do in either scenario. She didn't want to think or talk about it any more and was glad her friends behaved as if nothing out of the ordinary was going on.

As always, the three girls who worked on the dairy farm had eaten their breakfast and left a couple of hours before the rest of them came down. One wouldn't know there was anything untoward going on in the basement, as the housekeeper and Liza were carrying on as usual, preparing the breakfast and the packed lunches.

Jean was no longer making porridge – far too hot for that – and today it was to be scrambled eggs on toast. Having so many chickens meant there were always eggs available. Mr Pickering sometimes allowed them to take a jug of cream or a slab of butter home, as did Mr Root, who was the tenant of the dairy farm.

Conversation around the table was about the men locked up downstairs and they speculated when the authorities would come to remove them.

'Good thing we didn't have another air-raid last night,' Charlie said as she spread a very thin scraping of butter on her second slice of toast.

'It's safer out in the fields than it is here,' Daphne added. 'Pity the Germans are bombing more at night now.'

Today was her turn to take care of Star and she headed out first. She was just doing up the last buckle on the harness when the distinct sound of at least one motor vehicle interrupted her.

'Stay there quietly, good girl, I'm going to see who it is.' She patted the sleek grey neck of the horse, checked the brake on the cart was on, and hurried around to the front of the house, where she could see who was coming.

There was a lorry, an army one, as it was painted brown and camouflaged, travelling behind a large staff car, also camouflaged. Charlie and Sal joined her.

'Thank goodness, they've come to collect the prisoners. I know they couldn't get out, but I wasn't really comfortable knowing they were there.'

'I ain't that bothered about them Nazis,' Sal said with her usual happy smile. 'After Den, I reckon I can deal with anyone.'

There was the rattling of bicycles approaching from the rear. Usually, the three of them set out before the others as it was quicker on two wheels than in the pony cart.

'You'd better wait a minute, girls, you don't want to get squashed by the military,' Daphne said, pointing to the approaching vehicles.

The drive was about half a mile long. It was bordered on one side by the ploughed field that had once had potatoes in it and on the other by rhododendrons and other shrubs that Daphne didn't know the names of. Behind these was a strip of woodland that ran from the end of the drive to the boundary with Manston RAF base.

The car growled to a halt. A smart ATS girl turned off the engine, jumped out and opened the nearside passenger door. She actually saluted the senior officer who got out.

'Cor, he's a looker, ain't he? Ever so handsome. He must be important – look at the gold braid on his uniform,' Sal said quietly.

'Lady Harcourt obviously has important friends. I think I might have seen him before,' Charlie told them. 'But I've no idea who he is.'

The lorry rocked to a standstill and a dozen lethal-looking soldiers jumped out and, like trained dogs, stood in a row, at attention, waiting for a command.

* * *

Joanna had seen the vehicles approaching and knew at once that Peter had come in person. He was really quite predictable, and she was not surprised by his appearance so early in the morning. He'd obviously got her message and acted immediately.

She went down the front steps to greet him. If she'd expected him to smile, to show pleasure at seeing her, she would have been disappointed. He stood, face grave, back rigid, in front of her.

'Lady Harcourt, we've come to remove the prisoners of war from your premises.'

'Well, Lord Harcourt, I hardly thought you'd come for a social visit. I have to tell you that both of them are armed. They seemed eager to be taken into custody but I'm not sure I believe they were genuine. It was when they spoke in German that I had my doubts. Why change from English unless they were saying something they didn't want us to hear?'

He asked a few terse questions and she answered equally briefly. 'I'm sorry, Lord Harcourt, but I'm afraid you're going to have to move your vehicles as the land girls using the pony cart won't be able to get past.'

He nodded, spun round and with a flick of his gloved hand indicated to the drivers they were to move. The armed soldiers marched from their position next to the lorry to stand, ramrod straight, behind him.

'It really wasn't necessary for you to come in person but thank you for doing so. I'll get out of your way. I do hope no one gets shot.'

Joanna was mystified by his formality, as the last time she'd spoken to him, he'd been more like a friend. She retreated to the kitchen, where Jean and the twins were setting out the breakfast dishes. Elizabeth had yet to arrive.

'I don't think it's safe to be in here at the moment. Lord Harcourt has brought a small platoon of soldiers to arrest those men and I'm not exactly sure how they can do this without shots being fired.'

'I'll put everything on a tray and we can take it to the sitting room, Joanna. That's far enough away from whatever might happen,' Jean said.

'Shall I show them the outside entrance, Ma? Then they can enter from the boot room and the passageway at the same time.'

'You'll do no such thing, young man. Leave everything to the professionals.' Her son scowled for a moment; she thought he'd ignore her and go anyway. 'I explained to Lord Harcourt about the passageway, Joe, and he has half a dozen armed soldiers with him. You'd only be getting in the way.'

'I suppose so. Liza and I had better get to the study as Mr Kent will be here shortly. I'm hoping he'll give me a good mark for my essay.'

'Might I be allowed to read it after him?'

Joe beamed, his previous annoyance forgotten. 'Would you? I'd love you to see how I'm progressing.'

Jean carried one tray and Joanna carried the other and Elizabeth, who'd just come in, trotted along behind. The twins gulped down the remainder of their breakfast and vanished to the study.

Even with the sitting room door firmly closed, Joanna jumped at every noise, half-expecting there to be a fusillade of shots, pounding feet, a dramatic event of some sort. The time dragged by.

'I should think even a few inefficient soldiers could have arrested two German pilots by now, my dear. I don't intend to remain shut in this room a moment longer.' Elizabeth stood up and before Joanna could prevent it, her mother-in-law had whisked through the door with remarkable speed for someone of her years.

Jean had been reading a magazine and wasn't on her feet as quickly. 'I'll go, you stay here,' Joanna said. 'Better not to have all three of us roaming about at the moment.'

There was no sign of Elizabeth in the passageway and Joanna broke a habit of a lifetime and ran to the grand hall. She skidded to an undignified halt, almost ending up on her bottom. Peter was standing, relaxed and friendly, talking to the errant grandmother.

'Joanna, the two men have been apprehended without fuss and are already on their way to be interrogated and then placed in a prisoner of war camp,' he said.

'There, Joanna, I told you there was no need to skulk in the sitting room. I'm going to sit on the terrace. Perhaps you could ask Jean to make us some coffee and Lord Harcourt could join us before he departs.'

Not waiting for an answer, the old lady wandered off, leaving

Joanna alone with Peter. He was definitely laughing at her and this made her both annoyed and uncomfortable in equal measures. Not a good combination.

'Lord Harcourt, I thank you for your timely assistance. I'm sure that you have urgent government business elsewhere. Don't let me detain you.'

His smile vanished. He nodded, tight-lipped, and without saying a word turned on his heel and strode out. He was very cross indeed and Joanna suddenly bitterly regretted her outburst. She was about to run after him and apologise but something held her back.

Every day of her life, until David had left to fight in France, she'd spent at the beck and call of a man. Last September, things had changed, and she relished the independence and freedom of being in control of her own destiny. Going after him and apologising was something the old Joanna would have done – this new version of her intended to deal with things on her terms.

With a sigh of regret, she thought about John and wished with all her heart that things could have been different, and that her young lover could somehow have become a permanent fixture in her life. He hadn't wanted to dominate her or issued orders and expected them to be obeyed. He'd loved her, shown her nothing but respect, and had not wanted anything from her in return. But he was gone, and it was better that way for both of them.

She was halfway to the kitchen when, to her astonishment, the man she'd dismissed so rudely arrived beside her with the charming smile she'd expected to see earlier.

'I'm a complete ass, I apologise. I'm so used to everybody following my every order, women falling in droves at my feet because of my charm, wealth and undeniably handsome features, that being rebuffed by you was hard to take.'

He was more likeable when he was being like this, and Joanna smiled gently. 'And I apologise for being rude. I'm afraid I have an absolute aversion to being laughed at, however deserved it might be. However, I think it better if you don't stay now as you have a driver with you. Why don't you come for the small celebration we're having for the twins' fifteenth birthday next Saturday and stay the weekend?'

'I'd love to. There, you had to point out to me that I shouldn't leave my driver outside any longer than necessary. You are a good influence, Joanna. Do I bring gifts?'

'No, but if you can find a few luxuries at Fortnum & Mason or Harrods, that would be absolutely splendid.'

* * *

Bob had kept his head down and his thoughts to himself for the next few days. Daphne had pointed out the information he had was woefully incomplete; and he was determined to get the remaining kites in his hangar airborne as quickly as possible and then ask for leave before his next posting.

When he'd asked the officer in charge about a pass, he'd been told he could have three days when they'd completed their work.

'Do you have any preferences as to where you go next, Corporal?'

'I'd like to stay in Kent if possible.'

'I'll do my best. When do you expect to have the last kite airworthy?'

'By the end of next week, as long as we can get the spare parts. I think the other team will be finished around the same time; then the blokes with the diggers can start the new runways.'

'Sadly, I doubt that Manston will ever be fully operational again. Once the runway's functional, it will probably be just for emergency landings, refuelling and rearming. Would you be interested in returning here? With your experience and skill set, you would be an ideal member of the small team who will be based here.'

Bob didn't hesitate. 'Yes, sir, please put my name on the list.' If by some miracle they weren't related, then being close to the woman he still adored would make it easier to persuade her to be with him again.

He left the office, feeling more cheerful than he had since that dreadful day when he'd learned – or thought he'd learned – that he and Daphne were brother and sister. He understood now that it wasn't just losing Daphne that had thrown him, it was discovering his whole early life had been a lie. That he had been born someone else and not Robert Andrews as he'd always thought.

Daphne had said that whatever the outcome of their investigation, she didn't want to renew their relationship. But if by some miracle it turned out they weren't related, then he hoped to eventually persuade her to marry him. He knew this was a pipe dream, as what girl would want to tie herself to a man with his background? However, he wasn't going to give up as long as there was the faintest chance she'd come back to him.

He'd wanted a week off to begin his investigation, but three days was better than nothing. There was going to be some sort of social event at the village hall in Stodham tomorrow afternoon and everybody on the base intended to go. This sort of thing didn't interest him, so he'd never attended, but now things were different. This Saturday, he had an ulterior motive.

Perhaps it might be sensible to avoid meeting Daphne, but he wasn't going to miss an opportunity to speak to her. It had been she who'd suggested there could be reason to doubt the information and discussing this would be an excuse to talk to her.

As Bob collected his bicycle, someone called his name. It was the Home Guard captain.

'I say, Corporal Andrews, good news. Those German pilots were hiding in the cellar at Goodwill House. They've been apprehended. I thought you'd like to know.'

'Thank you for taking the time to inform me in person. One less thing to worry about.'

There was an ancient three-ton lorry on the base and those without their own transport piled in for the short ride to the village the next afternoon. Only two poor sods were left to man the telephones – everybody else was off for a knees-up.

As he had a motorbike, Bob could make his own way and return whenever he wanted. Several others were cycling and he swerved around them, inadvertently revving the engine noisily and causing two of them to wobble into the ditch.

He glanced over his shoulder to check the unfortunates were unharmed and then continued on his way. There was no ill feeling and the blokes were laughing. He arrived at the village hall a few moments after the local bus had disgorged a lot of eager partygoers.

There were a dozen land girls dressed in far from flattering beige dungarees and short-sleeved shirts. The glorious red hair of his quarry was easily identified amongst the group. He let them go into the hall before parking his bike out of the way.

There was a steady stream of villagers, families with children, older couples, and singletons as well as brown jobs – whom he viewed with disfavour, as there'd been a fight last time the RAF and army had met at one of these dos.

He dropped his shilling into the saucer and was about to make his way through the open doors into the hall itself when one of the ladies sitting behind the trestle table stopped him.

'Young man, what a coincidence. Your colouring is most unusual and yet today we have two of you here with identical russet hair and green eyes.'

'Is that so? I can't wait to meet this person.' He hurried past, not wishing to continue the conversation, as he could guess what the woman was thinking, and she might exclaim loudly that he and Daphne could be brother and sister. Red hair wasn't that uncommon, but the conker-colour and green eyes he shared with Daphne was.

He wasn't sure what to expect of this occasion and had expected there to be dancing, but the hall had been laid out with tables and people were settling down around them. As he dithered, not sure where he should sit or what to expect, the contingent from the base turned up.

'Crikey, it's a beetle drive. I've not been to one of those since I was a nipper,' Chalky said happily.

'A beetle drive? Never heard of one, but I'm ready to give it a go.' His mate explained they had to roll a dice and each number corresponded to a part of a beetle. He didn't follow this until he was seated and saw he had three sheets of paper, each with a hand-drawn picture of a beetle and each part of the beetle had been designated a number.

'Right – how does this work when there are so many tables doing the same thing?'

'The first one to cross off all the body parts yells *beetle*, and that person is the winner of that round. We're obviously going to have three rounds.'

'That won't last all afternoon, so what do we do after that?'

A stout lady sitting at the next table overheard his question. 'Then we clear the tables and we have party games. After that, there's tea and biscuits and then someone plays the piano and there are a few country dances.'

'Thank you, ma'am. Sounds like a fun afternoon.'

He couldn't see Daphne from where he was sitting, but just knowing she was in the same space as him was enough for the moment.

8

Daphne would never have agreed to go to the village hall if she'd known that Bob would be there. It wasn't that she didn't want to speak to him – although they hadn't made any definite plans to try to find out the truth, meeting again at some point was implied.

The fact that all the girls had been given a Saturday afternoon off to attend the event was nothing short of miraculous, and she was determined to enjoy herself and ignore him.

'This is a bit of all right,' Sal said as she gazed around the packed hall. 'I ain't never been to somethink like this. Never heard of a beetle drive but it sounds like a laugh.'

'The new area organiser, this Mrs Ramsbottom, is an absolute treasure,' Charlie said. 'It's her that's ensured that we have a few hours off. I know it says in the handbook we're entitled to time off every week but none of us have had any until today.'

'Even the girls working on the dairy farm are here,' Daphne said. 'It's about time we got what we're entitled to.'

Jill, a tall fair girl who worked on one of the market gardens, nodded. 'Don't forget, Daphne, that we'll have far more free time in the winter, as the days are shorter and there isn't as much to do.'

'That's true, but it's only right we get at least an afternoon free every week in the summer. Do you think we'll be laid off when there's no work? I can't see Mr Pickering wanting to pay us for doing nothing.'

A jolly lady in a floral dress that looked as if it had been made from a pair of curtains rang a bell from the dais at the front of the hall. 'Attention, everybody, it's time to start. You all know the rules – as soon as anybody on your table completes a beetle, they must shout out. Good luck.' She rang the bell a second time and Sybil – another market gardener – snatched the dice and rolled it.

Every table had six players, which made it fair, as they all got the same number of turns. For a while, Daphne thought she might be in with a chance, as she'd crossed off something every go. Then she had to roll several ones to complete the legs and she missed out every time.

Then a familiar voice yelled, 'Beetle!' Bob was the winner. The fact that he had to then walk to the front of the stage and receive his prize meant everybody could see him. It was as if every eye in the room turned to look at her and draw possibly correct conclusions.

'I say, Daphne, two redheads in here today. That's unusual,' Sybil said.

'Red hair and green eyes are not that unusual. I expect they both have Scottish or Irish ancestry,' Charlie replied.

Daphne smiled her thanks and was glad the bell rang for the second round. Nobody on their table won but they all had a good time. Whilst willing helpers were moving the tables to the edge of the hall ready for the party games, she slipped out. She'd managed to whisper to Charlie that she was going to leave, and her friend had understood.

It was a relief to be away from what felt like a hundred pairs of eyes looking at her, speculating. This was nonsense, of course, and she wished that Bob hadn't decided to attend. She'd been rather enjoying the event and without his presence would definitely have stayed until the end.

She had a choice to make. She could walk home and probably arrive at the same time as the next bus and save herself the fare or go to the café and have a cup of tea as she waited. She decided on the latter, but was disappointed to find the café closed. She supposed the owners were also at the village event. The streets were deserted, but from the noise coming from the nearest pub, it was doing a brisk trade.

Going into a public house unaccompanied was something she'd never do, so she'd no option but to start walking.

'Hang on, Daphne, let's get a drink. We need to talk.' Bob rushed up to her and although she'd intended to refuse, she found herself doing the exact opposite.

'All right, we do need to talk. Did you find it uncomfortable being stared at?'

He looked puzzled. 'Stared at? Wasn't aware anybody was staring at me.' Then he understood and nodded.

'Yes, someone on my table pointed out our red hair,' Daphne said.

'I'm sorry, I ruined your afternoon off. I don't suppose you get many of them.'

'This is the first. I really don't want to go into the pub. I'm going to walk back to Goodwill House.'

'Let me give you a lift. It won't be the first time you've travelled on the back of my motorbike.'

'It would be silly of me to refuse. Thank you.'

* * *

Travelling at speed through the countryside reminded Daphne of the many occasions Bob had taken her out of Chelmsford for a picnic. With her face pressed against his shoulder, her arms around his waist, for a few moments she could forget the reason they were no longer together.

They were back in no time, and she rather wished the ride had gone on for longer. She hopped off the back, and was about to say goodbye as she expected him to remain on the bike and drive away. Instead, he turned off the engine and put the bike on its stand.

'We still need to talk. Is there somewhere we can go?'

'There's a summerhouse we use sometimes as an air-raid shelter – we could go there.'

Daphne led the way and he followed without comment. He carried two scruffy wooden chairs out into the dappled shade of the overhanging trees and, with some reluctance, she joined him there.

'I've got three days' leave when I finish here. I'm going to speak to my mother and then try and find my birth mother.'

'I thought I'd try to wangle a day – say my father's ill or something – and speak to him about his affair. He won't like it, but he owes it to us to tell us the details.' She couldn't stop herself smiling. 'I'm beginning to think there's a slight chance we got this all wrong. Even if we don't get engaged again or anything like that, I'll be much happier knowing we weren't doing something wrong all those years.'

'I don't want you to get your hopes up,' Bob said. 'We have to be realistic, don't we? We look like close relations and there's no getting away from that.'

'Think about it – my being here is a coincidence, but do you really think we'd both be involved in a second one? My father had an affair, his mistress had a baby – that baby supposedly being you – and then your family moved into the same street as us and we fell in love. I just don't believe it.' As she spoke, things had begun to make sense in her head. They'd both jumped to a conclusion that could well be wrong.

'When you put it like that, it does sound highly unlikely. But we won't know the truth until we speak to the people concerned. That will have to wait until I get some leave in a couple of weeks. I'm glad you agreed to talk to me. Let's hope we can get to the bottom of this and be able to move on with our lives.'

* * *

Joanna was enjoying the peace in the house with only herself and Elizabeth at home. Everyone else had gone to Stodham for the event in the village hall, but it didn't appeal to Joanna. Spending it quietly with her mother-in-law was a far better option.

'Joanna, my dear, you're daydreaming. I've asked you twice if you'd be kind enough to fetch my spectacles. They are in my bedroom on the side table.'

'Yes, I'm sorry, I was just enjoying the silence in the house. It's always so noisy nowadays.'

Elizabeth snorted. 'I thought you wanted a house full of young ladies. Too late to repine, my dear. We've got them here for the duration.'

'I did, I do—' Her next words were drowned out as the house shook and the windows rattled as at least two full squadrons of fighters screamed overhead. She waited until they'd gone. 'Actually, I was thinking that being so close to the base, even when it's not fully operational, isn't pleasant. If the money stolen from us is returned, then what would you think about moving somewhere quieter and smaller until the war's over?'

'Move from Goodwill House? I should think not. Harcourts have lived here for centuries, and I intend to die here.'

'That won't be for a decade or more, but neither of us were born a Harcourt, so I can't see it matters where we end up. We won't be moving for a while, but quite possibly in a year or so. I'll fetch your glasses and then collect the afternoon tea Jean has prepared for us.'

Joanna disliked walking through the hall, as with boarded windows, it was gloomy. Despite every effort, her shoes still crunched on stray bits of broken glass that had somehow escaped the clean-up.

The front door was left open when it was fine, as the plaster needed to dry out completely from the soaking it had had when the Victorian wing had caught fire a few weeks ago. She paused at the door and looked out at the empty potato field. This had once been the park belonging to Goodwill House but was now arable land.

Meeting John, seeing the world from someone else's viewpoint, had changed her. If David hadn't died at Dunkirk, then she'd have spent the remainder of her life here without complaint. This wasn't her home, it had been his and was now Sarah's. But her daughter had told her she had no intention of living here, so why stay?

She was glad the crashed German bomber had been removed. Every scrap of metal was needed for recycling. She smiled wryly at the thought that a German plane could well become part of a British fighter or bomber at some point.

As she watched, a motorbike turned onto the drive. For a second, her pulse leapt, as John had ridden a big bike like this one. How was he? Did he miss her as much as she missed him? Then she saw it was the corporal, and Daphne was on the pillion. They vanished past the side of the house and she thought they might be coming in.

Glasses. She'd better retrieve them before she went to greet these unexpected arrivals. After handing the glasses over to Elizabeth, she hurried to the kitchen, expecting to find Daphne and the corporal in the kitchen, but it was empty. How odd – where had they gone?

She tipped the boiling water into the waiting teapot, removed the damp tea towel from the sandwiches, and took two jam tarts from the cake tin. After checking the tray was arranged attractively, she carried it into the sitting room.

'I wish we could use the terrace, Joanna, it's rather dull remaining in here all day.'

'There's no reason we can't sit outside if that's what you want, Elizabeth. I warn you, though, it's noisy with all the planes flying overhead.'

'I rather like to watch them. The Spitfires are so elegant. Like big silver birds in the sky.'

'Come along then. I'll take the tea. Can you manage?'

'Don't fuss, Joanna,' Elizabeth said. 'I'm old but quite capable of walking from here to the terrace without falling on my face.'

This proved to be the case and soon they were both comfortably settled on the terrace.

'Look, Joanna, there are people in our summerhouse. Whoever can they be?'

'It's Daphne and the RAF corporal with red hair. I saw them arrive a while ago.'

'You should have invited them in for tea. Do you think they could be related, as they certainly look very similar?'

'A lot of people have red hair, Elizabeth, so I think it very unlikely two strangers would turn out to have a family connection.'

This house, the grounds, the estates had become a burden. No one would buy the house, but perhaps she could give it to the War Office to use for officers, a convalescent home for wounded servicemen, something like that. Elizabeth might think she never wanted to leave Goodwill House but once established in a warmer, smaller home she'd soon realise the benefits. It would have to be a house big enough for Jean, the twins, Elizabeth and herself.

'What are you daydreaming about, Joanna?'

'I was thinking that we'd all be so much cosier elsewhere.

However, before you get agitated, we're not going anywhere unless the land girls are moved.'

* * *

Joanna was chairing a WVS meeting a few days later at which a discussion about sending further aid parcels to those living in the tunnels in Ramsgate was taking place.

'Lady Harcourt,' Mrs Thomas boomed from the rear of the hall, 'have you been down in the tunnels to see what else we might supply?'

'I have and it was quite extraordinary. People who lost their homes in the raid have brought down what furniture they had left and have made themselves a home. I saw double beds, sideboards, chests of drawers and armchairs in various curtained-off rooms throughout the tunnels. I think it's going to be like an underground town by the time they've finished.'

'Quite extraordinary – I can't imagine living like a troglodyte, whatever the circumstances. I think I'd rather pitch a tent in a field than live in a tunnel underground,' the redoubtable lady said firmly.

There was a chorus of agreement, and the consensus was that they didn't envy the townsfolk of Ramsgate their new accommodation. Joanna thought the people of Ramsgate had the right idea – the town engineer and the mayor who had devised this brilliant scheme were to be applauded.

The WI meeting that followed was mercifully brief and Joanna, Liza and Jean were able to troop out of the village hall in good time to catch the four o'clock bus.

* * *

'Look, Ma, Grandma is on the front step waving at us.'

Joanna raised her hand, acknowledging the old lady. It wasn't at all like her mother-in-law to show such enthusiasm and she hoped this wasn't another episode. Thankfully the bouts of confusion and wandering off had been less frequent lately.

'You two nip around to the back; I'll see what she wants.'

Elizabeth was waving something which looked like long, cream, important-looking envelopes.

'What have you got there? Is that addressed to me or to you?'

'They are for you. I've been sorely tempted to open them but have refrained. Hurry up, my dear, and tell me what is contained within them.'

'Let's sit on the terrace in the shade and then I'll do so.' Joanna put down her handbag, smoothed the skirt of her navy-blue frock under her bottom, and sat down. Elizabeth plonked herself on the nearest chair with scant regard for the creases she was going to get in her skirt.

'Oh, do hurry up, Joanna, the suspense is all but killing me.'

The first envelope contained a neatly typed letter from a man she'd never heard of writing on behalf of a bank she also didn't recognise. She quickly scanned the contents and sat back, her mouth slack, unable to quite grasp what she'd just read.

After taking a steadying breath, she turned to Elizabeth. 'The money stolen from the estate has been returned with interest by this bank. It seems that they have accepted full responsibility for the theft, as they own the bank in Ramsgate.'

'My word, I didn't expect to hear anything so soon. Forgive me for asking such a vulgar question, my dear, but exactly how rich are you now?'

'I've more than enough to keep us in absolute luxury. Here, read the letter for yourself. I'll be back in a moment with your tea and we can discuss it further.'

Fortunately, she wasn't asked to open the second letter in front of her companion, as this was even more perplexing. It wasn't from the bank – in fact, it wasn't anything to do with the stolen money. It was from a legal firm in London. They said they wished to speak to her in person urgently and wished to call on her at her earliest convenience.

She stared at the page and the words danced before her eyes. What possible reason could these lawyers have for wishing to speak to her? The telephone number was under the address and she asked the operator to connect her.

The person who signed the letter, she was told, wasn't available as he was out of town and there was nobody else who could help with her enquiry. She was told that his secretary would telephone her the following morning to make an appointment. Frustrated and annoyed, she replaced the receiver.

What this Giles Hoskins Esquire wanted would have to remain a mystery until the morning. There was nothing else she could do but contain her impatience and curiosity until the wretched man was back at his desk.

She hoped Elizabeth would forget about the second letter as she'd no intention of worrying her elderly relative. On returning with the tea tray, Joanna explained what she intended to do now she had more than enough in the bank to do whatever she wanted.

'I don't care how much it costs; I'm going to get the windows repaired so we can use the rest of the house. Is there anything you'd particularly like?'

'I miss having Jean looking after me. Do you think you could make enquiries in the village and see if there might be a suitable person to take Jean's place? I would much rather have somebody of my own, who is being paid, to do the menial tasks than relying on you and Liza to do them for me.'

'I'll look into it. Would you want them to live in or come each day?'

'I would prefer them to live in, but I fear there isn't enough room for them with the main bedrooms being out of service. However, once you can get the windows replaced, then things will be back to normal.'

Could things ever be normal with a war on? Joanna nodded, but until she knew the significance of the second letter, she couldn't really concentrate on anything else.

9

Daphne had been so busy on the farm, harvesting potatoes, weeding and hoeing between the Brussels sprouts and the mangelwurzels, that she'd scarcely had time to think about the conversation she'd had with Bob. He could have already left Manston and she wasn't sure if she was disappointed or pleased that he hadn't got in contact again. Time enough to think about him when she'd spoken to her father, and she was determined to do this at the earliest opportunity.

After a busy week, it was finally Saturday and for the second time, they all had the afternoon off. Tonight, Lord Harcourt was coming, and this meant everywhere had to be immaculate. The three ladies from the village had been busy and the parquet floor of the huge ballroom was looking super. The room was being decked out for the twins' fifteenth birthday party. All the girls had been invited on the understanding that they mucked in and helped get things ready.

'Daphne,' Charlie called out as she balanced perilously on top of a rickety stepladder. 'Do these balloons look all right here or should I move them to the other corner?'

'They look absolutely spiffing exactly where they are.' Daphne looked around the room, checking everything was in place. 'I bet this ballroom could tell a few tales of extravagant parties over the centuries. I bet having one for the twins will seem like a lowering of standards to the ghosts of Goodwill House.'

'Crikey, Daphne, don't talk about ghosts. I've seen me fair share of them in the past and I ain't keen to see no more,' Sal said as she attached the end of a paper streamer to the wall.

'You never mentioned that you'd seen a ghost. Do tell.' Charlie jumped to the floor and came across, her face alight with interest. 'I'd love to see a ghost. I've always said that if one believes in the Almighty, then it's perfectly reasonable to believe in ghosts.'

Fortunately, the three of them were alone in the ballroom as they'd volunteered to give up their precious afternoon to decorate in readiness for the event this evening. Talking about spectres with such enthusiasm might have upset some of the others – two of the girls were very religious.

'It'll be the beginning of October next Tuesday,' Daphne said hurriedly, not keen to talk about anything supernatural. 'Why don't you leave your ghost stories until All Saints Day? In my opinion, that's the proper time for spooky stories.'

'When's that? I ain't never heard of it,' Sal said.

'It's 1 November – and ghosts are supposed to appear the night before. I'm not especially superstitious, but I'd never go in a churchyard on that night. Why don't we get together and share ghost stories then?'

Charlie nodded. 'That's a terrific idea, Daphne. I love being scared out of my wits by tales of the unknown.' She gathered up the bits of dropped string and spare streamers before continuing. 'I wonder if there have ever been ghosts seen or heard here? Parts of this building are hundreds of years old – I think where we sleep was built in Tudor times. If we're going to go ghost hunting, then the attics above our bedrooms would be the best place to start.'

The conversation was interrupted by the arrival of Lady Harcourt, who came in to see how they were progressing. 'That looks absolutely wonderful, girls, very celebratory. There will be seven adults – not counting the twelve of you, of course – plus eight youngsters. Would you mind making sure we have enough seats and tables?'

'There's thirty chairs and eight tables, my lady, so I think we've got that covered,' Charlie said, pointing at the arrangement.

'Splendid, I knew I could rely on you three. By the way, I've managed to find a glazier and all being well, in the next week or two, every window will be replaced, which means you can move back to your original bedroom.'

'That's grand, thank you, Lady Harcourt, our original room was twice the size of the one we've got now,' Daphne said.

'Good show. Jean's organising the catering, as you know, so you can leave the buffet table to her. It's going to be such fun and I do wish my older daughter, Sarah, had been able to get time off from her studies and come too. She was eighteen last week.'

'I reckon she'd rather be here than in London, my lady. It ain't too clever there with all them bombs being dropped,' Sal said.

Her friend was about to continue, but Daphne shook her head, and fortunately Sal understood.

'Sarah's determined to remain at the Royal Free,' Joanna said. 'I just wish she could transfer somewhere closer to complete her studies, but she's an adult now and must make her own decisions.'

Lady Harcourt walked out and Charlie immediately ticked Sal off for being so tactless. 'Really, you should have thought before you jumped in with both feet. I'm sure Lady Harcourt doesn't need reminding how dangerous it is for her daughter to be working there.'

'Sorry, me and me big mouth,' Sal said. 'Have we done here? It looks ever so nice, don't it?'

'It certainly does. Daphne, did you check we've got a good selection of records to play for the party games and the dancing later?'

'I did, but I'll do it again if you like.'

'No, of course not. I'm being rather bossy, aren't I?'

Daphne and Sal exchanged a glance. 'Just a bit, but we love you anyway,' Daphne said with a smile.

'I'm a bit on edge, as this will be the first time I've seen James – I suppose I should now think of him as Dr Willoughby again – since I stayed there. I'm sure I wasn't imagining the connection between us, and I just don't understand why he hasn't spoken to me since,' Charlie said.

'If I was you, I would just behave as you did before you stayed there. Treat him formally, after all, he is our doctor. You've no need to be nervous or embarrassed. I just put it down to the fact that you were in such close contact. After all, you're a very pretty young woman and he's a man in his prime. I'm not surprised he flirted with you.'

'Thanks for your words of wisdom, Daphne, I'll do as you suggest and pretend nothing happened. Actually, nothing did really happen apart from spending time with him. He didn't make any physical advances and to tell you the truth, I was pleased that he didn't.'

There was no time to continue this interesting conversation as they heard Lord Harcourt's voice in the grand hall.

'Come on, let's go out of the French doors. That man's absolutely terrifying. He just has to look in my direction and my knees start knocking,' Daphne said as she led the way to the far end of the ballroom.

* * *

Joanna had sent the twins into the village so that they didn't see the party preparations. They would spend time with their friends and then would cycle back with four of the youngsters who lived in Stodham. The other four came from the opposite direction – no doubt they would cycle or walk to Goodwill House later.

Liza and Joe hadn't wanted any gifts, as they'd said they'd got more than enough already. Therefore, Joanna had put a substantial amount into their post office accounts, which they were delighted with. She expected at this very moment they would be drawing some out and treating their friends to afternoon tea at the local café.

In another couple of years, Joe would probably want to spend his money in one of the public houses. They were growing up too fast and she was dreading the day when her son would receive his call-up papers.

The ballroom looked exactly as it should and she was pleased with the three girls' efforts. As she was walking down the wide passageway, she heard Peter arrive.

'Good afternoon, Lord Harcourt, thank you for coming,' she said and was tempted to curtsy but thought that would be a step too far.

'Good afternoon, Lady Harcourt, I'm delighted to be here and thank you for inviting me.' He didn't offer his hand for her to shake, and she certainly wasn't going to step forward for him to embrace her. For a moment it was awkward, but then he laughed.

'Joanna, I managed to borrow a car but I don't have enough petrol to get back to London. I don't suppose you've got any hanging about in a corner somewhere?'

'I certainly do. There are several dozen cans full of it at the back of the barn. I don't want to be accused of holding onto something that's now rationed, so can you arrange for it to be collected?'

'Excellent, I'll fill the car up in the morning. I should hang onto the petrol. Presumably your husband bought it when it wasn't in short supply, so I don't see why his forethought should be penalised.'

'I'll stop worrying about it, then. I warn you that if anyone in authority accuses me of being a black marketeer, I'll send them directly to you.'

She rather enjoyed the verbal sparring with Peter, but he didn't interest her as a lover. Her cheeks flushed at her daring thoughts. John had changed her forever and she didn't regret their brief and passionate affair one bit.

Peter's eyes flashed dangerously. Had he misinterpreted her blush and believed it had been him that had caused her reaction? Oh dear! How could she defuse the situation without being rude? He stepped closer, and thank god, the dog bounced in, forcing him to step back hastily.

'Good boy, have you come to welcome our guest?' The dog ignored Peter, which made things a bit awkward. However, it gave Joanna the opportunity to distance herself from him.

'If you leave your overnight bag on the stairs, someone will show you to your room later. I'm afraid it's in the attic – half the bedrooms are unusable at present, as you can imagine.'

He took her cue and replied as if the moment hadn't happened. In future, she must make sure she wasn't alone with him. The fact that he was obviously interested in her was a worry but not one she was going to think about today. This evening was for her new son and daughter and she was determined that they should enjoy themselves.

* * *

Bob stood back with a sigh of satisfaction. 'That's it, our last kite ready to go. The ATA flyer's picking it up after he's delivered one from the other team.'

'A job well done, Corp, if I say so myself,' Chalky said as he too stepped away to admire their handiwork. 'We've got finished in half the time we expected. Nothing like the thought of a few days' R&R to get us going.'

Arthur had fallen off his bicycle two days ago and broken his arm and had been sent home to recuperate. Bob doubted he'd see him again. He, Chalky and Arthur had been working together for over a year and had become good friends, but the likelihood of them being posted to the same place a second time was remote.

'It's been good working with you, but it hasn't been the same since Jimmy died. I'll be glad to move on, won't you, Corp?'

'I will. I've got three days' leave as soon as this kite has gone. I'll stay – you go now. You've not seen your missus nor your kiddies for months.'

'That's good of you,' Chalky said. 'I'm already packed, and even though the bus doesn't call in here any more, I've still got my trusty bicycle. I'm not leaving it behind – they're like gold dust nowadays.'

Bob patted Chalky on the shoulder and that was that. No time for sentiment in the RAF and certainly not when there was a war on. Ground crew were the lucky ones – they didn't risk their lives every day as the flyers did.

He looked around the hangar for the last time. All the tools and unused parts were neatly boxed. The Hurry was waiting on the apron, there was nothing else to do apart from hand it over later today.

His kit was in his bag and all he had to do was attach it to the back of his motorbike. He was ready to leave Manston, possibly not for the last time but certainly for the immediate future.

He wasn't looking forward to visiting his adoptive parents – he could no longer think of them as his actual parents, which was probably irrational. They'd done a decent job of bringing him and his sister up, even if they hadn't been honest.

Not staying in contact with his sister, Mary, had been unkind, as it wasn't her fault his world had fallen apart so suddenly last year. It would have been a shock to her too and he'd not given her a second thought when he'd left. Whatever the outcome of his investigation, he would re-establish relations with his parents and his sister.

Mary was happily married to a train driver – a reserved occupation – and already had two kiddies. Had they been evacuated somewhere safer than Chelmsford as the town was perilously close to London? The Luftwaffe were making daily raids on cities all over Britain and it wouldn't be safe for women and children to remain in those places.

He'd had no contact with his family since he'd signed up last September but had stayed in occasional touch with a couple of his mates. This must have been how Daphne had discovered his whereabouts.

They'd not met since the social ten days ago, but he wasn't too worried about that. He might be leaving Stodham, but she was ensconced at Goodwill House for the duration and would be easy enough to get in contact with when he had some information.

The ATA bloke turned up as planned and Bob was able to load his bike and leave Manston by seven. As he passed the end of the drive that led to Goodwill House, some perverse instinct made him turn in and cruise up to the house. To his surprise, there were two cars and a pile of discarded bicycles already parked outside.

The front door was open and the sound of music and laughter drifted out. He certainly wasn't going to barge in unannounced and uninvited and was in the process of turning his motorbike when someone called out from the terrace.

'Young man, don't go. They are desperately short of males in the ballroom. I assume you can dance?'

He looked around and didn't see the speaker at first. Then he saw the old Lady Harcourt peering over the balustrade on the terrace above him. He grinned. 'I'm not invited, my lady. I just called in to say goodbye to my friend, Daphne.'

'Nonsense, young man. I'm inviting you, so come up here at once. Leave that noisy monstrosity with the other vehicles and escort me inside.'

He didn't need asking twice. Why not join in? Would he be the only one in uniform? He grinned. The land girls would be wearing dungarees or breeches, so perhaps not. The old lady beamed at him as if he was indeed a welcome guest and not an intruder at a private party.

'Excellent. Don't I know you?'

'You do, ma'am. I'm Corporal Andrews and I was here a couple of weeks ago when the German bomber crashed in the field.'

'One man in RAF uniform looks very much like another to me, but your extraordinary hair makes you memorable. We have a land girl with similar colouring. Are you related?'

'No, ma'am, but we are friends.'

'Come along, I want to rejoin the party. It's my adopted grand-children's fifteenth birthday celebration.'

The old lady directed him to the other side of the huge building and into a wide corridor that led to what had to be the ballroom. He stared around in awe. Imagine being so rich you had a special place to hold a dance.

'Here we are, thank you for your escort.' She released her grip on his arm and left him marooned in a room full of strangers. He squared his shoulders and fixed on a smile. He'd had bombs dropped on him and not flinched so wasn't going to be fazed by a load of posh folk.

'Good heavens, Bob, what are you doing here?' Charlie said as she came over to him. Her plummy voice carried and if he'd not been noticed before, now he was the centre of attention.

'Lady Harcourt, the senior one, dragged me in. I just came to say goodbye to Daphne and was about to leave when I was stopped.'

'Don't look so apprehensive, Bob, another man is always appreciated at a dance.' Imperiously she held out her hand and he'd no option but to take it. Thank god he was a decent dancer and wouldn't make a fool of himself.

He kept his eyes firmly on his partner, not daring to look around for the person he'd come to see. The record was a recent one from Glen Miller and perfect for a quickstep. He swept Charlie around the floor and was relaxed and enjoying himself by the end of the dance.

'Thank you, Bob, you're an excellent dancer.'

'I enjoyed it. I think I'd better apologise to Lady Harcourt junior for coming in uninvited.'

'She's dancing with the local doctor and I doubt she's even aware that you're here. However, Daphne has seen you and is on her way over.'

He turned and this time his smile was genuine. Even in brown dungarees, she looked stunning. 'I'm sorry, Daphne, I've finished my work at Manston and am on my way to Chelmsford. I've got three days' leave. I just came to tell you and got dragged in.'

'I'm coming with you. No, don't argue, I've got until tomorrow lunchtime free. Wait for me in the hall and I'll grab what I need.'

She was gone before he'd time to digest what she'd said. He'd come to say goodbye and instead he was taking her away with him. It made sense for them to go together but it was going to be torture being with her in the circumstances.

10

Daphne raced upstairs and threw the necessities for an overnight stay into her haversack. She was about to fly back downstairs when she hesitated. Did she really want to go with Bob? Travelling on the back of his bike for so many miles would be like the old days – would it reignite the same feelings she'd had for him back then?

It was the work of moments to change into her breeches, socks and brogues and then add the long-sleeved shirt, smart green jumper and tie. She wasn't keen on the porkpie hat but put that on as well. She was proud of her uniform and wanted her mum to see her in it.

Whatever the outcome, she couldn't miss this golden opportunity to go home. Her brother was overseas with the army and she'd never been close to her father. Mum, however, was someone she adored. If she had time, she'd go to Romford and visit her grandparents in the hope that they might be able to throw light on this mystery.

Mr Pickering was happy for her to go to matins on a Sunday morning as long as the three of them were there by midday to work. Bob would have to bring her back if she was to get to work on time. Her heart skipped a beat and a rush of excitement ran through her. Would she still be able to remain aloof from him if the reason for them being apart proved false?

He was waiting at the bottom of the stairs with his endearing, lopsided smile. 'Are you going to tell your mates that you're going?'

'No. As long as I'm back for work by midday tomorrow, I'm not breaking any rules. It's not like the armed forces, we can come and go as we please but would get the sack if we missed a day without permission. I'm hoping you'll be kind enough to bring me back.'

'I will, I've got three days before I have to report in Ashford. Let's hope I can get a tankful of petrol somewhere.'

'I'm sure Lady Harcourt will let you fill up here – she's got dozens of cans of the stuff stored at the back of the barn.'

'Then that solves one problem. Aren't you going to change into civvies?'

'I've changed into my best uniform. I'm proud of what I do and am perfectly happy for others to see me in my Land Army outfit.'

'Fair enough. I think it suits you,' Bob said. 'But you really should tell somebody where you're going in case they set up a search when they can't find you this evening. I need a few minutes to rearrange things, as at the moment my kitbag is tied to the pillion.'

'All right, I'll do what you suggest.' Daphne didn't go back into the ballroom but headed for the kitchen, hoping there would be somebody there she could tell, and she was lucky as Jean was busy making extra sandwiches.

She quickly explained. 'Would you tell Charlie and Lady Harcourt for me, please? I'll be back in time for work tomorrow. I couldn't miss the chance to see my mother as I've not been home since I signed up.'

'Don't worry, I'll make sure they know. Enjoy yourself and travel safely.'

Daphne was relieved to be outside without having been seen and questioned by Charlie or Sal. Jean didn't know the circumstances, which made it easier.

Bob had rearranged things so she could fit snugly between his back and the kitbag. 'That looks really comfortable, and I'll feel much safer jammed in between you and your bag.'

'Good thing it doesn't look as if it's going to rain. I don't suppose you've got a waterproof you could bring?'

She laughed. 'Even if I did have, there wouldn't be any room for it. I'm going to stuff my overnight bag in the pannier. I can remember telling you to get them and you finally did it.'

'And I recall that I usually ignored your suggestions as often as you made them.' He grinned, kickstarted the motorbike, swung his leg over and waited for her to hop on behind him. 'But as you can see, I actually did as you suggested, just this once.'

Sitting behind him her arms tight around his waist brought back happy memories. She leaned in and inhaled his familiar scent and something flickered inside.

* * *

They got through London easily enough, as there wasn't much civilian traffic now petrol was rationed. As they exited through the East End, the evidence of recent bombings was everywhere. Even so, housewives with headscarves, pushing babies in prams, seemed as cheerful as ever. East Enders were a tough lot, and a few bombs wouldn't make them give up.

Without being asked, Bob turned in to a roadside café – the sort of place that lorry drivers used. You could always get a decent cup of tea and a fry-up at one of these places and her stomach had been gurgling for some time.

'I need to find the Ladies'.' She giggled at his horrified expression. 'I know what it'll be like, but needs must. I can hardly nip behind one of those lorries like you can.'

She was obliged to hold her breath the entire time, but she would have burst if she'd not gone. He was waiting outside, trying not to laugh, and handed her a damp handkerchief. She didn't ask where he'd found the water.

'Here you are, you can wash your hands with this. I did as you suggest so don't have to brave that place myself.'

As expected, she was the only female customer in the café, but there were two waitresses, so she didn't feel too out of place. The food was hot, well cooked, and extremely good value. They didn't linger, but quickly cleared their plates, drank their mugs of tea, and headed out to the motorbike. Bob had parked it where he could keep an eye on it, which was a sensible move.

They travelled through the Essex countryside, through Shenfield and Ingatestone and entered Chelmsford along the familiar Moulsham Street. Bob turned left into Grove Road and her hands tightened around his waist. They would be in Mildmay Road in a minute or two, which was where both of them had lived until last year.

He sensed her agitation and coasted to a stop. He put his boots down to balance the bike and spoke without looking round. 'Are you sure you want to do this? I need to speak to my adoptive parents but...'

'No, I really want to get this sorted out. My worry is that talking about what happened all those years ago will just make it worse between my parents. I don't want to be the cause of them separating.'

'If they were going to do that, wouldn't they have done it years ago? I can take you to Romford and we'll go and see your grandparents together. That might be the best move.'

The constriction around her chest eased. 'Would you do that

for me? Yes, let's go back to Romford. Do you have enough petrol for all this shilly-shallying?'

'This is a very economical vehicle and I'll be absolutely tickety-boo until we get back to Stodham tomorrow.'

Joanna danced with Dr Willoughby once, as to not do so would have seemed ungracious. After that, she left him to the mercies of the land girls, who were overjoyed to have him partner them. Elizabeth had only remained in the ballroom for half an hour and then disappeared to return with the redheaded RAF corporal – goodness knows where she'd found him.

Peter had insisted he didn't dance and none of the girls dared to approach him. Mr Evans and the youngsters were much in demand.

The new arrival was immediately pounced upon by Charlie and acquitted himself creditably in a quickstep before he too abandoned the party, followed almost immediately by Daphne. Jean, bless her, had gone to the kitchen to replenish the buffet, which, although plentiful, had already been almost demolished by the ravages of the guests.

She wasn't sure who ate the most – the land girls or the youngsters.

'My lady,' Jean said a few minutes later, 'Daphne asked me to tell you that she's gone with that friend of hers to visit her mother. It seems he's finished at Manston and just called in to say goodbye.'

'That makes perfect sense. They grew up in the same street, so if he's returning to his family, then of course she'd take this opportunity to do the same. I'm assuming the young man will have her here in time for work tomorrow.'

Jean nodded whilst tapping her foot in time to the jolly music.

'Everybody's having a grand time. Lord Harcourt seems to be enjoying himself, despite not wishing to join in the dancing.'

'He certainly cuts a dashing figure in his uniform,' Joanna said. 'I don't think anybody's going to want to play party games, do you?'

'Don't give them a choice, just stop the music.'

This seemed rather unkind and Joanna wasn't prepared to interrupt the dancing. Then Peter arrived at her side.

'I hope the dancing is over. It's worse than doing hours of drill on a wet day in November.'

She laughed. 'You could have made a lot of girls very happy, but instead you left it to the vicar and the doctor. But I'm going to take pity on them. I've no wish to have the demise of the two who did participate on my conscience.'

Dr Willoughby was certainly looking rather flushed from all the exertion, and the vicar had collapsed, mopping his brow, at one of the tables.

She beckoned to Joe, who happened to look in her direction at just the right time. He grinned, appeared to be apologising to his partner, and then came across to speak to her.

'Please can we stop the music and have some quiet time before the older members of this party are reduced to a puddle?'

'Fair enough. It should have been party games immediately after tea. I'll get it organised now. Blind Man's Buff, Musical Chairs or Postman's Knock?'

'Good heavens, not Postman's Knock. Isn't that the game which involves a lot of kissing?'

'Pity, I think most of the land girls would be only too happy to kiss Lord Harcourt.' He grinned and walked over to the record player. He lifted the needle from the record and blissful silence descended.

Joanna had expected a chorus of protest, but instead there was a rush to the table where fruit punch and lemonade were being served. Joe let the noise subside before he banged the gong that many years ago had summoned the family to dinner. As the noise reverberated around the ballroom, the excited chatter stopped.

'Right, that's the dancing done. Now it's a game of musical chairs and then it'll be time to call it a night. Liza and I want to thank everybody for coming and making our birthday memorable. This is the first birthday party we've ever had, and we'll never forget it.'

There was a spontaneous round of applause and then Charlie organised some of the girls to set out half a dozen chairs facing in one direction and a similar number facing the opposite way.

Joanna was weak from laughing by the time the eventual winner was proclaimed.

* * *

Even with the extra hour, it would be dark soon, and Joanna wanted Liza and Joe's friends to be home by then.

The boarders, true to their word, started clearing up and she was confident the house would be back to normal before anybody retired. The vicar and his wife had come with the doctor and the three of them left, obviously having thoroughly enjoyed themselves like everybody else present.

Liza and Joe were escorting their friends to the end of the drive and Jean was supervising in the kitchen, which left Peter and Joanna to their own devices. Elizabeth had retired long ago.

'Jean's making us a pot of coffee and I've got half a bottle of excellent cognac. Would you care to join me on the terrace to share both?' she said.

'I certainly would. A stiff drink is exactly what I need. Thank you for inviting me – despite my whining, I've thoroughly enjoyed myself.'

'Thank you for coming, and the two boxes of biscuits you contributed were the most popular items on the buffet table.'

'I rather think the Harrods label made them seem better than they were.'

He insisted on carrying the tray and she led the way onto the terrace, smiling as she heard the voices of the young people walking together down the drive. Lazzy had gone with them and she could see him bouncing about, happy to be part of the group.

Peter poured out the coffee without being asked, handed hers over and then tipped a liberal amount of cognac into each glass. 'Here you are, you deserve it. This is the happiest house I've ever been in and it's all down to you.'

'Thank you, I appreciate you saying that,' Joanna said. 'Actually, there are one or two things I want to discuss with you. I'm so glad I've got somebody I can talk to about this sort of thing.'

He was alert, listening intently as she told him first about the good news from the bank and then about the mysterious letter from this Mr Hoskins.

'When's he coming? I might be able to wangle a day off and be here, if that would help.'

'His secretary contacted me this morning and he's coming on Monday. I'm none the wiser as to the reason for his visit.' She swallowed a warming mouthful of the brandy and closed her eyes to savour the heat as it trickled down her throat. 'Thank you for offering to come, but that's not necessary.'

'Why don't you get your solicitor, that Broome chap, to come? Never hurts to have a legal bod at your side.'

'I hadn't thought of that and it's the perfect answer. I will ring him first thing tomorrow. I hope, in the circumstances, he won't object to me calling him on a Sunday.'

* * *

Bob didn't need to ask for directions as he'd gone with Daphne many times whilst they were courting to visit her grandparents, Mabel and Alf Ransom. He liked the old couple, who were fiercely independent, and last time he'd seen them, about two years ago, Alf had still been working in Romford market on his tropical fish stall. The old bloke must be in his eighties – if he wasn't, then he certainly looked it.

It wasn't far from Chelmsford to Romford, no more than eighteen miles or thereabouts. He travelled down Roman Road, turned into Coatleigh Road and then first right into Honiton Road where the old couple lived.

They had a three-bedroomed detached house with a small front garden and a decent-sized one at the back that was more than big enough to grow vegetables and keep a few chickens. Alf had done well for himself, as well as inheriting a fair bit from a distant relative, and their house was a lot grander than the one that Daphne's parents lived in. It must have been a bit of a let-down for Mrs Taylor when she'd married Daphne's dad.

'Here we are, let's hope they haven't gone to bed,' he said cheerfully as he pulled up at the kerb in front of the house.

'Good heavens, Nanna and Grandpa won't be in bed yet, it's not quite seven o'clock,' Daphne said. 'I've been writing to them once a month and I know they'll be delighted to see us – well – to see me, anyway. I can't guarantee they won't refuse to let you over the doorstep.'

'Then I'd better wait here until you say it's safe to come in.'

She smiled but didn't disagree. 'They'll be in the kitchen listening to the wireless, but I expect they'll hear me when I knock.'

'Will they let us stay the night? I think it's a bit late to find a B&B on a Saturday night.'

'I hope so.' She rushed off up the immaculately weeded front path and he perched on the seat of his bike and waited to see what sort of reception she got.

After a few minutes, the door opened and Mrs Ransom appeared. He thought the entire street would have heard the old woman's squeal of delight when she saw her granddaughter. Seeing the two of them hugging made him regret that he'd abandoned his own family so readily last year.

The old lady yelled from the doorstep, 'Don't hang about out there, Bob, come in, why don't you?'

He waved his thanks, collected Daphne's overnight bag and his kitbag, and strode to the front door, which had been left open for him. He stepped in and inhaled the familiar aroma of pipe smoke, lavender water and cake. Mabel always had a cake available for guests, though god knows where she found the ingredients nowadays.

The front parlour was on the right – this was never used apart from for funerals, weddings and baptisms – on the left was the sitting room and directly ahead were the stairs leading up to the bedrooms. This house had indoor plumbing and a bathroom, which was a real luxury.

Alf appeared in the kitchen door, which was at the end of the passageway, his pipe in his hand as always. 'Good to see you, Bob lad, it's been too long. Take your things upstairs. Same rooms as usual. Ma keeps the beds made up just in case.'

'Good to see you, too, Mr Ransom, I'm sorry to come uninvited but we've things we need to ask you and I think we should have come a year ago and not left it so long.'

Bob grabbed both bags and bounded up the stairs. He and Daphne had stayed here often enough, and he knew the drill. She had the larger room that overlooked the street, and he took the box room at the back. He dumped the bags and returned to find Alf waiting for him.

'We never knew the truth of your jilting our granddaughter. Are you back together?'

'Sadly, no, but depending on what we discover from talking to you, you never know.'

The old bloke stood aside and Bob walked into the kitchen to find it empty, the door open, and only an ancient ginger cat asleep on a battered armchair.

'They'll be in the garden, son, too blooming hot in here when Ma's been baking. Nice bit of shade under the trees at the end.' He pointed to a table and four brightly painted kitchen chairs, where Daphne and her grandmother were already seated.

'They'll have tea, I'll bring us a light ale each. Too blooming hot for tea.'

Mrs Ransom, her stringy grey hair pulled up into a bun on top of her head, rushed to meet him and he was enveloped in a warm, welcoming hug.

'What a lot of nonsense, I've never heard the like. You and our Daphne, brother and sister? How stupid to think that just because you're adopted and have the same colouring you've got the same blood.'

He was surprised that Daphne had managed to explain so quickly but was relieved that she had. 'It wasn't me that thought this, Mrs Ransom, it was my mother. She'd had her suspicions ever since she saw Daphne when we moved into their street.'

'Sit down, Bob, and drink your beer. You look as if you need it. You're just the ticket in that uniform, and so is my Daphne in hers.'

'Thanks, I'm proud to be in the RAF and I know that Daphne feels the same about the Land Army.' He was glad to be talking trivialities as this gave him a few valuable moments to gather his wits.

'Daphne says her dad had an affair. First I've heard of it and I think my daughter would have told me, don't you?' Mabel was a small woman, but fierce, and you didn't upset her if you could help it.

Daphne shook her head. 'You'd have been the last person she'd have told, Nan. I was hoping you might have known the name of the woman he was involved with, but obviously not. This has been a wasted journey, Bob, I'm sorry to have dragged you here.'

'None of that, young lady, it's always a treat to see you both. Even though we can't help with your search, it's grand to have you both here,' Alf said.

'One thing I'm sure of, you're not brother and sister. It's just possible you might be second cousins or something, but nothing any closer than that.'

'I hope you're right, Nan, because neither of us likes the idea that we were doing something wrong.'

11
_____

Daphne was bitterly disappointed, as she'd pinned her hopes on her grandparents being able to give them some of the answers they so desperately wanted.

'Cheer up, Daphne love, you'll get your answers, just not from us,' her grandpa said as he took a swig of his favourite tipple.

'If you're worrying about dragging me on a wild goose chase, Daphne, then don't. I want to find out once and for all the truth of this.' Bob hesitated, as if not sure if what he was going to say would be well received. 'Look, maybe it would be better not to talk to your father at the moment. We can speak to my mother and get the details of my adoption and then go down that route.'

'That makes sense, because if I accused him of being unfaithful and he hadn't been, that would be an absolute nightmare. I have to be back at work tomorrow morning so don't have time to go with you.'

'That's not a problem. I'll take you back, fill up with petrol, and then go to Chelmsford. If I get any information that's useful, then I'll follow it up. I don't know when I'll get any leave again.'

'Do you know where you're going next?'

'Hawkinge, it's just outside Folkestone, only about twenty miles or so from Manston. As long as I've got petrol, I can get across to see you if I get a couple of hours free.'

Hornchurch base was close to Romford, so she wasn't surprised when a couple of squadrons screamed overhead. Her grandparents scarcely flinched – they just carried on sipping their drinks till the racket stopped and they could hear themselves speak again.

'Good job you're not one of those Brylcreem boys, son, you'll get through this lot without being killed.'

'I didn't have the education, or I'd have applied like a shot,' Bob said.

'I know, flyers are the bravest. Most of them seem scarcely out of short trousers, but they go up again and again knowing they might very well not come back,' Daphne said.

'Let's not talk about that. Tell me, love, what's it like working on a farm?'

Daphne was glad to change the subject and they continued to sit around the table chatting until her stomach rumbled loud enough for everyone to hear.

Nan leapt to her feet – she was remarkably spry for a lady of her age. 'What am I thinking? We've had our tea, but from the sound of it, you're both starving. How about eggs on toast followed by a slice of my cake? Having our own chickens means I've got plenty of eggs to spare.'

'That would be wonderful, Nan, we haven't eaten for hours.'

* * *

Bob delivered Daphne safely to the church by ten o'clock the following morning. He parked the bike out of sight and then told her he was actually coming in.

'I'm not religious, as you know, Daphne, but might as well sit in church with you as hang about outside.'

He followed her into the cool, gloomy interior of the parish church and several heads turned to stare, making her feel uncomfortable. She wished he'd remained with his bike.

Mr Evans, the bespectacled vicar, was popular with the parishioners, especially since he'd instigated a crèche for the little ones. His sermons were always interesting and commendably brief. They all trooped out just over an hour after entering.

Daphne hung back so she could speak to Lady Harcourt about Bob having a tankful of her spare petrol.

'Of course, he can have whatever he wants. He's exactly the sort of young man who should have access to it. How were your parents?'

Daphne was tempted to lie but didn't. 'We went to see my grandparents in Romford instead. Hopefully I'll get the chance to go to Chelmsford another time.'

She hurried off, not wanting to be waylaid by nosy villagers. Bob had the engine running and she scrambled on the pillion and they were on their way without any embarrassing comments or questions.

'The petrol's behind that big barn. Lady Harcourt said you can have whatever you need. Why don't you take a spare can? Then you can...' She'd been going to say *then he could come and see her* but stopped herself in time. Better to leave things as they were until he'd spoken to his mother.

'Can what?'

'Can use your bike as much as you want. I've got to change into my dungarees as we don't usually work in breeches and jumper.'

'Then I'll fill up and get going. Are you sure Lady Harcourt won't mind if I take an extra can?'

'I'm certain. Anyway, I'll tell her this evening. Thank you, I enjoyed seeing Nan and Grandpa. Drive carefully. Goodbye.' She raised her hand and hurried off, for some reason finding it hard to leave him. She sent up a quick prayer that Nan's prediction was correct, and she and Bob weren't closely related.

By the time the others arrived, Daphne had harnessed Star and the mare and cart were waiting to leave for Fiddler's Farm. Charlie and Sal were back in a flash and jumped into the rear of the cart.

'Good show, now we'll be in good time. It'll be hoeing and weeding in the back field I expect,' Charlie said happily. 'I love hoeing.'

'It ain't as bad as weeding, I'll give you that, but it's back-breaking work,' Sal said. 'It'll be the spuds next week and we're dab hands at that.'

Daphne had learned to drive the cart but had yet to drive the massive Shire horses. Maybe she'd get a chance when the potatoes were lifted. They arrived half an hour early and the farmer was waiting in the yard for them. When they'd first started here, Mr Pickering had been unpleasant and lazy, but now he was a changed man and couldn't be more helpful.

'Good, I was hoping you'd be early. I've got a surprise for you.'

Charlie and Sal jumped down and Daphne guided the mare into the open barn, applied the brake and then followed them. The horse would be fine as she was for a few minutes. She was as eager as them to discover what the surprise was.

'Come with me, girls,' he said and they trooped after him to the closed barn. He pulled open the double doors with a flourish.

'A tractor!' Charlie said. 'Where did you get it? How did you get it? You'll be the envy of the neighbourhood.'

The farmer beamed. 'I put in for one last year and to tell you the truth had forgotten about it until it turned up this morning. It's reconditioned – not brand new – but good enough for me.'

'Do we get a go on it?' Sal asked.

'I'll teach Charlie first and then she can show you two.'

'Does that mean you'll get rid of your horses?' Daphne would hate to think that these magnificent beasts would end up as dog meat.

'I should think not, my missus would have my guts for garters if I did. Those two are her pride and joy and were bred by her own dad. I'll do the heavy work with the tractor and keep the horses for pulling the carts.'

As there wasn't a lot to do, Pickering suggested that Charlie had her first lesson immediately. 'Will you two do the milking this afternoon? I reckon if I have an hour with Charlie, she'll be good as gold to drive it.'

'Shall we leave the hoeing until tomorrow, Mr Pickering?' Daphne said. 'Then Sal and I can take care of the livestock and the dairy work before we leave this evening.'

'Fair enough, you get on with it and I'll show Charlie how this tractor works.'

* * *

Joanna had been accompanied to church by Peter, as well as Elizabeth and the twins. He'd kindly offered to drive them in his car – he'd not brought a driver this time. On the return journey, there was the sound of snoring from the rear.

'We're home, Elizabeth, time to wake up.'

She was answered immediately. 'I wasn't asleep, Joanna, merely resting my eyes. I suppose Sunday lunch will be delayed as Jean attended church this morning.'

'I'm sure it won't be, as it's far too hot for a roast.'

Peter gallantly helped her mother-in-law out of the car whilst Joanna hurried in to make the telephone call to her solicitor as she had not done it before they'd left for church.

The operator connected her and Mr Broome answered immediately. 'Good morning, Mr Broome, I'm so sorry to call you on a Sunday but I have a dilemma and hope you can help me.' She quickly explained about this unknown person coming for a visit the following morning.

'I drive past Goodwill House on the way to the office, so it will be no imposition to call in. If he's coming so early, it must mean that either he's local or he's stayed the night in a hotel in Ramsgate.'

'Yes, Mr Broome, I thought so myself. Thank you offering to help. I must admit that I'm rather curious to know why this person is coming all the way here from a prestigious legal firm in London.'

Peter had remained on the terrace with Elizabeth and seemed to be getting on splendidly with the irascible old lady. Sitting outside was a rare treat at the moment. But there never seemed to be quite as many bombers and British fighters flying overhead on a Sunday. This might be a coincidence, but she liked to think even the Nazis – atheists, so she'd read – respected Sunday.

Jean was straining a large saucepan of potatoes in the scullery sink when Joanna went to the kitchen area to find her. 'Shall we eat outside? It won't take a moment to lay up a table and it's far too pleasant to be indoors.'

'I was thinking that myself,' Jean said. 'Joe and Liza are picking soft fruit for dessert and there's still a jug of cream left over from yesterday. The rabbit pie's done to a turn. We're having it hot, but the girls will have it cold with salad tonight.'

'It'll be delicious however we eat it. I'll do the table.'

When her husband, David, had been alive, Joanna wouldn't have dreamed of doing this. He'd expected her to be aloof from the staff and considered any domestic work beneath her. He'd been gone just over a year and, she was ashamed to admit to herself, she scarcely recalled his features or his voice now.

Peter left immediately after lunch and asked her to let him

know the reason for this visit and she promised to do so, but she didn't invite him to come down again and he didn't suggest it. He was charming, intelligent, and attractive – not to say handsome – but he didn't interest her in that way. She'd occasionally detected what might almost be called a predatory gleam in his eye when he looked at her and she didn't want to encourage him.

* * *

The following morning, Joanna dressed with more care than usual. She paused to inspect her appearance in the full-length mirror. The burgundy frock was elegant, the handmade lace collar indicated it was an expensive gown, and her smart black court shoes set the outfit off perfectly.

She was wearing a pair of her precious silk stockings and had only two other pairs in her underwear drawer; there was no chance of getting them replaced. She sincerely hoped she wouldn't be reduced to drawing a seam with gravy browning up the back of her calf as she'd seen recommended in a recent copy of *Woman's Own* – 3d well spent in her opinion. This magazine was full of excellent recipes and advice for dealing with the shortages.

Obviously, those in the bombed cities would be suffering far more deprivation than they were at Goodwill House. In fact, country dwellers had an advantage over those in towns and cities as they had access to fresh food. They were also less likely to be bombed. Her household were fortunate to have so much and she vowed to do more in future for the less well-off.

Satisfied her hair was secure in its French pleat, that her lipstick wasn't smudged, or her nose shiny, she was ready to descend. Jean had, she thought, found the perfect dresser-companion for Elizabeth and the woman was coming for an interview that afternoon.

Mr Broome arrived at the front door at the same time as she

stepped into the hall. The door was left open during the day, so he'd no need to knock. Joanna smiled a greeting at him.

'Good morning, Mr Broome, thank you again for coming.'

'I'm as intrigued as you are, my lady, and am only too happy to be of assistance whenever you require it. There are other matters I wish to discuss with you, which is why I'm so embarrassingly early.'

He must've been aware that she'd only just come down and wouldn't have had her breakfast yet. 'If you'd care to go to the study, I'm sure you remember where it is from your previous visits, then I'll collect us a tray of tea and toast.'

Jean had everything ready and Joanna carried it through. As they munched freshly made toast with far too little butter and a scraping of jam, he gave her the best possible news.

'Am I to understand, Mr Broome, that the money promised by the bank has already arrived with you?'

'It has, my lady, and you must decide how you wish to invest it. I don't advise leaving it in your bank account, as it will do far better elsewhere. I suggest that munitions and manufacturing would be the most advantageous.'

'I'm sure they would, but I wish to put it into war bonds. I know they pay below the market value but investing with the government to help pay for the war is my patriotic duty, don't you think?'

'It is, and I applaud you for it. Do you intend to put all of it in the same place?'

From his tone, she gathered immediately that this would be an unwise move financially. 'No, I thought half in war bonds, a quarter in whatever stocks and shares my bank suggests and the remainder somewhere accessible.'

'I'll arrange for somebody from the bank to come and see you,' Mr Broome said. 'I guarantee whoever comes will be knowledgeable and you'll be able to trust them absolutely.'

'Thank you. I'm seriously considering moving to somewhere

smaller and easier to manage but obviously won't do so as long as the Land Army billet their girls with me. If they decide it's too dangerous so close to Manston and put them elsewhere, then I'll close this house for the duration.'

'I think that's a sensible plan, my lady. Things are only going to get worse and once Manston has been repaired, it will be a target again.'

'I know and I would prefer to be living somewhere not so vulnerable.'

Liza and Joe were in the library with Mr Kent doing their morning schoolwork and the house was quiet. Two of the three ladies from the village who worked on rotation doing housework and so on would be upstairs. This meant there was nobody to take the tray back to the kitchen apart from herself – but she was happy to do so.

'I won't be a moment. I think I can hear a car approaching – the puzzling visitor will be here in a few minutes.'

* * *

Bob rode his motorbike down the side of his parents' house in Mildmay Road. It seemed strange parking it in the same place he'd always done before he'd abandoned his family so abruptly. He then went in through the back gate, which was always unlocked.

He'd wanted to arrive when his mum and dad would be eating Sunday lunch – regardless of the weather, it was always a roast of some sort followed by a heavy steamed pudding or crumble. If he'd come before or after, his dad might have been in the pub or on the allotment and he wanted to speak to both of them.

The kitchen door was open and an appetising smell of roast potatoes and onion gravy wafted through. He'd not stopped to eat and hoped there'd be enough for him.

He hesitated for a second, took a deep breath and stepped in. 'Hello, Mum, Dad, we need to talk.'

He wasn't sure what sort of reception he'd get, as he'd left after saying unforgivable things to his mother. Dad hadn't been there but would have been told. Mum dropped her cutlery with a clatter, pushed her chair back so violently it tumbled to the lino and threw her arms around him.

'Bob, my boy, my son, I'm so glad you've come home. I've missed you so dreadfully.'

He couldn't speak, his eyes welled, and he returned her hug. Whatever happened between him and Daphne in the future, at least one thing was now restored. He'd got his family back and it was entirely his own fault they'd been estranged for over a year.

'I'm so sorry, Mum, I shouldn't have said what I did. I should have waited until I was calm and spoken to you sensibly.'

'That's all right, love, you're here now. Mary will be made up that you're back. You're going to go round and see them before you go, aren't you?'

'I certainly am. I'm glad that Mary and her family are still living around the corner, I thought they might have been evacuated when the bombing started.'

'Not been any bombs dropped on Chelmsford so far, Romford and the base at Hornchurch have been attacked, but not here. They don't bomb civilians deliberately, do they? All the factories and that are on the other side of town.'

Now wasn't the time to tell her that Ramsgate had been bombed six weeks ago and hundreds made homeless, and many innocent people killed or injured. Coventry, Manchester, Liverpool and other cities were being bombed most nights and it wasn't just industrial sites and RAF bases that were being attacked. Even if the Luftwaffe wasn't supposed to drop bombs on civilians, it was inevitable that many went astray.

'Welcome home, son, it's good to see you. Sit yourself down and your mother will get you something to eat.' Dad hadn't changed – shirt sleeves rolled up neatly, clean-shaven and his gardening trousers held up by a piece of string. This always infuriated Mum, as Dad had a perfectly good leather belt in his drawer.

He didn't need inviting twice and joined his dad at the table. A large helping of roast potatoes, carrots, runner beans and onion gravy, accompanied by a smaller portion of what looked like rabbit, was put in front of him.

'That looks as good as always, Mum. I've missed your cooking and I've missed you.'

'Eat up then, we can have a good chinwag afterwards. Are you staying the night?'

'I don't have to report to Folkestone until they day after tomorrow.'

'Good thing you've got your old bike, son, but I'm surprised you've got any petrol to put in it. Must be easier if you're in one of the services because you can't get any for love or money round here.'

'Don't talk to him now, you old fool, let him eat. Good thing I made plenty.'

Bob was happy to enjoy his meal and leave the difficult discussion until later.

12

Daphne was impressed with the speed with which Charlie had learned to drive the tractor. Sal was going to have a go next, but Mr Pickering said he wanted Charlie to get on with harrowing a field before either she or Sal got a chance to learn. With Charlie footling about on the tractor, there was extra work and it was really far too hot to have to rush about. It must be lovely sitting in a tractor and not having to do everything by hand.

Charlie often seemed to consider herself better than both of them and this was beginning to grate. Since she'd spent two weeks at the doctor's house, Charlie admittedly was more relaxed, but things hadn't been the same between the three of them.

'I'm off to the back field with me hoe,' Sal said cheerfully. 'Ain't you coming with me?'

'No, Charlie asked me to clean out the chicken shed before I join you,' Daphne said. 'Not sure which is worse. It shouldn't take me too long; the shed was only done a few days ago.'

'Charlie's got a bit bossy again, ain't she? Why should she be telling us what to do?'

'Never mind, someone has to do it and it might as well be me. See you later.'

Sal left her to it and Daphne headed for the poultry shed. She was on her second wheelbarrow full of manure when she heard male voices coming from the pigpen. Perhaps the pigs were being sold – they were certainly big enough to leave the sow.

In order to get the manure in her barrow on top of the pile, she had to push it up a plank and then empty it into the muck already there. She was almost at the top when the most hideous screaming came from behind the barn, making her lose her balance. They were killing a pig.

With a despairing cry, Daphne toppled sideways into the manure heap and the contents of the wheelbarrow landed on top of her. The stench was appalling, she could feel herself slowly sinking into it. If she didn't get out quickly, then she might suffocate.

She kicked the wheelbarrow aside and it fell down the steaming mound and ended up with a clatter on the cobbles. Then she carefully rolled sideways until she could hook a foot over the plank and slithered, ignominiously, down to the ground to land in a smelly heap.

Her boots were full of manure, her clothes were covered in the wretched stuff, it was in her hair, up her nose and inside her shirt as well. She stood, trying not to breathe through her nose, trying not to cry.

She wasn't sure what to do but knew she'd no intention of continuing to work the way she was. Then Charlie arrived.

'Good grief, how incredibly unfortunate. Have you got any spare clothes here?'

'Of course I haven't, what a stupid thing to ask,' Daphne said. 'I'm going to wash the worst off at the pump and then borrow a bicycle and go home and change.'

'You can't go now; you'll have to wait until lunch break. There's no need to bite my head off, Daphne. It's not my fault you fell into the manure.'

'No, nothing's your fault, is it? Go away and let me sort this out for myself. You can swan about on that tractor for a few more hours and leave everything else to us – you've been Mr Pickering's favourite ever since you concussed yourself by stupidly falling over a chicken.'

Her friend recoiled and it wasn't just because of the awful smell coming from Daphne. 'I'll leave you to it, then. I'm not swanning about, as you put it, I'm harrowing a field and my job is just as useful as yours.'

Daphne didn't care there were men somewhere about the yard who could see her in her bra – she was desperate to get clean. Her boots came off first and she emptied them and then filled them up with water and emptied them a second time. Better to squelch than to stink.

She pulled down the straps of her dungarees and removed her ruined shirt. She then stuck her head under the pump while she pulled the handle up and down vigorously. The water was icy, but it did the trick and after ten minutes she'd removed the manure from the places that mattered. She then washed her shirt before putting it back on. The fact that she was abandoning her duties and taking a bicycle without permission didn't bother her.

She sped down the lane and onto the narrow road that led to Goodwill House and just prayed that nobody would see her the way she was. She threw the bike against the wall in the yard, hooked off her boots and turned them upside down outside the back door and then rushed in.

There were back stairs – put there for the servants – and she used those instead of using the main staircase. She pushed the plug into the bath and turned on the taps. It took her a quarter of an hour to remove the disgusting debris. The bathwater was a nasty colour and smelled even worse.

She found the cloth, scrubbed it clean and then got in again. There was a jug that the girls used when they wanted to wash their hair over the sink and she grabbed it. Only after she'd tipped clean water a dozen times over her naked body was she ready to get out.

After wrapping a towel around her, she scooped up her discarded clothes and nipped down the passageway to her bedroom. She only had her breeches to change into as they were issued just one pair of dungarees. Fortunately, she had a second shirt, and a spare bra and knickers, as well as socks.

She roughly dried her hair and then pulled it back and pinned it. She tucked her fawn shirt into her jodhs and fastened the leather belt that held them up. Most of the girls had had to make extra holes in the belt since they'd started working on the land.

Finally satisfied she was fragrant, Daphne was ready to return to the farm. She was going to be hot dressed as she was, but she had no option. How on earth the powers that be thought the girls could manage with only one pair of dungarees each, she'd no idea. With a bundle of smelly clothes under her arm, she retraced her steps and headed for the laundry, where she put everything in a galvanised tub to soak.

She'd been gone more than an hour and might well get a ticking off from Mr Pickering, but it would be worth it. He could always dock her wages by a shilling but even that she didn't mind. Better to lose out financially then have to walk around smelling the way she had after falling into the manure heap.

* * *

Joanna had arranged for Jean to answer the door and bring this unexpected visitor to the study rather than go and get him herself.

She was, after all, Lady Harcourt and now a very wealthy woman. She had a moment's regret that David had died thinking he'd lost the family fortune – maybe if he'd known the truth, then he wouldn't have been so ready to rejoin his regiment.

Both she and the solicitor were standing in the middle of the room, waiting to greet her guest. She tensed as she heard heavy footsteps approaching – whoever it was must be a big man to make so much noise.

Jean had been well briefed and stopped at the door. 'My lady, Mr Giles Hoskins to see you.'

'Thank you, Jean. Please bring the coffee through at once.'

She half-expected Jean to curtsy and was glad she didn't, as then she'd have laughed and spoiled the impression she'd decided to create.

The man standing behind Jean walked in. He was of average height, sharp featured and had thick, wavy grey hair. Exactly as she'd expected a London barrister to look.

'Good morning, my lady, thank you for agreeing to see me.' The man stared pointedly at Mr Broome and she introduced him.

'Shall we be seated? Whatever it is you have to tell me, it must be important, and I'm eager to know what has brought you down from London.'

He put his briefcase on a side table and took the seat she indicated. She hid her smile behind her hand after watching him prissily adjust his trousers before he sat. David had done this, as he'd said it made sure the creases remained intact.

They sat in silence, awaiting the arrival of the coffee tray. Obviously, what he had to say shouldn't be heard by a servant. Jean was a friend and Joanna knew that unless it was something detrimental to the good name of the family, she would share whatever she learned with when this meeting was over.

After handing Mr Broome and Mr Hoskins a coffee, Joanna sat down and looked expectantly in his direction. He took her cue.

'Lady Harcourt, your husband died at Dunkirk.'

'That's correct.'

'A Peter Randall Harcourt assumed the title, did he not?'

'Yes, he did. I'm at a loss to know what any of this has to do with you.'

'I'm sorry to have to inform you, my lady, but another claimant to the title has come to light.'

Whatever she'd expected him to say, this hadn't been it. 'Someone else has a better claim than Peter? I don't believe it.'

'We've been looking into the claim, and it appears that it is valid. I'm afraid Mr Harcourt isn't the new Lord Harcourt at all – he will be informed of it this morning.'

It took her a few moments to assimilate this extraordinary piece of information. It was Mr Broome who asked the questions she should have done.

'Who is this new claimant? How is it that he has only just stepped forward? Lord Harcourt, Lord Peter Harcourt, had no expectations of assuming the title but was assured that he was directly in line.'

'The gentleman who has actually inherited the title is Lord Stephen Harcourt. He is your deceased husband's second cousin, whereas Mr Peter Harcourt is his third cousin.'

Joanna recalled having been told that this Stephen Harcourt had pre-deceased David. How could he have suddenly been resurrected? 'This man was listed as dead, Mr Hoskins.'

'He was indeed, my lady. He was thought to have died at Dunkirk, like your husband, but obviously he didn't.' He cleared his throat.

'Where has this person been for four months?' Mr Broome asked.

'He was severely injured and in the chaos his tags were lost, so he was unidentified. Believe me, my lady, you are not the only person to be shocked. His wife and children held a memorial service for him.' He shook his head. 'However, his wife, it seems, never believed he was dead and continued to search for him. His remains were not identified or recovered.'

'How awful for them, but they must be overjoyed to have him back,' Joanna said. 'I'm still, like Mr Broome, wondering why it has taken so long for him to recall who he really is.'

'He was disfigured horribly and unrecognisable. He was unable to speak and, therefore, didn't inform his nurses and doctors of his true identity.'

'What changed?'

'His wife eventually discovered the poor fellow languishing in a rehabilitation facility. She identified him immediately and arrangements were made to take him home, where he is being nursed. As soon as this happened, the family lawyers were obligated to remove the title from Mr Peter Harcourt and ensure that the new Lord Harcourt is established as the holder of this ancient title.' He shifted uncomfortably on his chair. 'This was the first time we knew about an infant, we think Stephen Harcourt has a son as well as his daughters. He, of course, should have taken the title not Mr Peter Harcourt.'

'You wrote to Lady Harcourt ten days ago. Why has it taken so long for this information to be given and why in god's name didn't you just put it in the original letter or telephone?' Mr Broome was rather cross, and Joanna wasn't quite sure why.

'I understand your concern, sir, and will explain. There is something else, something that I couldn't risk putting into a letter and certainly not have a telephone operator overhear.' He paused and she wasn't sure if it was for dramatic effect or because the news was so shocking that he couldn't bring himself to speak it.

'Well, man, spit it out,' Mr Broome said.

'I've given you the official version, but despite what I've said, I have grave misgivings about the validity of this claim. I have a nasty suspicion that it is fraudulent and being orchestrated by the wife. At no time did we discuss the title with her as, as far as we were concerned, Stephen Harcourt was dead and had no male heirs. Peter Harcourt automatically inherited.'

Joanna was shocked and even Mr Broome was rendered silent for a moment. She still couldn't see how such a deception could be managed.

'Surely there are other relatives who can identify this man and reveal if he is an impostor, even if he is disfigured,' Mr Broome said.

'And his children – they must know if the man who purports to be their father is in fact him,' Joanna added.

'If only it was so simple. His in-laws are deceased, and his mother and sister have moved to an unknown location and cannot be contacted. The wife says she thinks they are in Scotland but isn't sure.'

The lawyer no longer referred to this woman as Lady Harcourt, which was significant in itself.

'And his daughters?' She was determined to get an answer on this point.

'They are too young to be reliable. Their father had been away for almost a year, and they have not been allowed to see him as he's too unwell to have small children in his room.'

Joanna poured out more coffee and this was accepted gratefully. 'If you think the man's an impostor, why not just expose him?' Mr Broome said.

'I would do so with alacrity, but the wife has friends in high places and I could be dismissed.'

Joanna was baffled by this new development. It seemed an

extraordinary length to go to just to claim a title and no land or wealth. It was also nothing, really, to do with her.

* * *

Bob offered to help with the washing-up but was shooed away by his mother. 'Why don't you and your dad go down the pub for a half?'

'I'd rather go to the allotment. There must be things I can help you with, Dad.'

'There are, son, it's been that dry, things will need watering. Next thing you know, the blooming government will be rationing that as well as food and petrol.'

'Don't be more than an hour, love, I'll have the tea in the pot waiting for you both.'

Bob squeezed his mother's shoulder as he walked past, and she beamed at him. How could he have been so unkind last year? She was a good woman, loved him and he loved her. He understood why she hadn't told him about the adoption, as pretending he and Mary were their natural children must have made them feel closer as a family.

The allotments at the back of the gardens were quiet – no doubt folk were still recovering from their Sunday lunch. He preferred it that way, as it gave him a chance to speak to his dad without having to upset his mum with his questions.

'We'll sit on this old bench then, shall we, son? Then you can ask me what you want. I'll tell you anything I know.'

'Thanks, Dad, I'm sure you understand why it's so important to me that I know everything you do. Daphne and I were torn apart last year and by an accident of fate, we met up again the other week and we both realised a year hadn't made any difference, at least to me. I'm not so sure about Daphne. I can't believe she's my sister – I couldn't feel the way I do about her if she was.'

'Then let's hope you get the answers you want, son,' his father said. 'We tried for kiddies of our own, but the doctor said your mum couldn't have them. We talked about it and decided to take in two little ones that couldn't stay with their birth mums.'

'Obviously Mary and I don't have the same parentage – you know what I mean – but can you tell me anything about the woman who gave me up?'

'She was a married lady who'd been having a relationship with a married bloke. Her man had been injured at Ypres and she had three other children so couldn't keep you.' His dad stopped and looked at him with tears in his eyes. 'I'm sorry, son, talking about you as if you were a parcel to be handed about. We loved you the moment we set eyes on you. We didn't meet your birth mother, a woman from the church she attended arranged everything. I think your mum might have some paperwork to show you.'

'Right, I understand. But why did Mum think I might be related to Daphne apart from our similar colouring?'

'Your mum discovered that Daphne's dad had been having an affair with a married woman and his mother had red hair like you do. This could have meant your colouring came from him. She was worried right from the start about the pair of you getting together and we should have told you and not kept your adoption secret. We couldn't love either you or Mary more, even if you'd been our natural children.'

'I know that now, but losing Daphne the way I did ruined my judgement,' Bob said. 'I apologise for the way I spoke to you both.'

'Water under the bridge, son, it didn't matter what you said, we knew you'd come back to us when you'd calmed down. Shall we get back – I should think that the tea's ready, don't you?'

The allotments were only a five-minute walk from the house and Bob returned feeling more optimistic about things than he had an hour ago. It was beginning to look increasingly unlikely that they would be able to disprove Mum's belief that he and Daphne were siblings, but at least he now had his family back in his life. Tomorrow he'd go round and spend some time with Mary before going in search of the woman who'd arranged his adoption all those years ago.

His mum put a brown manila envelope on the table alongside the teapot – despite the hot weather, still in its knitted cosy – and the three cups and saucers.

'I found what papers I had, Bob, and you're welcome to them,' she said as she pushed it towards him.

He tipped the contents on the table and spread them out. There wasn't much to look at, but his eye was drawn immediately to the handwritten letter.

Dear Mrs Andrews,

I will be expecting you and your husband to collect the baby on Monday. His mother will bring him round at nine o'clock, so you must both be here no earlier than ten o'clock and no later than eleven.

It wouldn't do for you and the baby's mother to meet. As you can imagine, this is a difficult time for her and she wouldn't be giving the baby up if she could afford to keep him.

Her husband accepted him, even knowing that he wasn't his child, but it is financial necessity that has brought them to this adoption.

When the baby is old enough, if you decide to tell him, make sure that he knows he was loved by his natural family for the first nine months of his life.

I look forward to seeing you and Mr Andrews next week. I will have the legal paperwork to hand when you arrive.

Yours sincerely,
Freida Canning, Mrs.

Bob sank into the nearest chair, clutching the paper, and tears trickled unheeded down his cheeks. Now he had even more reason to find his natural mother – he wanted to let her know that he'd had a happy life.

He brushed his cheeks dry and then looked at the other pieces of paper. There was just the legal document relating to his adoption, his baptism certificate, his confirmation record, and a snap of himself as a small baby. He couldn't see the person who was holding him, but he guessed it was his birth mother.

'Thank you for keeping these. If I'd stayed when you told me, I could have saved us all a lot of time.' He swallowed the lump in his throat before continuing. 'I'm going to look for Mrs Canning and hopefully then be able to speak to the woman who gave me up so reluctantly.'

His mother was crying, and he immediately embraced her. 'Don't worry, Mum, you and Dad will always be my real parents. You brought me up and loved me. I'll only find out the truth about who was my actual father if I speak to my birth mother. I want to be with Daphne and unless I do this, I never will be.'

Bob's mum hugged him back and then pushed him away. 'Go on with you, you big softy, we know that. Sit down and drink your tea then you can tell me what you've been up to this past year.'

* * *

Bob rode away the following afternoon, having spent an enjoyable morning with his sister and his niece and nephew. His bulky kitbag had been left with his parents, as he intended to return there tonight before heading back to Hawkinge the following evening.

He was on his way to St Mary's Church in the hope of being able to discover the whereabouts of Mrs Canning. Mum had said she was a lady of middle years so could well be dead by now.

The church was still there and he found it with no difficulty. He walked in and saw two ladies polishing the wooden pews.

'Excuse me, I wonder if you can help me. I'm trying to locate a Mrs Freida Canning. I think she used to be involved with this church, but she'll probably be in her seventies by now.'

The nearest lady with a headscarf pinned over her hair and a floral wraparound apron around her ample girth nodded. 'Freida is still hale and hearty, but she doesn't live around here. She moved to live with her daughter a few years back.' She turned to her companion. 'Somewhere the other side of Colchester, wasn't it, Vera?'

'It was, but I don't know the exact address. Let me think a moment.' Vera, similarly dressed but tall and thin, closed her eyes and pursed her lips. Bob waited, holding his breath, praying she would give him something to go on.

'Her son-in-law works in a shipyard. It's on a big river and the church in the village is called St Mary's too. I can't remember anything else.'

'That's going to be enough, I think. There can't be that many shipyards on a river close to Colchester. Thank you so much.' He dipped into his pocket and dropped a handful of coins into the charity box as he rushed out.

It shouldn't be difficult to discover the name of the river – he doubted there'd be more than one big enough to sustain a shipyard. This river would have to run into the sea. He would head for Colchester, find a map of the area and possibly by the end of the day he'd have the answers he was looking for.

13

Daphne returned the borrowed bicycle and was about to grab a hoe from the barn and run to the back field where Sal would be working. She hoped Charlie wouldn't be there, as they'd parted on bad terms. Then she realised she'd left the chicken shed half-cleaned and had to do that before doing anything else.

The thought of pushing the wheelbarrow up the plank again filled her with horror. Just the smell of the midden made her stomach turn over. She hurried to the shed and stopped in astonishment. Someone had finished cleaning it and everything was pristine.

The doors to the field where the chickens spent their days were now open and several of the nest boxes had hens contentedly laying their daily eggs. It had to have been Charlie, as Sal wouldn't know about the drama. How kind of her after they'd had words.

On Sunday they brought their own packed lunch as the housekeeper at Fiddler's Farm had this day free. The church clock had struck two on her way over, so she'd missed her lunch break. Her greaseproof-paper parcel of sandwiches had gone from the shelf where they stored their lunches safe from marauding chickens.

Missing her lunch had been worth it to be clean. She collected a hoe and hurried to the field where her friends should be working. She saw them coming down the row towards her and waved, but with their heads down, they didn't see her.

'Hey, you two, I'm back. Thank you for finishing the chickens for me, whoever did it.'

Both girls looked up and, and to her relief, both waved. She ran down the field to join them.

'Blimey, what a palaver! We've put your butties under the hedge with the flasks. You get them down you, no need to start until we get to the end of this row,' Sal said.

'Thanks, I'm starving after all the unwanted exercise.' Daphne left them to it and ran back to find her lunch. She settled in the shade of the hedge and devoured the spam and mustard sandwiches with enjoyment.

She was waiting with her hoe when they reached the end of the field ten minutes later. 'Charlie, I'm sorry for being so nasty to you. Thank you for finishing the cleaning for me.'

Charlie looked away. 'Actually, it wasn't me. Mr Pickering must have done it. I came down here immediately after you left.'

Daphne frowned and wished she hadn't apologised. 'I see. Thanks for nothing, then. I'll thank the person who did help me when I finish here.'

She smiled warmly at Sal, after all, this was nothing to do with her, and turned her back on Charlie. When she started hoeing, Sal stepped in beside her on the next row, which meant Charlie wasn't beside her, which was how she wanted it.

The two of them worked well together and after a while, her anger subsided and she was able to chat to Sal and laugh about what had happened.

'Glad I weren't there when they was killing a porker. I've got to like them. They ain't got a sow, so I reckon they bought those in as piglets.' Sal stopped and leaned on her hoe as she digested this unpalatable information. 'That means they'll all be for the knacker's yard and a new lot will be coming in, don't it?'

'I'm afraid so, but that's how things work on a farm. The posters they put up about joining the Land Army make it seem glamorous, but it's hard work and the exact opposite, isn't it? Thank goodness I wasn't wearing what I've got on now when I fell in the muck.'

'Why don't we ask Jean to run us up a spare pair of dungarees each? That'll make life a lot easier, won't it?'

'It certainly will. It doesn't really matter what they're made of or what colour they are, I don't suppose Mrs Ramsbottom will care as long as we look smart when we're out and about.'

They reached the end of the row and moved along so that Sal would be working next to Charlie and not her. It wasn't really fair for Sal to be at odds with Charlie as well, and once the shift was over, she would sort it out.

It was well after six o'clock by the time the field was done. Her back was aching and her hands sore where the wooden handle of the hoe had rubbed. She would have worn her work gloves, but these had been lost in the manure heap and she certainly wasn't going to go rummaging about for them.

'Sal, would you harness Star whilst I go and find Mr Pickering and thank him? I also need to apologise for missing an hour.'

Charlie overheard this and said sourly, 'It was more like an hour and a half, Daphne, and you'll be very lucky if he doesn't stop your wages.'

Daphne ignored the dig – she didn't want to have a row here. Much better to sort it out when they were on their own.

The farmer was busy in the dairy and looked up with a grin when she came in. 'Should have warned you about the pig, Daphne.'

'I'm sorry I sloped off to get clean. I'll understand if you want to knock off a shilling.' She smiled back. 'Thank you for doing the chickens.'

'Forget it, you couldn't carry on working the way you were. I'd better warn you that the other pigs will be slaughtered over the next week or so. Then the sties will need a good scrub and disinfecting before the new piglets arrive.'

'Sal's upset about them going but understands that's how things work. I'm sure it won't stop her eating a nice rasher of bacon with her breakfast or a lovely ham salad for tea.'

'You get on, Daphne, I'll not be taking anything out of your wages. You girls work hard for me, I appreciate it, and wish I could pay you more.'

'Thank you, we do our best.' Mr Pickering was very jolly today, which wasn't like him. 'Are you going to see your family this week?'

His smile lit up his face. 'No, they're coming home. They miss being here as much as I miss them. There's quite a few families returning to Stodham, even though bombs could still be dropped on the village.'

'Golly, no wonder you're pleased,' Daphne said. 'If there's anything extra you'd like us to do, you only have to ask. Will they be coming back by train?'

'No, there's enough of them to fill a coach and we've got together to hire one. We just need to find petrol to fill the tank. Even with the right amount of points, the driver can't get any.'

'You could always try asking Lady Harcourt, I know she's got quite a few cans stored at the back of the barn.'

'I didn't know that. Would you do me a favour and ask her for me? I'm not comfortable speaking to grand ladies like her.'

'I'd be happy to, Mr Pickering.'

Daphne hurried back to clamber into the cart, glad she could do something for her boss in return for his help and understanding today.

* * *

Joanna couldn't believe that a woman could be so desperate to have a title in the family that she'd stoop to a deception of this kind.

'I'm not exactly sure what you expect me to do about this, Mr Hoskins.'

Mr Broome had other questions. 'This is complete nonsense. This Stephen Harcourt was a member of the armed forces, that means that dozens, if not hundreds of people would have met him before he went to Dunkirk and whilst he was there. All they've got to do to disprove or prove this man's an impostor is to get one of them to identify him.'

'Believe me, Mr Broome, I tried to arrange this,' Mr Hoskins said. 'The man, who I think is indeed an impostor, is the same colouring and build as the man he's impersonating. No one has been allowed to see him apart from his nurses and wife, which means there's been no opportunity to ask him to identify himself.'

'Then you must find the missing mother and sister. I doubt they'll be prepared to perjure themselves and risk going to prison if this man is, in fact, not who they say he is.'

'Now you have the nub of it, my dear sir, I cannot instigate such a search for fear of losing my position, but I'm hoping that you and Lady Harcourt will do so.'

Joanna considered this suggestion and then nodded. 'Mr Hoskins, I'm prepared to finance the search...' Then she heard the telephone jangling in the distance. 'Excuse me, I must answer that as everybody else will be busy.' She left the two men to discuss how the search should be conducted and she hoped they would come up with some sensible suggestions.

'Goodwill House, Lady Harcourt speaking.'

'Joanna, I expect you now know why this odd gentleman was coming to see you.'

'Peter, I intended to ring you as soon as I had a moment. I'm so sorry...'

'Sorry? What have you got to be sorry about?' Peter said. 'I don't give a damn about the title – I didn't want it anyway, as you know – but I do care that this could cause you difficulties.'

'That's not the worst of it.' She quickly explained and he listened without comment.

'Good god! In which case, I *am* concerned. If this Hoskins chap has asked you to search for the missing relatives, then the matter's serious. I can't get away as I'm snowed under at the moment with work. What I can do is use my position to speed up the search. As soon as I hear anything relevant, I'll let you know.'

'Have you told everybody that you're no longer officially Lord Harcourt?'

Peter chuckled. 'I've not used my title at work – I've got my rank and that's more than enough. Don't worry, Joanna, if this man's an impostor, we'll rout him out. Sorry, I'm expected at a meeting in ten minutes.'

The line went dead. She was left holding the receiver, not having, as far as she was concerned, finished the conversation. Thoughtfully, she replaced it in the cradle and returned to the study.

Both men stood up at her entrance, which she thought was rather antiquated but charming. 'That was the previous Lord Harcourt. He's going to make enquiries on our behalf.'

'Good show,' Mr Hoskins said. 'I believe he's something important in the intelligence service. Just the man for the job. I must take my leave, my lady, and return to my chambers. Any correspondence from me in future will be taking the official line. I cannot be involved in this further.'

'Thank you for taking the time to come here,' Joanna said. 'I assume that you'll be informed if any information that disproves this claim emerges from our investigations.'

'I'm sure I will. Can I ask you not to contact me directly? Nobody knows that I came here; as far as my head of chambers is concerned, I'm visiting an elderly aunt in Surrey. Good day to you both.' He nodded, and didn't wait to be shown out, but strode off.

'Well, that was unexpected, my lady,' Mr Broome said. 'I'm glad I was here to support you. I too will initiate discreet enquiries about this woman and her family. I have contacts in Hampshire who will be invaluable in this search.'

'It's hard to comprehend that a woman would kidnap a stranger and then fob him off as her husband.'

'It seems beyond belief that the authorities, those that run the Manorial Register, would just take this woman's word that the injured man is who she says he is.'

'She must have trawled through all the hospitals and so on until she found someone returned injured from Dunkirk who fitted the description of her husband,' Joanna said.

'It all seems very far-fetched, not something that could stand the scrutiny of lawyers, so maybe we've got it wrong, and this man really is the missing lord.'

'Perhaps Peter could demand to speak to this patient? After all, he has a reason to be concerned.'

'He could, but I doubt that he would want to,' Mr Broome replied. 'What bothers me is that this man, if he isn't Lord Harcourt, might well suddenly succumb to his injuries. As long as he was alive when your husband died, the title stays with that family. We need to find out about the possibility of there being a male heir.'

Her solicitor departed, leaving her more confused than before and she headed to the terrace to share the news with Elizabeth.

'At last, my dear, I've been beside myself with curiosity this past hour as to why this unexplained visitor came to see you,' her mother-in-law said as Joanna walked out into the sunshine.

After hearing the explanation, her mother-in-law clapped her hands. 'How terribly exciting – just like an Agatha Christie novel.'

'Good heavens, I do hope not, as they always include a murder.' She'd not mentioned to her mother-in-law that Mr Broome might have suggested exactly the same thing could happen to Peter.

* * *

Bob hadn't been to Colchester before but did know it had a magnificent Norman castle and a lot of Roman remains – he'd been a bit of a history buff at school. He thought the station would be a good place to make his first enquiries.

He cruised to a halt outside the down line platform and spotted a uniformed guard. 'Excuse me, mate, are you local?'

The bloke grinned and walked over. 'Decent bike you've got there, always wanted one myself. How can I help?'

'I'm looking for a village with a shipyard on a river close to Colchester. Any suggestions?'

'Crikey, that's easy. You want Wivenhoe, there's a couple of ship-yards there as well as yacht builders, but I don't know the names. I do know the river's the Colne.' The young man gave excellent direc-tions and Bob rode away, confident he was going to find Mrs Canning sometime today. The woman would be involved with the local church, so all he had to do was go there and ask.

It was a short run, no more than four or five miles, to Wivenhoe and he rode through fields and woods and farmland before arriving at the top of the hill where the houses started. Park Hotel was the first building he saw on the left.

He headed down the hill, over a bridge and then on his left he saw the church. There had been several shops in the lower part of the village, but he thought there were probably more pubs in this place than he'd seen anywhere else. He'd passed two on the outskirts of the village and another two on the way down the hill.

Adjacent to the churchyard was the Falcon Hotel, which offered all sorts of delights, according to the board outside, including pyramids and pool. Maybe he'd drop in for some lunch there and find out what the 'pyramids' were.

The churchyard was well-tended, the headstones clean and no weeds encroached on the graves. The door was open, and he could hear women's voices inside. Was his search going to be over so easily?

He walked through the porch and stepped into the dim interior. This church was similar to the one he'd been in earlier today, probably with Norman origins and rebuilt a hundred or so years ago. The stained-glass window behind the altar was superb and he stood for a few moments, watching the way the light filtered through the coloured glass and then played over the altar.

'Good morning, young man, can I be of assistance?' A smartly dressed woman in her forties – obviously not the person he was looking for – came over with a frosty smile. She wasn't here to polish the brass.

'Good morning, ma'am, I'm hoping that you can help me find somebody I'm looking for. It's Mrs Frieda Canning. I'm pretty sure she moved to Wivenhoe a few years ago and as she was very active at her previous church, I think she would probably be involved here as well.'

'Why do you wish to find her?'

'I'm sorry, ma'am, but that's really none of your concern. Could you tell me, please, if you know her or not?'

The woman took offence and stared at him as if he was something unpleasant stuck to the bottom of her elegant court shoe. 'In which case, I'm not prepared to give you any information.'

He nodded and walked out, well satisfied with this exchange as it proved that Mrs Canning was indeed a member of this church. All he needed to do was find someone less pompous to give him the address he wanted.

It was now a little after one o'clock. He would go into the Falcon Hotel and see if he could get himself a bite to eat. There might well be someone there who knew this Mrs Canning.

He had to duck his head in order to go in and he stood in the reception area admiring the beams and leaded windows. There was a brass bell resting on a countertop and he walked across and rang it. The place was so quiet, he doubted there were any guests, which probably meant no food available either.

'Hello,' a cheerful female voice called from behind him. 'Are you looking for some lunch?'

He turned to see a young woman, probably not more than seventeen or eighteen years of age, standing in a doorway.

'I am, I'm not fussy, just hungry. I'm assuming I can also get a beer.'

'You can have both. We don't do hot meals at midday, but I can make you a tasty ham salad. Come through, you've come in through the hotel entrance and the pub is at the other end of this building.'

He followed her and was greeted by the sound of laughter, clinking glasses and an overwhelming smell of pipe and cigarette tobacco.

'Would you like to sit in the garden? There's plenty of shade and from your expression, you don't smoke.'

He grinned and nodded. 'Thanks, that will be perfect.' She pointed to an open door through which he could see sunlight and greenery.

There were a couple of men in the small garden who looked up and smiled and then returned to their conversation. He took one of the free tables in the shade and was surprised and impressed that his beer arrived a few minutes later and his lunch within ten minutes.

The girl handed him the neatly ironed napkin in which were wrapped his cutlery and then put down the cruet set. 'This ham is from a local farm and all the salad as well.'

'Before you go, miss, I'm wondering if you could help me. I asked in the church but was given a flea in my ear.'

She giggled. 'I bet you met Mrs Gibson. She's a real tartar. What do you want to know?'

He told her and she nodded. 'I know exactly who you mean. She's a lovely old lady and comes in here with her family occasionally. I'm pretty sure she lives in Alma Street, although I don't know which house. I seem to remember she said they were close to the hardware store. You cut through the churchyard and go out of the back entrance, turn left and then left again and you should be in roughly the right place.'

'Thank you, I'll go and look for her after lunch. If this tastes as good as it looks, then I'm in for a treat.'

He left the girl a shilling as the meal had been excellent, and a tip to thank her for being so helpful. She'd agreed he could leave his bike where he'd parked it. He thought he might as well knock at the first house in Alma Street.

The door was opened by an elderly lady, with crimped grey hair and a friendly smile.

'I apologise for bothering you, ma'am, but would you by any chance be Mrs Frieda Canning?'

'I am. And you are?'

'I'm Robert Andrews. You arranged for me to be adopted twenty-three years ago and I urgently need to know who my birth parents are.'

14

Daphne didn't want to deliberately ignore Charlie and just talk to Sal, so she decided to talk to neither of them. Her silence rubbed off and they too remained quiet. The atmosphere in the pony cart was difficult and she knew this was mostly her fault. It wasn't fair for her to involve Sal in her disagreement with Charlie.

She was relieved when Sal expertly guided the mare into the yard. Charlie was gone before either she or Sal could move.

'I'll help you with Star. I don't want you and Charlie to fall out because of me. I'm going to talk to her and sort it out. I don't know what I've done to cause her to be so snappy with me.'

'It ain't you, she's not been herself since she thought herself in love with the doc,' Sal said. 'He ignored her at the party, didn't even dance with her once and I weren't the only one what noticed. Ain't he supposed to be clever like? The way he behaved towards her was blooming rude.'

'That explains it. It must have been humiliating for her after saying that there was something going on between them. Hopefully, we can smooth things out because we can't work together properly like this.'

'She never told no one else about it so I don't reckon the other girls would have thought nothing of it,' Sal said. 'Them girls what did mention it to me just said the doctor should have danced with everybody.'

'I'm going to finish washing out my dungarees and get them on the line. With luck, they'll be dry enough to wear tomorrow morning,' Daphne said and headed for the laundry. Sal accompanied her.

'Look, they're good as new and bone dry on the line.' Daphne removed the wooden pegs and carefully smoothed her dungarees so they wouldn't need ironing. 'I wonder who did this for me?'.

'We're ever so lucky to be living here despite the racket from the base and all that.' Sal looked towards Manston. 'Mind you, there ain't much going on there at the moment. Did you have a good visit with your ma and pa?'

'We went to my grandparents' instead. Unfortunately, they didn't know anything useful, so Bob was going to speak to his parents. I'm glad he's going to make up with them because even if we can't be together, he won't lose his family as well.'

When she came down after changing into her dungarees – which were much cooler than her smart uniform – everyone was sitting around the table and there were bowls of steaming, parsley-covered new potatoes, tomatoes, beans, and lettuce set out down the centre. At every place, there was plate with a serving of succulent freshly cooked ham.

This reminded her of the pigs on the farm and her near-death experience in the muck heap. She joined them and launched into an account of what had happened and by the end, everybody was laughing, apart from Charlie, who just about managed a half-hearted smile.

It wasn't their turn to clear the table, so Daphne was on her feet immediately and caught up with Charlie as she was about to go into the ballroom.

'We need to talk, Charlie, we can't be at odds. Come onto the terrace and we'll talk this through.'

Daphne had her hand on Charlie's arm and her erstwhile friend looked pointedly at it. 'I don't believe there's anything to talk about. As soon as the glass is put back in the windows in our old bedroom, you and Sal can move back. I don't want to share with either of you.'

'Come on, that's being silly. We've been good friends up until now, and the fact that things didn't work out with you and the doctor mustn't make you so bitter with everybody else.'

'My personal life is none of your business, Daphne. You and Sal have more in common and it's better if I share with somebody else, someone more like me.'

'Like you? Stuck-up and bossy, you mean?'

'No, someone who comes from the same background as me,' Charlie said. 'I find Sal vulgar and you irritating. I'm going to ask Mrs Ramsbottom if I can transfer to a different team.'

Daphne forgot her good intentions, that she'd wanted to restore the friendly relationship between them and lost her temper. 'And I find you overbearing and patronising. I doubt that anyone else will want to work with you, as we certainly don't. You're Mr Pickering's favourite since you were injured, and it'll be better for us if you go somewhere else.'

Charlie stalked off and for a second, Daphne was glad to see her go, but then her eyes filled and she regretted every angry word she'd spoken. She ran after her and dodged round, blocking Charlie's path.

'I'm sorry, I didn't mean any of that and I'm sure you didn't either. I know you're unhappy and if it's not because of Dr Willoughby, then what is it? Let us help.'

Sal joined them on the landing. 'We're good mates, we work well together, I ain't going to let that go down the pan without a fight.'

For a moment, the matter hung in the balance and then Charlie deflated like a spent balloon, from angry and superior she became just a young woman who was desperately unhappy about something.

'Let's go to our room. I'm sorry too. I've been an absolute beast and you're quite right to say that something's upset me. I should have told you. I'm going to tell you everything now and I hope you'll still want to be my friend when you know.'

* * *

Joanna explained to her children and to Jean about there being a new Lord Harcourt, but didn't mention the very real possibility that this person had no claim to the title. Time enough for that revelation when the investigation was completed.

That afternoon, the glazier turned up to measure the windows and shortly afterwards, the carpenter arrived. The window frames were irreparably damaged in more than half the rooms involved, so this tradesman was as important to the restoration as the glazier.

She went out to speak to the pair of them when they'd finished. 'How long is this going to take, do you think, Mr Finch?'

The man sucked on his pencil stub and looked gloomy. 'It's like this, my lady, it's a lot of glass you need and that's in very short supply.'

'I am aware of that fact, Mr Finch, and you assured me you could replace all of them if I was prepared to pay the exorbitant amount you quoted.'

'I didn't understand until now what's involved. I'm afraid you'll have to make a choice. It won't be possible to do all of them – at least not this year.'

Joanna did some rapid mental calculations. It was October already and winter was just around the corner. The drawing room was too big to heat, so better to have the bedrooms done so they could all return to where they should be.

'Do the first floor and the windows in the hall. I'll need a new quote, obviously, as your original one included replacing all of them.'

He scowled and she stared frostily at him. 'Mr Finch, if you don't want to do the job then I'll find someone more amenable to do so. Good afternoon.'

He muttered something rude and stomped off. The carpenter, a much younger man, who hadn't been introduced, watched him go. 'Don't worry, my lady, he's a bad-tempered old codger and you're better off finding someone else. I'll do the windows. Sam Trust at your service.'

'Delighted to meet you, Mr Trust. I'm afraid Mr Finch was the only glazier I could find prepared to do the work.'

'My uncle could help you out. He lives in Dover. I'll get him to contact you if you like?'

'Excellent. The windows have to be replaced and repaired before the glass can go in anyway. Can you start immediately?' Joanna asked.

'You'll need a quote first, my lady. I could charge you something silly if you didn't have it in writing.'

'Your name is Trust and I'm sure that applies to your business practices also. Give me the quote when it's done but start as soon as you can. Do you do this on your own?'

He gawped at her as if she'd sprouted horns. 'I've another man and boy, my lady. This isn't a one-man job. There's the scaffolding has to go up first. I'll get that done tomorrow.'

'Thank you. Do you have all the measurements you need?'

'I do. This is a grand old house and I'm going to try and find timber from similar buildings to do the work where I can.'

Elizabeth had wandered into the hall and overheard this conversation. She, thankfully, ignored Joanna's naïve assumption that work could be done without anything being written down and focused on the fact that the drawing room wasn't going to be restored.

'I insist that the drawing room be brought back into use, Joanna. I refuse to sit in your pokey little sitting room for the rest of the war.'

'I'm sorry, Elizabeth, we've no choice. Bedrooms must be done first. We can't use the drawing room in the winter anyway, as it's too expensive to heat and there's a fuel shortage.'

'We're wealthy again, so surely that means we can have what we want when we want it?'

'Before the war, perhaps that was true, but not now. Rationing applies to us in the same way it does to those less fortunate. If you're suggesting I go to the black market, you shock me. Harcourts never consort with criminals.'

'We have a noisy horde of girls living here, we've adopted two urchins from the East End, I can't see why bending the rules to repair this lovely house is wrong.'

'Then we shall have to differ on that point, Elizabeth,' Joanna said. 'Isn't it exciting to think we shall be able to move back into out proper rooms in a few weeks?' Her change of subject didn't work.

'Poppycock! This family is going to rack and ruin. David must be turning in his grave – wherever that might be.'

This wasn't like the woman she'd come to love but it reminded her of the bitter and unpleasant person who'd arrived at Goodwill House a few months ago.

* * *

Bob smiled hopefully at Mrs Canning, expecting to be invited in so they could talk. Instead, she shook her head and frowned.

'I'm sorry, but you've had a wasted journey, Mr Andrews. It will do none of you any good to reopen old wounds.' She started to close the door, but he stepped forward and put his boot in the way.

'I'm sorry, ma'am, but you don't understand. I'm in love with a girl who it seems could be my half-sister.'

Her expression changed to sympathetic and less dismissive. 'Good heavens, I think you'd better come in and tell me how this has come about.'

When he'd finished, she nodded. 'I can see the necessity to speak to your birth mother. If I knew the name of your natural father, then I'd tell you immediately and that would settle things one way or the other. Unfortunately, I was never told that detail and certainly didn't pry.' She stood up. 'I won't be a moment; I think I've got the name and address of the couple who so reluctantly gave you up to be adopted. It's highly unlikely they still live there after twenty-three years, but you might be lucky.'

She returned triumphant. 'Here you are, I've written it down. Good luck with your search, Mr Andrews. What a frightfully awful coincidence to be involved with someone who might be a close relative.'

He hadn't been offered a drink – in fact, the woman was obviously eager for him to leave. Perhaps her daughter didn't know that her mother had been involved with private adoptions all those years ago.

After using the outside facilities at the pub and collecting his motorbike, Bob was ready to return to Chelmsford. He still had the spare can of petrol in a pannier and could hear quite a bit of petrol sloshing about in the tank when he rocked the bike.

He opened the throttle on the straight stretches of road, enjoying the speed. He was glad that he was wearing the flying goggles and helmet he'd bought, along with a few other things, when an unfortunate flyer had gone for a Burton and his personal belongings had been auctioned off to help his family. Without them, he'd have been unable to see clearly.

Chelmsford was deserted. Where the hell was everybody? They must be in the shelters and he hadn't the foggiest where the nearest public shelter was so all he could do was get off the road and take cover down a narrow passageway between two shops.

If a bomb dropped on either of the shops, he'd be a goner, but he was safe from a Luftwaffe fighter who might be looking for a stray civilian to strafe. He hadn't heard the siren as he approached the town, so that must've gone off some time ago. Hopefully, this meant the bombers had already passed overhead without dropping their load and the all-clear would sound soon.

He was right and the continuous howl began almost immediately. The air-raid warning undulated so there was no question of civilians or service people confusing them. He walked his motorbike out of the passageway and was on his way as shoppers and residents emerged.

In order to reach the address he'd memorised, he had to go past the Great Eastern Railway Station and then cross Mill Road. Town Field Street should be easy enough to find once he'd done that. Although this was a fair distance from his own home, he still thought it strange that he'd been adopted from a local family, which made the chance that he and Daphne met far higher than it could have been.

Of course, Mrs Canning hadn't known the name of his father, otherwise she might have been more careful. Also, his parents had lived in a village some miles from Chelmsford and only moved when he was school age. Therefore, no one involved could possibly have known what might happen.

He rolled to a halt outside the house. His heart was trying to escape through his throat – he'd never been so nervous. Was knowing better than living in ignorance and hoping? Definitely. He marched to the front door and knocked more loudly than he'd intended.

He heard children playing in the garden at the back, which meant this wasn't the family he was looking for but maybe they might have information that would help him in his search. The door opened and a harassed housewife, a toddler on her hip, managed a half-hearted smile.

'Can I help you?'

'I don't think so, but I'm going to ask anyway.' He quickly explained the reason for his visit and she shook her head sadly.

'I'm sorry, mister, we've only been here two years and the family that was here before had youngsters like us.'

'Thank you, it was a faint hope, but I had to come just in case.' He was turning away, disappointed and with no clear idea where he should go next, when she called him back.

'We rent this house, try the landlords. Give us a minute and I'll fetch me rent book. I'm pretty sure their address is written on that.'

Whilst she was gone, he pulled out a ten-bob note from his wallet. She needed it more than he did.

'Here you are, I don't have a pencil or no paper, can you remember it?'

'I've got both, thanks.' He stepped to one side and propped his notebook on the wall whilst he copied down what he hoped would be his last and most useful call of the day. He then slipped the money in the rent book and handed it back. He didn't want the woman's thanks but wanted her to find it when he'd gone.

He checked his watch. Damn it! Too late to visit the landlord's offices in Duke Street. Time to go home and update his parents, as they were almost as invested in this search as he was. They were eagerly awaiting his return and listened to what had happened without interrupting.

'That's grand, son, I reckon you'll get the information you want tomorrow,' his dad said.

'I was thinking, Bob, why don't I go and see Daphne's dad? I'll be discreet...'

'God, no, Mum, don't do that. If he is my natural father, that's not the way for him to find out. I promised Daphne I wouldn't involve her parents in this unless absolutely necessary.'

'If that's what you want, I'll not go. I was thinking, love, that if you were his son by this woman, wouldn't he have made quite sure you and Daphne didn't get engaged?'

'That has occurred to me too. The only explanation is that he never knew his mistress, my mother possibly, had a baby. I have to be at my new posting before curfew tomorrow. I'm going to be waiting on the doorstep of Chalmers & Sons at nine o'clock. If they can give me the information I want, I've then got a few hours to try and find this family.'

* * *

With his belongings strapped to his pillion, Bob left in time to be waiting when the offices opened the next day. He'd tipped the contents of the can into his petrol tank and was confident he'd be able to get back to his new base near Folkestone without running out.

He was leaning on the door when the two ladies who worked there arrived. 'Hang on a minute, love,' the older one, a friendly grey-haired woman, said to him. 'We'll be open in a jiff. We don't often get someone so keen first thing.'

They were true to their word and he was beckoned in almost immediately. He seemed to have told his story a dozen times in the last few days and he hoped this might be the penultimate one.

'You're in luck, Corporal Andrews, I know exactly where to look. We have records that go back to the last century.' The grey-haired lady seemed to be in charge and bustled off whilst the younger woman smiled nervously.

He was obviously making her uncomfortable. 'I'll wait outside. If you'd be good enough to write the address on a bit of paper and bring it out to me, that'll be really kind.'

She nodded but didn't answer and was obviously relieved to have him out of her small office. He didn't think of himself as a particularly overwhelming sort of bloke, but his uniform and his bright red hair might seem a bit alarming to a young miss like her.

He didn't have long to wait before the girl opened the door, shoved a piece of paper in his hand and closed it again hastily. He looked down. The family he was looking for had remained tenants of this company until five years ago.

Their last address was in Regina Road, a small turning off Victoria Road, and he was pretty sure he could find it without getting lost.

15

Daphne and Sal followed Charlie into the bedroom. The two of them sat on Daphne's bed and Charlie took the one adjacent, which was her own. Sal had a bed jammed up against the far wall, as this room really wasn't big enough to take three of them, whereas the one they'd had to vacate after the broken windows was perfect.

Charlie started to speak but kept her head down, which wasn't like her. She was a direct sort of person and always looked you in the eye when she was talking.

'I told you that I had to leave my uncle's farm where I'd grown up. I didn't tell you why and didn't think I'd ever have to, but I got a letter last week which changes everything.'

'You don't have to tell us if you don't want to, Charlie, but we're listening if you want to continue.'

'Thank you, Daphne, I don't deserve your support after the way I've treated you recently. There's no excuse, as you've got absolutely nothing to do with what's bothering me.'

'For gawd's sake, don't keep us waiting. Tell us what's wrong,' Sal said in her usual forthright way.

Finally, Charlie looked up and Daphne was shocked to see the tears in her friend's eyes. 'My cousin raped me.'

'Bleeding Nora! The bastard – did you report him to the bobbies?'

'I told my aunt and instead of supporting me, they said I'd encouraged him, and it was my fault. I was thrown out of my home with scarcely time to pack my belongings. I was fortunate that I had a reasonable amount in my post office savings book and wasn't entirely destitute. This was four years ago. I found myself a bedsit in London and got a job in an office. I hated it but I was anonymous, didn't have to mix with anyone and it gave me time to recover.'

Charlie rubbed her eyes on her sleeve, took a deep breath, but was having difficulty forming the words. Daphne moved to sit next to her friend and put her arm around her shoulders.

'But I found out last week that my cousin attacked someone else and this time there were witnesses and the parents of the girl had him arrested. My aunt wrote to me and apologised for not believing me and begged me not to go to the police.'

'What a cheek,' Sal said. 'You go and tell them what he did to you. It ain't going to be fun, but your cousin will get what he deserves if you're another witness.'

'I don't understand why she'd write and tell you this,' Daphne said. 'You wouldn't know anything about it if she hadn't alerted you, would you?'

'I'm sorry, I didn't explain it very well. The vicar's daughter, Jennifer, and I were good friends and I still write to her. She told me about it first, and my aunt's letter arrived the next day. I'm not sure what to do as having to relive it in public isn't something I relish.'

Daphne now understood why Charlie had been drawn towards the local doctor. Her horrible experience at the hands of her cousin would have made her wary of young men. Dr Willoughby was a lot older than her and had made no physical advances. She probably felt safe with him.

'Why don't you send a written statement to the police? Tell them you've no intention of appearing in court but are happy to have your statement witnessed and co-signed by a solicitor. I think that Lady Harcourt's chap would be a good person to go to.'

'That's good advice, Daphne. If Mr Pickering will let me borrow his bicycle, then I can race down to the village and telephone from the kiosk there.'

Daphne grinned. 'I didn't bother to ask so I don't think you need to either – you know you're Mr Pickering's favourite!' She clapped a hand to her mouth. 'I promised him I'd ask Lady Harcourt if they could have some of her petrol to go in the coach that's collecting the families from Norfolk. I'd better do it now. Won't be a tick – shall I bring you up some cocoa?'

'Ta ever so, that'll be just the ticket,' Sal said.

Daphne located her ladyship in the small sitting room and was relieved that her autocratic mother-in-law had already retired. The old Lady Harcourt terrified her. She hesitated outside the door and was beckoned in.

'How can I be of assistance, Daphne?'

She quickly explained and Lady Harcourt nodded. 'I'd rather it was used for a good cause than remain as a fire hazard behind my barn. Please tell Mr Pickering the coach can come and fill up whenever he likes.'

'I'll do that, thank you, my lady.'

'Before you go, my dear, did you enjoy your visit to your parents?'

'We decided to go to my grandparents in Romford instead,' Daphne said. 'Bob has promised to take me to Chelmsford next time he gets a twenty-four-hour pass.'

'Tell him that he can fill up his noisy motorbike at the same time he collects you,' Joanna said. 'By the way, you'll be pleased to know that the carpenters will be starting work tomorrow. With any luck, the three of you will be back in your original bedroom next week sometime.'

'Golly, that's good news. We're a bit cramped in the other room.'

When she returned carrying the mugs of cocoa, Sal was in the bathroom. 'Here we are, no biscuits to go with it tonight, I'm afraid.'

'Not to worry,' Charlie said. 'I'm glad we've got a few moments to ourselves, Daphne. I really am sorry for behaving like an absolute cow to you. Am I forgiven? Are we friends again?'

'Of course we are, you goose. Drink your cocoa and stop talking nonsense.'

* * *

Mr Pickering was delighted when Daphne took the good news about the petrol to the farmhouse the following morning. 'Thank you, that's a load off my mind. In case you girls were wondering, my missus will carry on making your lunch, but you'll have to come here to collect it.'

'That's so kind of you. Charlie has to make an urgent telephone call, so will it be all right for her to use your bicycle to go down to the village in her lunch break?'

'None of you has to ask to borrow my old bike, Daphne. You're good girls, hard workers, and my farm's looking grand because of you,' Mr Pickering said.

'Thank you, we love it here. Forgive me for asking, but are the rest of the pigs going to be slaughtered? I don't want to fall in the muck heap again.'

He laughed. 'Not until next month and then the other four nearer Christmas. Folk do like a nice piece of ham on the Christmas table.'

'Sal will be pleased. Are you getting any piglets to grow on for next year?'

'I certainly am. I'll talk to Sal about what she needs to do. Can't let the little buggers go in with the old ones or they'll be eaten alive.'

* * *

Joanna, as chair of the WVS, was being kept busy as the bombardment of London and other cities at night, and coastal cities and ports during the day, continued. They were always on call to offer tea and support to families in need. Their latest project was to unpick a sack of unwanted woollen naval socks and re-knit them as rollneck jerseys for the sailors. Liza was in charge of distributing the hosiery and appeared to be enjoying the task.

Mrs Thomas, not exactly a friend, made a point of sitting next to Joanna during this knitting-bee in the village hall, which was quite unprecedented.

'My lady, I'm sure that you're aware the majority of the families evacuated to Norfolk earlier in the year have now decided to return. Don't you think that this is foolhardy and premature?'

'Although the Luftwaffe fly over us day and night and continue to drop the occasional bomb on Manston, and have also dropped a few more bombs on Ramsgate, none have fallen anywhere near the village,' Joanna said. 'Therefore, Mrs Thomas, I think on balance it will be better for the families to be reunited than kept apart.'

'I see. It's only the younger children returning with their mothers, as far as I know, and the older children are remaining in situ. This means that the school won't be re-opening and we can continue to use it as a temporary shelter for those made homeless in Ramsgate who don't wish to live underground.'

'Yes, I'd heard that too,' Joanna said. 'I suppose that because the older children were evacuated with their teachers, they're not as homesick as the others might be.'

'I suppose it will be pleasant to have children in the village again. The place seems far too quiet and dull without them.'

Joanna smiled. The last person she'd expected to express such a view was the redoubtable Mrs Thomas. 'Mrs Evans will be pleased to have more candidates for her Sunday school.'

'Having a crèche at the rear of the church wasn't something I approved of initially, but I must admit, on this occasion, I was premature in my judgement.'

Good heavens! Mrs Thomas admitting she was wrong – now that was a first. Whatever the reason for this *volte face*, Joanna rather liked this new version.

'I wonder if we could perhaps have an impromptu garden party to welcome them home. I would suggest doing it at Goodwill House, but I'm not sure it's the best place, being so close to the base. As you're on the village hall committee, Mrs Thomas, do you think we could use this venue?'

'What a splendid idea, my lady. I have my diary in my handbag. Excuse me for a moment and I'll go and check which days are available. Do we know exactly when the wanderers return?'

Liza was handing out socks to the lady sitting next to them and heard the question. 'They'll be here Monday next week, Ma, which gives us the weekend to prepare.' She abandoned the socks and sat in the empty chair, which meant that Mrs Thomas would have to find somewhere else to sit.

'Can I help with the party? Joe and I like making things look pretty. We could use the bunting from the parties we've had. There are still plenty of balloons left over too.'

'You don't need to ask, my dear, nobody will fight you for the privilege, I can assure you. Look around – most of the members are almost the same age as your grandmother. I hardly think they'll want to be involved in something so energetic.'

'I only come because you do, I don't really like being the youngest here,' Liza said. 'The WI meetings are even worse, but I'm going to stick it out because it's my duty.' She hesitated and then continued firmly. 'I've decided I'm definitely going to train to be a nurse. I don't have the brains to be a doctor like Sarah, but I'm quite clever enough to be a nurse.'

This wasn't a surprise to Joanna as her daughter had mentioned it a couple of times. 'I think that's an excellent idea. I seem to recall that passing the St John's exams means that you're already well in advance of what's required in the first year of training.'

'That's what's decided me. Dr Willoughby said that I've only got a few more exams to take and then I'll be fully qualified as a first-aider. He said that he'll be my reference when I apply. I'd like to train at the hospital in Ramsgate, then I can get home when I get a day off.'

'Perfect. You have to be seventeen to start, so you've got plenty of time to get your school certificate and complete your training with St John's. Sarah was able to join two thirds of the way through the academic year because of having passed those exams.'

'Dr Willoughby said all nurses do a three-month preliminary course and if they pass that exam than they can start working on the wards,' Liza said. 'He thinks I won't need to do the preliminary instruction, which would be a bonus.'

'Has Joe said anything more about his plans to join the RAF as soon as he's old enough?' This was something that worried Joanna, as the mortality rate for airmen was staggeringly high.

'You'll not change his mind on that, Ma, he's got all the pamphlets and talks of nothing else but becoming a pilot.'

'In which case I hope that his eyesight or hearing isn't A1 and he can't fly. I won't be so worried if he's ground crew. I no longer expect the war to be over by then, which is sad.'

Mrs Thomas trundled back, diary clutched to her ample bosom. 'I doubt that the mothers of the children would appreciate being asked to attend a party on their first day back. Therefore, I suggest that you book the village hall for Saturday the twelfth. That will give them sufficient time to resettle into village life.'

'Also holding it on the Saturday means those who would normally be working might have a few hours free,' Joanna said. 'My land girls now have Saturday afternoon off most weeks. I'm sure I can persuade some of them to help arrange party games for the little ones.'

'Mr Evans must announce the event in church on Sunday and ask for donations of suitable food. I'm sure then you'll have sufficient for a small spread.'

'Liza, would you be an angel and ask Mrs Evans?'

'I'll do it now.' The girl stepped around Mrs Thomas with a polite smile and dashed off. Her daughter and the vicar's wife had become good friends, despite the disparity in age. Liza was now a member of the choir so couldn't help with the crèche at the back of the church on Sunday mornings. However, she was often at the vicarage in the afternoon taking care of the children so he and his wife could get on with parish business.

Jean drifted across and took the empty seat. 'I just wanted to tell you that I've just heard someone has been asking questions about Lord Harcourt and Goodwill House.'

'What sort of questions?'

'About the estate, how often Lord Harcourt visits, that sort of thing.'

Jean knew about the new claimant and the investigation into the wife and the poor soul who she claimed was her husband.

'Thank you for telling me, but I don't think there's anything they can discover that will help their claim,' Joanna said.

Jean didn't smile, in fact she looked very serious indeed. 'It occurred to me, my lady, that if our Lord Harcourt died then this woman's son would automatically inherit the title.'

Joanna stared at her friend. 'Good gracious, Jean, that's a bit far-fetched, don't you think? I cannot believe for one minute that a mother, a wealthy woman with so much to lose, would even contemplate something so appalling as murdering a complete stranger in order to obtain a title for her son, let alone murder Peter.' She smiled as she recalled the news she'd received from Mr Broome. 'Anyway, it's academic as there's no son, only two daughters.'

Jean looked relieved. 'You'd be surprised at what people will do to get something they desperately want.'

She spoke with such vehemence that Joanna thought that maybe Jean had experienced something similar before she'd come to live at Goodwill House. Now wasn't the time to ask Jean to divulge any secrets, but she stored the information away, hoping that one day she'd know.

'It beggars belief. I think I could possibly kill to protect those who I love but certainly not for something like this.'

'I should think not, Joanna, and neither would I. But there are people in this world, even those from good homes with the best education, who are quite capable of doing something so despicable.'

As soon as they got home, Joanna called Peter. She had his private number, the one for his Kensington flat, and asked the operator to connect her. He picked up the receiver immediately.

'Peter, it's Joanna...'

'Excellent, we must be telepathic. I was about to call you. I've got news that isn't helpful. The two women, the missing mother and sister, that we were trying to locate have sailed to America. Zero chance of speaking to them now.'

'That makes me more convinced that there's something nefarious going on here. Although, I suppose, relocating somewhere safer does make sense.'

'It would, but for it to happen at exactly the same time as the new Lord Harcourt was discovered is decidedly suspicious,' Peter said. 'Sorry, I haven't even wished you a good evening! Did you ring for an update or something else?'

'This might seem unnecessarily alarmist, but Jean's convinced that this woman is dangerous.'

'Exactly what are you suggesting?'

'It sounds ridiculous, but could this woman murder the man she's claiming to be her husband so he can't speak up?'

His rich, deep laughter echoed down the line. 'Murder? That's a bit far-fetched. She just wants to be known as Lady Harcourt, it will give her and her daughters added status.'

'If you don't mind not being Lord Harcourt, then shall we forget all about this investigation?'

'I agree, but before we do that, I'm arranging for a medical officer to visit this Lord Harcourt. The wife can't refuse as he's still officially a soldier. She'll be told that until someone has seen the patient and confirmed his identity, then he can't be officially discharged. I can't see that she can object to this unless she has something to hide.'

'Why don't I go too?' Joanna said impulsively. 'Again, she's unlikely to refuse to meet the widow of the late Lord Harcourt if she's coming to pay her respects to the new one?'

'I'm not entirely happy about you going but it's absolutely none of my business,' Peter said. 'As you say, what's more natural than for you to contact her? If they refuse to allow either the army medic or you to visit, then that will raise red flags.'

'Peter, you're still a Harcourt and part of this family, even if only as a third cousin removed or whatever it is. As soon as I have a date for this visit, I'll let you know and perhaps we could meet for dinner. I intend to stay overnight in London so that I can catch up with my daughter, Sarah, for a few hours. As you know, she's in her second year at the Royal Free doing her medical training.'

'I'd like that. I'll tell you when my chap has arranged to visit. Thank you for your input. Goodbye, hopefully we'll meet in the not-too-distant future.'

Thoughtfully Joanna replaced the receiver. What on earth had she been thinking? The very last person she wished to see was this new Lady Harcourt or her injured husband. She also wasn't sure that inviting Peter to have dinner with her was a sensible plan. She'd seen the gleam in his eye when he'd looked at her and didn't want to give him any encouragement.

She was still in love with John, thought of him several times a day, and prayed that it would be longer than a few weeks before he was sufficiently well trained to be on active service as a pilot in the RAF. Their passionate, but far too brief, love affair had been the first time in her life that she'd been truly happy. Although she accepted that she could never be with him, she knew she'd never love anybody else in the same way and therefore would never remarry. A marriage without love was something she'd experienced once with David and had absolutely no wish to experience again.

16

Bob cruised to a halt outside a row of neat, detached houses in Regina Road. This wasn't the kind of home a family in desperate financial need would occupy – the rent for such a property would be too much. This was a wasted journey, but whoever lived here might be able to give him the information he wanted.

He kicked his bike onto the stand and stood for a few moments, assessing the neighbourhood. The lawns were mowed, hedges were clipped and where there was a picket fence, it was undamaged and painted.

It was impossible to tell if this was the sort of place that held families of all ages. He checked the numbers on the doors and saw that he wanted the third one along. He frowned as he marched up the front path. His natural mother and her family had definitely moved to this address and he couldn't fathom how they'd been able to afford it.

He knocked, this time more softly than on the previous door. There was silence and then he heard light footsteps approaching.

It swung open and he clutched the door frame. The dazed woman facing him blanched, and only his quick reaction prevented her from falling backwards in a dead faint. There was no doubt about it – this was the woman who'd given him life.

As he gently held her, his heart was singing. The woman was a redhead, just like him. Surely this meant that he and Daphne weren't related after all and it had just been a horrible coincidence.

'I'm sorry to turn up unannounced. I think you've guessed who I am.'

There was a scuffle further down the passageway and a man, his face etched with pain, hobbled into view.

'Gordon Bennett! You must be the nipper we gave up all those years ago. You look just like your mum.'

The woman he was cradling recovered her composure. 'I can't believe you're here. I've not stopped thinking about you all these years and praying that you were happy.' She stepped away, mopping her eyes on the corner of her pinny. 'Come in, we want to hear everything about your life. I want to know why you've come to find me.'

He followed her down the passage into a sunny kitchen similar to the one in his parents' home. 'My name's Robert Andrews, but I'm called Bob.'

This seemed the most sensible way to start the conversation. Despite his initial joy that he'd got the answer he craved, he was now less certain, and needed to hear it confirmed. Speaking about this woman's infidelity in front of her disabled husband was going to be difficult.

'I'm Angela and that's my hubby, David Johnson. Sit down, I'll make you a cuppa.'

'I'm just going to water the beans, love, leave you two to catch up. Glad to meet you, Bob.' He shuffled away and Bob thought what a gentleman this veteran was.

'I'm sorry to be so direct, Mrs Johnson, but there's something I need to know, and I couldn't really ask you when Mr Johnson was present. What was the name of my birth father? I've no intention of contacting him but there's a possibility his daughter, the woman I'm in love with, could be my half-sister. Was his name Taylor? I don't need to know anything else.'

'No, it wasn't,' she said. 'Are you sure you don't want to know his name?'

'Absolutely. I've got a mum and dad; I don't need any others.' He realised this sounded harsh and wished he'd chosen his words more carefully.

'Of course you don't,' Mrs Johnson said. 'I always wanted to know you were well, have prayed most nights that one day I might find out and God has answered my prayers. My husband was gravely injured and could no longer be a true husband to me and, although this is no excuse for how I behaved, when I met your father, I couldn't resist.' She smiled, and it was strange staring into the face of someone who looked so like him. 'I don't regret it because you were the result.'

'What sort of man was he?' Bob asked.

'He was a good man; his wife was an invalid, so we had that in common. It didn't last long, and I ended it before I knew I was expecting, so he doesn't know anything about you.'

'I know that you only gave me up because you already had three children and couldn't afford to bring up another one. Do my siblings have the same colour hair as you and me?'

'Your sister, Alison, does, but Billy and Reg are dark like their dad used to be.'

'It's just good to finally know a little about myself.'

Over tea and biscuits, he explained about his abandoned wedding. They told him how they came to be living in such a smart house.

'We had a bit of luck about fifteen years ago. David inherited a nice sum of money from a great-aunt he didn't know existed. We were able to rent this house and provide for our family.'

There was an awkward silence as they each considered what might have been if they'd kept him. Bob was suddenly glad that they hadn't; he was happy with his life and would never have met his beloved Daphne if he'd remained in this family.

When he left, he shook hands with David and kissed Angela on the cheek, knowing that he'd probably never see either of them again. He hoped that Angela could now stop worrying about the baby she'd been forced to give up, as she knew he was happy.

He perched on his motorbike for a few moments, gathering his thoughts. He could scarcely believe that his life had been turned upside down so suddenly and so wonderfully. If he hadn't taken his team to assist Lady Harcourt, he might never have bumped into Daphne and gone in search of the truth.

Now all that remained was to convince his beloved girl that they were meant to be together and persuade her to become his fiancée once more.

* * *

Daphne put the last of her personal items into the chest of drawers she was sharing with Sal, delighted that the three of them were back in their original bedroom. Lady Harcourt had kept her promise that their room would be restored first.

'It's like a new beginning, isn't it, girls? After sending my sworn testimony to the court, I finally believe I can move on. Mr Broome was exceptionally kind and refused to charge me for his services,' Charlie said happily.

'You're right,' Sal said as she flung herself full length onto her bed. 'I'm like a pig in clover. For the first time in me life, I'm proud of what I'm doing. I got money in me purse, two good friends, and am free as a bird.'

'I agree,' Daphne said. 'Which reminds me, I wonder why Bob hasn't contacted me as he must have discovered something about his parentage by now.' It had been a week since she'd gone to Romford with him.

'I honestly think that in this case, no news is good news, Daphne. I wouldn't be surprised if he turns up with your engagement ring in his pocket,' Charlie said.

'I wouldn't accept it if he did. But I'll always be fond of him and would be relieved that we hadn't been breaking any taboos when we were engaged.'

'I ain't having none of that malarkey, Daphne. We both know you're still in love with him.'

'Then you know more than I do.' She busied herself rearranging the items on top of the chest of drawers, hoping they didn't see her tell-tale blush. No matter how much she denied it, she had a nasty suspicion they were right.

'If you've quite done fiddling, we need to get a move on if we're going to be able to do anything useful for this welcome home party. Mr Pickering's so happy to have his family back. His wife isn't at all what I expected. I like her, but she's no doormat, is she?' Charlie was right.

'I think that's why the poor bloke went to pieces when she left. She keeps him in order, and he didn't know how to carry on without her in charge. Things won't be quite so relaxed in future. Didn't you notice – she's not keen on him spending time with us?' Daphne said.

'I'm not surprised. Must've been a bit of a shock for her to find three stunningly beautiful young ladies working on the farm, the only thought in their pretty little heads to seduce her husband and steal the farm away from her,' Charlie said dryly.

They were laughing as they thundered down the stairs and dashed to the stable yard to collect the bicycles they were borrowing to get them down to the village. Daphne was a bit cross that they were the only three girls who'd volunteered to help out at the party to welcome back the reunited families. As she and her friends owed Lady Harcourt a favour for getting them moved back into their lovely bedroom, she was happy to help.

They were pedalling merrily to the village when the sirens began to wail ahead and on the base. They scarcely had time to register this when several squadrons of fighters screamed overhead.

'Quickly, let's get over the gate and into that field. Then we can shelter against the hedge. Our bikes will be safe enough as they won't be seen from the air,' Charlie yelled over the noise. They had to get off the road, as they would be an easy target for a Junkers, a German fighter-bomber, if one of them managed to get past the Hurricanes and Spitfires.

The dogfights seemed to be taking place nearer Folkestone and Dover than Stodham. They huddled where they were for half an hour and the noise of the battle receded. Charlie stood up, shaded her eyes with her hand and stared into the sky.

'I can't see anything. I think it's safe to carry on, but I'll have to go into the middle of the field where I can have a better look.'

'Don't be daft, Charlie, it's not safe until the all-clear has sounded,' Daphne shouted but her friend ignored her advice.

Suddenly there was a roar of engines and what looked like a huge grey blanket appeared right overhead. The Junkers 88 was no higher than the ceiling of their bedroom. How could it have got past the fighters so easily?

All three of them were wearing their khaki dungarees and the gunner must have thought Charlie was a soldier because he opened fire. Daphne cowered back, helpless to assist her friend, who was now face down on the grass.

Then two Spitfires skimmed over the hedge and what happened next was inevitable. The enemy bomber burst into flames and crashed with a massive explosion half a mile away. Sal moved quicker than she did and got to their friend first.

'Charlie, are you hurt? For gawd's sake, say something,' Sal gasped as she dropped to her knees beside the worryingly still form.

Then Liza suddenly hurdled the gate and was running towards them. The girl was a first-aider so was exactly the right person to take charge. Daphne saw Joe race past, head down, hopefully heading for the doctor's house, which was only a five-minute bike ride away.

Daphne touched Sal on the shoulder and her friend looked up and nodded, then shuffled backwards.

'I can't see no blood, no bullet wounds, but she ain't conscious.'

'Let me see.' Liza carefully ran her hands down Charlie's arms and legs, and checked her spine and her neck before carefully turning her over.

Sal said something very rude, and Daphne didn't blame her. There was blood seeping through the right leg of Charlie's dungarees. A lot of blood. Liza immediately put pressure on the wound. Daphne wasn't good with this sort of thing and swallowed bile.

They stood by helplessly whilst a girl several years younger than them coped beautifully with this potentially life-threatening injury. 'Don't look so worried, it's not as bad as it seems. There's a lot of blood, but I'm pretty sure no major blood vessels have been damaged. I'm keeping pressure on and you can see that already there's nothing else coming through.'

'Why is she unconscious? Did she hit her head when she went down?' Daphne asked.

'Shock can render a patient comatose for a while. Her colour's good and I think she's coming round.'

Liza was a revelation. Up until now, Daphne had thought her the less able of the twins, but how wrong she was.

'My leg hurts like the very devil,' Charlie said quite clearly.

'The bleeding German shot you. What were you thinking of? You should've stayed under cover like what we were.'

The sound of a car approaching at speed meant that Dr Willoughby would be there in a moment. 'I'm going to undo the gate so he can bring the car right in. I'm pretty sure you'll have to be taken to hospital this time, Charlie, but at least you don't have to wait for an ambulance.'

Daphne ran across and had just untied the rope and pulled the gate back when the car slowed. The doctor expertly steered it into the field. It bumped and juddered across the grass and rocked to halt next to Charlie, who was now sitting up and looking a lot better despite the injury to her leg.

Dr Willoughby jumped out with his medical bag in his hand, and five minutes after his arrival, Charlie was safely on the rear seat with the bullet wound neatly bandaged.

'I'm taking her straight to the hospital,' he called out of the window as he reversed the car before driving across the field and back through the gate.

Liza got to her feet, smiling. 'That was good fun. I can't go to the hall like this, I'm going to have to go home and change. Will you tell my mother what happened and that I'll be there as soon as I can?'

'We will. Can you ask someone to collect Charlie's bike? She borrowed it and it will be wanted tomorrow.' Daphne brushed herself down and then she and Sal reclaimed their abandoned bicycles. 'We'd better get a move on, or we'll be late.'

'Blimey, that were exciting,' Sal said as she followed her through the gate and back into the lane. Daphne carefully fastened the bit of rope around the post, just in case there were some lurking cows she hadn't spotted at the far side of the field.

'Exciting? More like terrifying. Charlie could have been killed.'

'You might as well leave that open, Daphne, them fire engines and that will need to go through here to put that blooming plane out.'

'I'm sure there's a gate closer to where that Junkers crashed,' Daphne said. 'I expect you can see the smoke and flames for miles. I wonder what happened to Joe? I thought he'd come back after taking the message to the doctor.'

'I reckon he's gone on to tell Lady Harcourt. Ain't it funny that our Charlie has been injured twice and both times the local doc has come to her rescue?'

After the excitement they'd just been through, nothing the children could do at the party bothered Daphne. On the way home, she and Sal stopped at the doctor's house. His housekeeper informed them that Charlie would remain in Ramsgate Hospital for a few days but was in no danger.

'That's a relief, isn't it, Sal?'

'I reckon the doc will fuss round her and maybe this time the two of them will make a go of it.'

'After what Charlie told us the other day, I doubt it. I don't want her to leave, and if they get married, that's what will happen.' Daphne couldn't help thinking about Bob. If he'd got the news they both wanted, would she agree to marry him?

* * *

Bob had scarcely had time to stow his kit when he'd arrived at RAF Hawkinge last week before he was in a hangar with three other blokes repairing a Spit. This base, just outside Folkestone, was under the control of fighter command and was now a satellite airfield linked to Biggin Hill sector station.

The men he was working with were efficient, but they were

already an established team and closed ranks on his arrival. He was the senior NCO and they followed his orders when he gave them but made no effort to let him into their circle.

This didn't bother him. He just kept his head down, did his job, and when he had a moment to himself, thought about how he was going to approach Daphne with the good news.

Kites weren't permanently based here but arrived from Biggin Hill and other bases in the same sector at five o'clock when he and his ground crew were just crawling out of bed. The flyers were scrambled from Hawkinge and came back to refuel and rearm as and when. At the end of the day, they returned to the somewhat safer Biggin Hill or Hornchurch.

The visitors, for that's what they were, remained with their kites to eat their breakfast, their chutes dumped on their tailplanes ready to be grabbed when the order to scramble came over the Tannoy.

This base was similar to Manston in appearance. Every building was camouflaged with green and brown paint and wherever you looked, there were thousands of sandbags piled up. There were machine-gun posts, dugouts and shelters around the airfield perimeter.

Bob had been there just over a week and hadn't had a moment to telephone Goodwill House. He decided it might be better to wait until he had a few hours free – god knows when that would be – and go and see Daphne in person. This wasn't the sort of conversation a bloke could have over the telephone.

He was busy doublechecking the spare parts that had just arrived when he was interrupted.

'Oi, Corp, we're done here. We thought we'd nip over to the NAAFI for a cuppa and a wad before starting the Hurry.' This was yelled at him from the other side of the hangar by the least likeable of the three men in his team.

Bob was about to tell them to get on with their bloody work, but they vanished before he could do so. They'd all started work at six and it was now just after eleven. They'd had a break at nine o'clock and weren't entitled to another until midday.

He could put them on a charge when they came back, but that would just make him look as if he wasn't doing his job, and they knew it. He ran to the far end of the hangar, hoping they might still be near enough for him to yell at. Even these three wouldn't disobey a direct order.

They were walking briskly across the strip towards the distant buildings where the NAAFI was situated when he heard the scream of two Junkers JU87 Bs, known as Stukas, at the edge of the airfield.

These gull-winged dive bombers flew across the Channel at sea level so could avoid being detected by radar. This meant no one on the base was prepared, no siren had wailed, and there were no fighters being directed to Hawkinge by those in command.

These murdering bastards opened fire on his men, who were running for their lives. He watched in helpless horror as they were mowed down. Then the Stukas dropped their bombs, missing the runway but hitting a hangar and another building. Pieces of red-hot shrapnel sliced through trees and buildings and there was so much smoke, he could no longer see his men.

He'd started to run towards them before the bombs had landed. These men might be disrespectful, but they didn't deserve to die. As he tore across the strip, he sent up a hasty prayer to whatever god might be listening that his men had just flung themselves to the ground and weren't, in fact, mortally wounded.

17

Daphne and Sal had to stay later at Fiddler's Farm over the next few days, as they had Charlie's work to do as well.

'If I see another blooming turnip, that'll be too soon for me. Thank gawd this field's done,' Sal said as they trudged back to the barn at the end of another long day.

'Mrs Pickering is doing the deliveries to the village and taking care of the livestock now, which makes our life a lot easier,' Daphne said.

'I miss them porkers, but as they're for the knacker's yard in the next few weeks, I'm glad I don't have to see them every day.'

'The late crop of potatoes is coming up next week. As Charlie didn't have time to teach either of us how to drive the tractor, I suppose we'll be using the horses again.'

'It needs two of us picking the spuds and one with the team. I don't see that we can clear that field on our own.'

'Pickering will have to drive the tractor or the horses whilst we pick the spuds up. How long do you reckon Charlie will be away?'

Sal chucked her hoe on the pile of miscellaneous farm implements without bothering to clean it.

Daphne was going to point this out but then decided to follow her lead. Things might be better on the farm, but if Mr Pickering didn't mind if his tools were left in a dirty heap in the barn, it wasn't up to her to mention it.

'It's been a lot easier since we've got our own bicycles and don't have to bring the horse and cart. I noticed Joe riding Star the other day – I suppose she needs exercising now.'

Sal was already astride her cycle and pedalling down the track so didn't answer. Daphne caught up and together they rode home. It was already past eight o'clock and their supper would be congealing, as the other girls would have eaten at seven.

'That's the third time you've almost run into the ditch, Daphne, why do you keep looking up all the time?'

'I'm checking for Germans. That plane just turned up from nowhere.'

'I was thinking that maybe we could cycle to Ramsgate tomorrow night and see Charlie?'

'We'd have to leave a lot earlier, as visiting time's between six and eight. I'll speak to Mr Pickering if I get a chance tomorrow morning. There's a bus goes past the end of the lane just after six.'

'What about getting back? There ain't no buses after eight o'clock.'

'Then we'll have to have a very brief visit. After hoeing a field all day, I don't think I'll have the energy to cycle that far,' Daphne said as they turned into the long straight drive of Goodwill House.

* * *

Mr Pickering was happy for them to leave in time to catch the bus the following evening. 'Give Charlie my regards and ask her when I can expect her to be back at work.'

'I don't suppose she knows, Mr Pickering,' Daphne said. 'But I doubt it will be for at least another week. How are we going to manage the potatoes with just the two of us?'

'I've arranged for a couple of girls from another farm to help out. They're just hedging and ditching at the moment and won't be missed.'

'That's good. Thank you for letting us leave on time tonight. See you tomorrow.' Daphne hoped he didn't take her remark the wrong way, as she wasn't being impertinent, but he grinned and strolled off. He was a changed man from the grumpy, scruffy person he'd been when they'd first arrived.

She and Sal jogged down the track to make sure they were waiting to wave down the bus when it came past. Daphne wondered if she'd ever be so dependent on another person that their absence would make her fall apart. Mr Pickering had done so when his wife and children had been evacuated to Norfolk.

The bus groaned to a halt and luckily there were plenty of seats. They took the first two and were barely settled when the bus drove off. The conductor wobbled to their side.

'Where to, ladies?'

'Ramsgate hospital, please. Could you tell us what time the last bus leaves this evening?'

They gave him the coppers, he clipped two tickets and handed them over before answering. 'The last one's at seven-thirty. It'll be full, mind you, with folk coming back from work, so I reckon you might have to stand.'

'Thank you, that won't matter as long as we can get back and don't have to walk,' Daphne said as she handed one of the tickets to her friend.

The conductor returned to his position by the driver so he could chat to him through the sliding glass window.

'That's good, ain't it? I reckon we'll have almost an hour to spend with Charlie,' Sal said. 'Pity we ain't got anything to give her, but we've plenty of best wishes and love from the others.'

'She's a bit accident-prone, don't you think? This is the second time she's needed medical attention and we've only been here a few months. Neither of us have had injuries.'

Sal laughed, turning several heads in their direction. 'My ex, Den, tried to murder me and your Bob thought you was a German and nearly brained you, so I reckon we're about even with our Charlie.'

'I'm trying to decide whether no news is good news where he's concerned. It's been more than a week and still he hasn't written or telephoned.'

'He'll be wanting to see you in person, I expect.'

The bus picked up a few youngsters and a couple of housewives in Stodham. They'd have a long walk home if they were going to the pictures, as it wouldn't finish until long after the bus departed.

They weren't the only passengers getting off at the hospital, but they were certainly the scruffiest. Gumboots and grubby dungarees were hardly suitable for going into an immaculate ward.

'I hope the ward sister lets us in dressed as we are. The others are in their Sunday best.'

'I don't give two hoots,' Sal said. 'No snooty sister is going to stop me seeing Charlie. Don't say nothing about being smartly dressed on that notice, do it?'

'No, it's just saying there's to be no smoking by visitors or alcoholic beverages to be brought onto the premises.'

'That's all right, then. She'll be in the women's medical ward, I reckon. Ain't that an arrow pointing to it over there?'

Sal's reading had improved no end since Daphne and Charlie had been helping her when they had a few spare minutes in the evenings.

'Don't you think we should ask at reception in case she's somewhere else?'

'If it ain't the right place, I'm sure they'll soon tell us where to go.'

Sal headed off and Daphne trotted along behind, worried her friend was going to cause a scene of some sort and that was something she really hated.

There was a staff nurse in a starched white apron standing guard at the door of the ward they thought Charlie might be in. Daphne stepped in front of Sal in order to prevent an incident.

'We are here to see Miss Charlotte Somiton.'

'She's in the end bed. She already has a visitor, so I'm afraid you'll have to wait until he goes, as only two visitors are allowed at a time.'

'Thank you. Would you be so kind as to inform this visitor that we are waiting? We have to catch a bus back to Goodwill House in half an hour.'

'Oh dear! I can see why you're anxious to get in. I'll see what I can do.'

The nurse beckoned over a student and sent her with a message.

'I reckon it's that Dr Willoughby. Can't think of any other bloke what might be visiting, can you?'

Sal was proved right, as this gentleman arrived at the door with an apologetic smile. 'I'm on duty here tonight and thought I'd pop in and see how Charlie was getting on. I'll come back later.' With a friendly smile, the doctor walked briskly down the corridor.

'He ain't wearing a white coat so I reckon he weren't telling us the truth,' Sal said gleefully.

'It's none of our business. Let's get in and spend what little time we've got with our best friend.'

There were ten metal beds down either side of the ward, all

immaculate, not a wrinkled counterpane in sight. The lino was so highly polished, it was hazardous. Charlie was sitting up in bed watching the door and waved to them.

'Thank you so much for taking the time to see me. I've just had Dr Willoughby in for a few minutes, but I'd much rather talk to you two.'

There were already two plain wooden chairs standing in military precision by the bed and Daphne looked around anxiously before daring to move one so they could both sit down. 'How are you? You look tickety-boo. Mr Pickering sends his best wishes and also wants to know when you're coming back to work.'

'I had twenty-four stitches in my leg. They don't come out for another four days and I'm not allowed out of hospital until they do. Then the consultant said I must have at least another week's convalescence before I'm allowed to return.'

'Blimey, we didn't realise it were so serious,' Sal said. 'We should have bought you a clean nightie and that but thought you'd be coming out tomorrow.'

Charlie grinned and pointed to her ugly nightgown. 'This is hospital issue, not exactly flattering and far too hot for this weather. The doctor has kindly offered to call in first thing tomorrow morning and pick up what I need. I didn't like to ask him to take back my dirty clothes. Do you think you could do that for me, please?'

Sal was already looking in the small wooden locker next to the bed. 'I've got them. Someone's already folded them up neat as you like. We'll sort out what you need and make sure it's downstairs when the doctor comes. You ain't going to be paid whilst you're off – can you manage?'

Charlie nodded. 'Remember I told you I had a bit of a nest egg and I've still got half of it. Do you think you'll be able to come and see me again? I was the only one without any visitors the last two nights.'

'We get Saturday afternoon free so can come for a proper visit then. We'll make sure we bring you something nice to eat if we can find anything in the shops. I've got plenty of points to use,' Daphne said.

'Could I ask you both another favour? Would you please ask Lady Harcourt if she'd mind if I come back to Goodwill House to convalesce? I won't need any assistance from anyone, but I'll still be underfoot for a week at least.'

'I'm sure she won't object. It was different when you were almost unconscious last time,' Daphne told her. 'You can sit on the terrace with the old Lady Harcourt and keep her entertained.'

The half an hour sped by and both she and Sal embraced their friend before hurrying out, arriving just in time as the bus was already approaching the stop. The conductor had predicted there'd be no seats available. By the time they got on, it was like playing sardines inside, and Daphne and Sal had to squeeze onto the end of the line.

'Golly, let's hope this bus doesn't have to stop suddenly as we'll all go flying.'

'I ain't going anywhere,' Sal said with a grin. 'I'm jammed in good and tight.'

* * *

Joanna was delighted to hear that Charlie was progressing so well and reassured the girls their friend would be welcome back whenever she was ready to come home.

'I'll ask Jean to put something tasty in a tin and it can go with her nightwear and toiletries when Dr Willoughby calls in tomorrow morning.'

'Thank you, my lady, that's kind of you. I'm going to write a note so that Dr Willoughby can deliver it for me with the other things, telling Charlie the good news.' Daphne smiled happily and rushed off to eat her somewhat belated supper.

Joanna had asked Mr Broome to make the necessary arrangements for her visit to Guildford, as she thought it better not to contact this new Lady Harcourt herself. He'd agreed to do this as long as he was allowed to accompany her. Did this mean she couldn't meet Peter for dinner? She wasn't sure if she would be pleased or disappointed if this was the case. She heard from her solicitor the next morning.

'My lady, the other Lady Harcourt agreed with considerable reluctance to allow us to visit the invalid on Friday afternoon. I hope that's convenient.'

'Yes, it's ideal, as my daughter has the following morning free. A rare occurrence, and it means we can spend time together. I'll be remaining in town overnight but will be grateful to have your company for the visit.'

'I'll get my secretary to book our train tickets and we must just hope that they're running smoothly that day,' Mr Broome said. 'I was in Town last week and the journey took three hours.'

'In which case, Mr Broome, I suggest that you have seats booked on the first available train. I'd rather be early than late.'

'I'll certainly do that, my lady. I'll let you know the train as soon as it's booked. Do you want my secretary to reserve your return for Saturday morning as well?'

'Thank you, how kind,' Joanna said. 'That will make life so much simpler.'

There was time for a letter to reach Sarah if she asked Joe to take it down to the village immediately. Before writing this note, she rang the Savoy and booked a room for the night. She then contacted Peter's office and left a message with his very efficient secretary that she would be in London on Friday evening and staying at the Savoy. They might as well eat there, as they had an excellent restaurant. The food was, so Mrs Thomas had told her, very good, despite there being rationing.

A letter arrived for her on Thursday morning and she immediately recognised the bold, scrawled black writing. It was from Peter.

Dear Joanna,

I'm delighted that you're going to be at the Savoy this Friday. I've taken the liberty of booking us a table for dinner at seven.

I'm assuming that you will be safely returned from Guildford by then. The medical chap will be visiting on the Monday following – the Harcourt woman refused to let him in any sooner.

I'm still not sanguine about you going but if you have your solicitor chappie with you then you should be safe enough.

I look forward to having dinner with you on Friday.

Yours sincerely,

The letter was finished with a scrawl that was barely recognisable as his name. She smiled and folded the paper back into the envelope. Should she be worried about the doctor from the army not being given access to the patient?

* * *

Bob's eyes were streaming by the time he reached his men as the buildings were on fire. He dropped to his knees. The smoke was clearer at ground level. He knew at once that there was nothing he could do for these poor blokes.

They'd been mowed down mercilessly and each of them had received half a dozen or more bullets in the back. Their uniform jackets were blood-soaked. He checked for a pulse on each of them just to be absolutely sure and then stood up slowly, his heart heavy.

For these three to have died in such a way was unbearable. Being shot in the back was the worst form of cowardice by those German bastard murderers. Jimmy gone, and now these men he barely knew.

God – would he have to notify their families? He didn't even know if they had loved ones, as in the short time he'd been working with them, they'd exchanged no personal information.

Bob coughed, cleared his throat, and slowly regained his feet, moving like an old man, not one of barely twenty-three. There was nothing he could do for these men apart from standing guard until the wagon from the morgue turned up.

As the smoke from the fires began to dissipate, he could see the devastation the Luftwaffe had wreaked on the base. The three corpses at his feet were far worse than any crater on the edge of the strip or holes in the hangars. In the distance, he could hear voices shouting, vehicles moving – so it wouldn't be long before someone came in his direction.

His stomach lurched as the distinctive roar of an approaching fighter returning to the base filled the air. He and his men were marooned in the middle of the runway and not only could he be killed, but far worse, the kite and its flyer might well perish too. Visibility was still poor, he couldn't see more than a few yards on either side through the swirling smoke. Whoever was coming in to land would be flying almost blind and relying on his instruments.

No point in shouting, no one would hear him. The sensible thing to do was run for his life, but he couldn't do that. He had to stop the fighter landing. This was paramount. The unfortunate blokes at his feet were past caring but he had to prevent a prang and a further fatality.

He ripped off his jacket and ran towards the noise. He waved the garment frantically above his head in the vain hope this might be enough to warn the flyer to abort his landing.

The engine sound was distinctive. It was a Spit. It was very close – too close. As he emerged from the smoke, he could see the kite coming directly at him. The look of horror on the flyer's face meant he'd been seen. He flung himself face down on the strip and the Spit screamed over his back. He felt the heat from the engine. The noise deafened him. He was spattered with oil but was still alive and the Spit had safely soared back over the runway.

He collapsed in an undignified heap to await the arrival of the ambulances and fire tenders that were now racing in his direction.

18

Daphne didn't have time to dwell on the lack of communication from Bob, as she and Sal were too busy hoeing the last field of turnips. Friday morning had an autumnal nip in the air and everyone had on their smart green jumpers when they sat down for breakfast. Porridge was back on the menu; this was appreciated by everyone as it was tasty, especially with a dollop of homemade jam or honey.

'It'll be winter before we know it,' one of the girls said happily. 'The nights are already longer and we don't have to work so much.'

'Will we get laid off, do you know?' Daphne asked the girl.

'Crikey, I'd not thought of that. I can't afford to pay my board and lodging here if I'm not working full-time.'

'I'm going to ask Jean. If she doesn't have the answer, then I'm sure she'll ask Lady Harcourt for us.' Daphne picked up all the empty plates and carried them through to the kitchen – one never went back and forth empty-handed.

'Have you come for more toast, Daphne?' Jean asked as she turned, rosy cheeked, a toasting fork in either hand, each speared through a slice of yesterday's bread.

'Actually, I've come to ask you something. I'm not sure you know the answer, but I'm hoping you can find out for us.' She explained and Jean nodded as she removed the hot toast from her forks and dropped it onto a breadboard and quickly sliced it in half. Daphne knew the drill and put each piece into the waiting silver toast rack.

'I'll take this through; it's so much better when it's hot.'

'Thank you, Daphne. I won't be able to ask Lady Harcourt today or tomorrow as she's going to be in London. However, I'll certainly do so as soon as she returns.'

She relayed the housekeeper's answer to those sitting around the table.

'I ain't bothered if we don't know for a week or two,' Sal said as she munched through a piece of toast liberally spread with dripping and sprinkled with salt.

'The girls working on the dairy farm will be kept all year round,' Daphne said as she sat down again. 'Although that's an advantage, I wouldn't want to be working the strange hours that they do. I expect the cows will still need milking even if it's pitch-dark at four o'clock in the morning.'

If they were laid off, would they be evicted? She doubted that many of them could pay their sixteen shillings board and lodging in full, if at all, if they weren't working.

'What will happen if we can't afford to pay our way here?' Daphne said.

It was Sal who reassured them. 'Crikey, they ain't going to let us trained girls go, are they? I reckon the Land Army will help out.'

* * *

As usual, the sirens went off twice that morning. Daphne and Sal raced for the shelter of the trees. They'd no intention of being shot like Charlie had been. At midday, they cycled back to the farm, hoes balanced over one shoulder, to collect their meal.

Today, Mrs Pickering invited them in. Daphne and Sal exchanged a worried glance, thinking they might be in trouble for some unspecified reason, but followed her anyway.

Daphne was relieved to see that places had been laid for both of them. The children, Peter and Rose, were perched on cushions and both smiled shyly in their direction.

'Wash up in the downstairs WC, girls, don't be long as I'm about to serve.'

Mr Pickering wasn't there but his cutlery was at the head of the table so presumably he'd join them. Daphne and Sal sloshed water over their faces, scrubbed their hands with the brush – no soap, as that was on the ration too.

'What do you reckon this is all about, Daphne?'

'I haven't the foggiest, but you know I love my food, and something smells absolutely scrumptious.'

'Good thing we ain't been with the pigs, as no amount of washing would make us smell nice enough to sit down at the table.'

Chicken and ham pie and creamy mashed potatoes with freshly picked vegetables was just the ticket. There was little conversation whilst they ate with enjoyment. Even the little ones tucked in without any assistance.

'That was a magnificent lunch, sweetheart,' Mr Pickering said. 'Shall I ask the girls whilst you get the afters?'

'You do that, love, I won't be a tick. Peter, Rose, you come with me. You can carry one plate each if you're very careful.'

The children squealed with delight and scrambled down from their high perches. Obviously, being involved in domestic work of any sort was still a treat for these children.

'Now, girls, you must be wondering why we asked you in today rather than eating your meal at the table outside.'

'We certainly are, Mr Pickering. I think that spread would have tasted just as delicious wherever we ate it.' Daphne beamed at him.

'Right. Well, we were wondering if you and Sal would like to live here instead of at Goodwill House? It would save you the travel and it's going to be nasty cycling in the dark during the winter.'

Daphne's first thought was that he'd just confirmed they wouldn't be laid off. Her second was that he hadn't included Charlie in the invitation.

'That's very kind of you, but it wouldn't be fair on Charlie for us to move and leave her on her own. Otherwise, I think we'd seriously think about it. Thank you for asking us.'

Sal didn't say anything but nodded her agreement. He glanced almost nervously at the scullery door, where his wife and children were pottering about.

'It's like this, my wife's not too taken with Charlie. She says that I talk about her too much, show her special favouritism and she doesn't want her living here.'

Sal had been silent up to this point, but now joined in. 'Dr Willoughby's interested in Charlie, I reckon they might make a go of it.'

Before Daphne had the chance to tell him Sal was just speculating, Mrs Pickering returned, having overheard the remark.

'In which case, he wouldn't want her living here and she won't want to come anyway. Please think about it, there's no rush, but perhaps you'd like to look at the bedroom you'd be sharing if you did come.'

It would have seemed impolite to refuse after being given such a tasty meal, so when the last mouthful of apple crumble and custard had gone, Daphne and Sal were given a conducted tour of the house.

The children had followed them and insisted that they look at their bedroom too. This was similar to the one they would occupy but instead of a large chest of drawers, there was a big wooden toy box.

'It's a lovely room, thank you for showing us. We have to get back to work or your daddy will be cross with us,' Daphne told them with a smile.

They skipped off and she and Sal were glad to slip out without further questioning.

'I ain't in no hurry to start hoeing, I'm too full. Eating so much when you've got to work all afternoon ain't a good idea,' Sal said plaintively as she rubbed her rounded tummy.

'As he doesn't check, we can go as quickly or slowly as we like. There was no bathroom upstairs or loo. I suppose that means you have to have a chamber pot under the bed and then empty it in the morning.'

'Reckon so – we're spoilt at Goodwill House. I'd rather cycle in the dark than live at Fiddler's Farm. Another thing, did you see the bit of soap with little black bits in it?'

'I didn't – was it significant?' Daphne asked.

'You catch fleas with a bit of wet soap. Works a treat, that does.'

Daphne shuddered. 'Another reason not to move – fleas wouldn't dare live somewhere so grand as Goodwill House!'

'That bedroom were ever so nice though, weren't it? More room, lovely comfortable beds as well.'

'It certainly was, Sal, if we didn't mind the fleas. But we'd have to muck in with the family and wouldn't have any privacy apart from in the bedroom. It might be pleasant up there now, but in the winter it'll be freezing, as I'm sure you noticed there's no fireplace.'

'No, I never saw, but I reckon you're right. Better we stay where we are. I wonder why they really asked us? Seems a bit odd to me.'

'Absolutely. We're a trio – we'll not leave Charlie, will we?'

* * *

Joanna discovered Mr Broome in the café enjoying *The Times* and a pile of hot toast. He jumped to his feet so suddenly his toast flew off the table to land, as it always did, butter side down.

'I apologise, my lady, as the train isn't due for three quarters of an hour, I thought you'd not be here for a while.'

'Please sit down, Mr Broome. Such a shame about your toast.'

'I'll order some more. What would you like? Or have you already breakfasted?'

'I haven't. I was too nervous to eat,' Joanna said. 'I'll have a pot of tea, nothing else, thank you.'

A waitress, possibly younger than Liza, was already on her knees, clearing up the mess. Mr Broome apologised – he seemed to be doing that a lot lately, or perhaps he had always done so, and she'd just not noticed.

'I'll get you fresh toast, sir, in a tick. And another pot of tea for your lady friend.'

The girl grinned up at him and then whisked away, leaving him apologising for the third time in as many minutes.

'I'm so sorry, my lady…'

'Please, Mr Broome, none of this is your fault and there's absolutely no need to apologise. Perhaps you would feel more at ease if you called me Joanna.'

His mouth rounded. He shook his head. 'Good heavens, that would never do. I always keep things professional with my clients.'

The tea and toast arrived, which smoothed over an awkward moment. Joanna hadn't meant to offend her companion, but she obviously had. Before her affair with John, she wouldn't have dreamt of suggesting such informality, but she was a different woman now.

Mr Broome appeared to have recovered his aplomb and she smiled politely and waited for him to continue. 'Forgive me for asking, my lady, but why are you nervous about visiting Lord Harcourt?'

Joanna shook her head. 'If the patient is actually who she says he is, it will be sad, and if he isn't, then it will be even worse.'

'I do believe that the whole thing is quite likely a massive fraud and that the unfortunate person unwillingly impersonating Lord Harcourt could be in danger.'

'Lord Harcourt changed his mind about that and I wish I could share his optimism.'

'That the medical officer has been denied access until Monday is suspicious,' Mr Broome said. 'I think we should detour to the War Office, my lady, and try to find someone who might have met this Lord Harcourt previously.'

'It's fortunate that we're catching an early train. We're not expected at Crawley Hall until the afternoon. As long as we arrive in Town by midday, we should have ample time. With any luck, Lord Harcourt will be in his office.'

Mr Broome munched through his toast with enjoyment and Joanna drank two cups of tea and watched him eat.

He then insisted on carrying her small overnight suitcase, despite her being quite capable of managing it for herself. It really wasn't worth arguing over something so trivial when she had far bigger things to worry about.

Their train hissed and puffed, stopped and started, but by some miracle managed to arrive only twenty minutes later than the scheduled time. Mr Broome dashed ahead to find a taxi, leaving her to arrive at a more ladylike pace.

On emerging from the station in London, Joanna stopped in delight. The vehicle Mr Broome had managed to obtain was perfect. 'Good heavens, what a splendid cab. I have seen these old cabs but never had the opportunity to ride in one. I just adore the way half the roof goes back like a perambulator hood.'

He held the door open for her and she skipped in, wishing the weather was slightly more clement so the hood could be opened. It would have blown away her smart cloche but that would have been a small price to pay.

Joanna enjoyed every moment of the bumpy journey and insisted that the taxi wait for them. She was determined to travel in it to Waterloo. The impressive War Office building was situated in Horse Guards Parade, not far from Whitehall. This time, it was she who dashed off, leaving her companion to follow or not as he wished.

'Good morning, I am Lady Harcourt and I wish to speak to Lieutenant Colonel Harcourt most urgently. Would it be possible for someone to see if he is here today?'

The smart ATS girl in her khaki uniform nodded vigorously and snatched up the receiver of the telephone on her desk. She passed on Joanna's request and smiled.

'Someone's coming down to collect you, my lady.'

A young lieutenant arrived at speed and slid to a halt in front of her. 'Lieutenant Humphrey, my lady, come to escort you. Would you care to come this way?'

He led her down a wide passageway and up an equally imposing staircase and then, three doors down, he stepped aside and bowed as he showed her into a large room in which three typists clattered away and there was the constant ringing of telephones.

Peter was standing in the open door of his inner sanctum. He came forward to take her hand.

'This is an unexpected pleasure, Joanna. Come through, you can tell me why you're here.'

As the door closed behind them, she heard Mr Broome's voice, but Peter didn't suggest that he join them. When she'd spoken of her fears over the telephone, Peter had laughed, but this time he took her seriously.

'Actually, after dismissing your fears so casually, I thought about it and decided to make further enquiries. It's fortuitous that you've come here. The lieutenant who brought you up here served with Stephen Harcourt. I'll send him with you. I wish I could come as well, but I'm too busy.'

'Presumably Lieutenant Humphrey knows of our concerns?'

'Good god, I should think not.' He sounded so like Mr Broome had earlier that Joanna laughed. He raised an eyebrow but she didn't explain. 'He thinks he's going to pay his respects to a wounded comrade who he thought had perished along with the rest of his brigade. Humphrey was serving elsewhere at the time of the explosion.'

'Oh dear, that rather complicates things, don't you think? If this young man identifies himself as someone who knew the patient personally, it could cause all sorts of problems if what we suspect is true.'

'But it could also prove our suspicions are incorrect. If this Lady Harcourt is happy for Humphrey to visit, then we've no further need to investigate.'

Previously he'd been anxious to keep her away from possible unpleasantness and now he was actively encouraging her to walk into it. She laughed again.

'Peter, I'm rather confused. Am I visiting the genuine article to pay my respects or going in order to uncover an impostor?'

He grinned and raised his hands as if surrendering. 'God knows – but as long as you've got your solicitor chap and my lieutenant with you, then I'm not concerned about your personal safety.'

* * *

Bob took a few moments to register the fact that he was still alive – but more importantly that the kite that had been about to land was also intact.

'Hey, you cretin, what the bleeding hell do you think you were doing?' An irate sergeant was standing over him, not an iota of sympathy or admiration in his expression.

Slowly Bob pushed himself to his knees and then stood up, looking around for his discarded jacket. 'My men were shot. Their bodies are in the middle of the runway. Sod off, I'm going for a drink.'

'Jesus wept! I'm sorry, Corporal, I just thought you were playing silly buggers.' The man wiped his brow and offered his hand.

Bob took it. For some reason, he was cold. Had the weather changed unexpectedly? Then Sarge gripped his elbow and bundled him into the nearest ambulance. 'Shock, nearly got himself killed saving an incoming kite.'

By the time they reached the small hospital, his teeth were chattering and he couldn't think coherently. He was cocooned in a warm blanket and a medic pushed a couple of tablets into his mouth, gave him a drink and told him to swallow.

'Get him back to his billet, he needs to sleep. He'll be ticketyboo in the morning.'

Willing hands guided him outside and into a waiting car. He leaned back against the seat, unable to talk, still trying to process what had happened. He scarcely recalled being ushered into the room he shared with another corporal. By the time he'd stripped off his uniform, his eyes were heavy.

'Here, Corp, you've got to take these before you go to bed.'

The orderly pushed another two pills into his mouth and obediently Bob swallowed them. He washed them down with half a glass of water.

He awoke the next morning disorientated, sluggish, his mouth dry and a niggling pain behind his eyes. He needed the bog so rolled out of bed and had to lean on the wall before walking unsteadily to the door.

Usually the billet was noisy, but it was eerily quiet. He never removed his wristwatch so he glanced down at it. Crikey – he'd been asleep for almost twenty-four hours. He needed to get a grip, have a shave and a wash, get himself dressed and over to the admin block to make his report.

It took him longer to get sorted than it normally did. When he'd finished his ablutions, his head had cleared a bit, but it still felt as if he was wading through treacle. His stomach was growling in protest. For a moment, he couldn't remember where he'd left his motorbike – was it at the hangar or outside his billet?

It didn't really matter, as he wasn't in any fit state to ride it at the moment. Food first and then maybe he'd be ready for the grilling he was going to get from whichever officer was in charge. The mess was half-full, but as he didn't know anybody here, nobody waylaid him.

He grabbed a tray and walked somewhat unsteadily to the serving hatch. It didn't really matter what he had, as long as it was filling.

'You're Corporal Andrews, aren't you?' The speaker was a pretty WAAF, and she was beaming at him.

'I am.' Why was he finding it so hard to speak, to concentrate?

'You're a real hero. Everybody's talking about it. Flying Officer Gentry, the pilot whose life you saved, wants to speak to you. He's somewhere up there at the moment but he said he'll come and find you before he goes back to Biggin Hill tonight.' She'd pointed to the ceiling, but he knew what she meant.

Bob somehow turned his mouth into a smile. 'I need to eat and then get over to admin. The men I work with died and I must—'

'Sergeant Benson has taken care of everything. You just eat your lunch. You find a seat and I'll bring it over. I expect you'd like a nice mug of tea too.'

He wasn't used to being made a fuss of and would normally be uncomfortable with all the attention, but for some reason today he didn't care.

He nodded and wandered across the room to an empty table, as far away from everybody as he could find. His head felt as if it was stuffed with cotton wool and even though he was ravenous, what he really wanted was to go back to bed.

'Here you are, Corp, lovely sausages and mash with onion gravy. I'm pretty sure it's real pork in the bangers and not just bread-crumbs.' She plonked a piled plate on the table and then another WAAF arrived with a huge helping of spotted dick and custard. A third set a steaming mug of good, strong tea in front of him – just the way he liked it.

Bob ignored them all and started eating and they got the message and drifted away, leaving him in peace. He thought he'd be able to devour every scrap but abandoned his first course half-eaten and ignored the pudding. The strong tea was just the ticket, though. He left his dirty dishes on the table and walked out. Used plates were supposed to be returned to the hatch, but he couldn't even be bothered to go back and do that.

Outside in the fresh air, his head cleared a bit and he was able to look around and take in what he saw. The crater at the edge of the runway had been repaired overnight and the fire damage was no longer visible. Amazing what a dozen erks could do with a few cans of paint and a bit of elbow grease.

He wasn't looking forward to having to talk about what had happened. How was he going to explain why his men were wandering across the runway when they should have been at work? He didn't want to besmirch their good names. In fact, he didn't want to talk to anyone about anything.

19

Joanna was hardly reassured by Peter's somewhat ambivalent attitude to the risk that she might be taking by visiting Crawley Hall.

'I have a taxi waiting, Peter, is your lieutenant ready to accompany us?'

'If you wait downstairs, I'll just have a quick word and send him out, I promise he won't be more than five minutes. Use the time to tell the solicitor chappie not to reveal the real reason that you're going.'

She was all but bundled from his office and was now regretting that she'd arranged to have dinner with him this evening. He was far too fond of giving her orders and she'd had quite enough of that from David when he was alive.

'Mr Broome, a lieutenant's coming with us. Shall we wait in the taxi for him?'

He understood immediately that she didn't wish to explain the circumstances where they could be overheard. Once they were outside on the pavement, she quickly briefed him.

'Makes sense, my lady, to have an armed escort. Also, better that he truly believes he's going to visit an injured comrade.'

The taxi driver had turned off the engine and was lolling against the luggage space, smoking an evil-smelling cigarette. In these old-fashioned vehicles, there was no front passenger seat, just an empty section for suitcases next to the driver.

'I wonder if any cases ever fly out when the taxi goes around the corner too fast.'

The taxi driver grinned, revealing he had more spaces than teeth. 'Never happened, missus, this old girl don't go fast enough.'

'That's a relief. I'm sorry to have kept you waiting. Also, there'll be another passenger accompanying us to Waterloo.'

Mr Broome opened the door for her, she ducked her head and scrambled in. Despite the age of the vehicle, the leather seats were still in good condition and there was more room inside than there was in a modern taxi.

'The cabbie will be delighted to have been kept waiting, my lady, as the meter will still be ticking and he won't be using precious petrol.'

She took her place on the right of the rear seat and the solicitor settled on the left, leaving a large space between them. The young officer bounded in and folded down one of the jump seats.

'I apologise for keeping you waiting, my lady, and thank you for allowing me to accompany you. I can't tell you how happy I am to think that my dear pal Stephen actually survived the explosion.'

The taxi lurched into motion and the young man, so busy talking that he hadn't braced his feet, slid sideways and ended in a heap on the matting that covered the floor. Joanna hid her smile, as it would be unkind to laugh – the poor fellow was already embarrassed enough. He scrambled back, red-faced, and, to give him credit, resumed talking as if nothing untoward had occurred.

'I was told that Stephen has been so severely injured that he's almost unrecognisable and isn't well enough to be able to identify himself. However bad he is, I'll be able to recognise him because he's got a large mole on his shoulder that looks like a horse—'

Mr Broome interrupted the flow of words. 'One can be quite certain, sir, that this was how Lady Harcourt was able to eventually find her missing husband. I have such admiration for a wife who is so devoted that she doesn't give up, despite being told by the War Office that her husband has perished.'

Joanna had no wish to join in this conversation so pointedly looked out of the window. London was drab and depressing nowadays. Sandbags piled high everywhere, people carrying gas masks over their shoulders, the plate glass windows of the shops crisscrossed with brown sticky tape in the hope that if they broke, they wouldn't fall outwards onto pedestrians.

There didn't seem to have been much bomb damage on the route they were taking. One must suppose the taxi driver deliberately avoided those places. The East End was getting the worst of the bombing and they weren't going there, thank goodness.

The lieutenant was like a puppy, desperately wishing to please, but becoming tiresome by doing so. When the cab pulled up outside Waterloo Station, he almost fell out in his eagerness to be the one to open the door and offer Joanna assistance.

She ignored his outstretched hand but smiled her thanks.

'Do you have a travel warrant?' Mr Broome asked.

'I do, sir, and I've been instructed to purchase your tickets. My lady, do you wish to sit in the ladies-only compartment or in first class with us?'

Joanna thought this a strange question. 'First class, of course. We'll wait under the clock.'

Mr Broome hailed a porter and discovered that the next train to Guildford would be leaving in fifteen minutes – perfect timing, as long as buying the tickets didn't take too long.

The station was thick with smoke, the smell of coal, the hiss of steam from the engines, but she didn't dislike it. This was the first time she'd travelled on a train anywhere but to and from Ramsgate and she was so looking forward to seeing a different part of the country. Surrey, so she'd heard, was a pretty county, full of houses as magnificent and old as her own.

The journey should take an hour and a half. Joanna closed her eyes after becoming bored with the scenery that sped past the window, as she didn't wish to be involved in a trivial conversation with the other two. Out of respect for her, she believed, both gentlemen remained silent until an inspector tapped on the door to tell them the next stop would be Guildford.

She quickly picked up her overnight bag before either man could grab it but was quite happy to walk first through the sliding door into the narrow passageway outside the compartment.

The train rocked to a standstill and she stepped aside to let the young soldier open the door. This involved lowering the window by the leather strap and then leaning out to grab the handle on the outside. She'd tried this once when a schoolgirl and had ended up swinging in a most undignified fashion over the platform so was quite happy for one of the men to do it for her.

Once more, their unexpected companion rushed ahead, saying he would find a taxi, giving her a valuable few minutes to talk to Mr Broome.

'Peter told me Crawley Hall's about five miles from Guildford, in a small town called Farnham. I doubt that we'll be able to catch a bus there, so let's hope the lieutenant's successful.'

Joanna glanced at the station clock and saw the time to be a little after midday. She'd had no breakfast and it looked as if she'd get no lunch either. She certainly wasn't going to suggest that they found somewhere to eat.

She blinked as she stepped into the sunshine and was surprised and impressed that a taxi was available. She and her solicitor sat in the back and the officer was obliged to sit next to the driver. The closer she got to their destination, the more nervous she was. Whatever the outcome, the visit was going to be stressful.

Daphne thought things seemed different without Lady Harcourt in residence at Goodwill House. Everything worked like clockwork, even the old lady seemed cheerful enough, but somehow things were more subdued. Jean assured everybody that her ladyship would be back the following evening and there was a general sigh of relief.

'When's Charlie coming back?' Sandra, who worked with Joyce on a neighbouring farm, asked as they were clearing the table after breakfast.

'Not until her stitches come out, which won't be for several days,' Daphne said. 'We're going to need you and Joyce until then. Thank you for helping us out.'

Sandra frowned. 'We didn't have any choice. I warn you that we're not happy about this, we like working where we are so don't expect us to enjoy being at Fiddler's Farm.'

Sal ignored this sour comment. 'Too bad. The two of you have just got to lump it.' Then she smiled. 'Can either of you drive a tractor?'

Joyce stopped frowning and looked more cheerful. 'We both can – we haven't got horses where we are. Has Mr Pickering got one now?'

'He has, but I ain't learned how to use it and neither has Daphne. Would you learn us whilst you're there? Charlie was supposed to do it, but she never got round to it.'

'We'd love to show you, wouldn't we, Sandy?' Joyce said eagerly and now even her grumpy friend was almost smiling.

'Will your boss be happy for us to do that and not be in the fields?' Sandra asked.

'He wants both of us to be able to drive the tractor. He's not getting rid of the horses, as he's going to use them for the hay cart and deliveries and so on. One of you start with Sal and the other can work with me,' Daphne told them.

They all had bicycles and set off together. With their snacks and bottles of water in haversacks slung across their backs, they pedalled to the farm – not exactly best of friends, but certainly better than it had been first thing.

Whilst they were putting the bikes away tidily in the barn, Mrs Pickering appeared. This was unusual, as she'd never come to the barn before. 'I noticed that you girls don't bring your gas masks. It's against the law not to have them with you at all times.'

'Mr Pickering said we didn't need them as we're not going to get gas dropped on us – if they do use it, it'll be in the city.' Daphne spoke more sharply than she'd intended, but gas masks weren't Mrs Pickering's concern. She was just the farmer's wife. 'We brought them at first but obviously we couldn't work with one around our neck and more often than not, we forgot to take them home with us. Mr Pickering said it wasn't worth bringing them.'

'I see. If my husband said you didn't need them, then I'll say nothing more. Have you decided about moving in here for the winter?'

Daphne wished this hadn't been mentioned in front of Sandra and Joyce, but there was nothing she could do about it. The two of them were listening avidly and would no doubt tell everybody else what they'd heard when they got back tonight.

'Thank you very much for your kind offer, but Sal and I have decided to stay where we are. Cycling in the dark and the cold won't be a problem for us.'

Mrs Pickering looked less than pleased, pursed her lips in disapproval, and stalked off.

'Blimey, who pulled her chain? I reckon we won't be getting no nice lunch in future. Good thing we bought two sandwiches today.' Sal didn't seem unduly bothered by this change in Mrs Pickering, but Daphne was worried. Something had happened, something to do with them, and she wanted to know what it was.

Sandra exchanged a knowing glance with Joyce. 'Everybody thought things were tickety-boo here, what with you getting a lunch every day and all that. Seems we were wrong.'

'The hot meals were done by the housekeeper that Mr Pickering employed whilst his wife was away,' Daphne said. 'Things are obviously going to be different now she's back. In case you're wondering, we never had any intention of leaving Goodwill House. Why would we? I don't think there could be better accommodation.'

'Too true. We're all as happy as Larry where we are – why would anyone want to move? I expect Mrs Pickering just wants the extra money,' Sandra said.

'They seem to be doing all right, but maybe that's why she invited us.' Daphne could hardly say their main reason for refusing was that Charlie wasn't included, as that would just add more to the speculation and gossip. 'We'd better get a move on. Sal, do you think you can learn to drive that Ferguson in an hour?'

'I reckon so. Ta for letting me go first.'

Sandra was going to teach Sal and then would exchange places with Daphne and Joyce this afternoon. By lunchtime, she and Joyce had cleared the weeds from a third of the huge field.

'I'll be glad to leave the hoeing to the others. Do you think I'll be able to master the art of driving that beast in a couple of hours?'

Joyce nodded. 'I did, so I'm sure you can. Neither Sandra nor I can handle a team of horses or drive a pony cart. If we're still here when you start lifting taters, would you teach me how?'

'I'd be happy to, but Sal's better than I am with the horses, so I'll leave it to her. We didn't stop for a mid-morning break and I'm starving. Two rounds of spam sandwiches and a drink of water will be like a feast.'

Sal was waiting for them, beaming and pleased with herself. 'I'm a dab hand with the tractor now, ain't I, Sandra?'

'Took to it like a duck to water, it was a pleasure to teach you.'

'Mrs Pickering went out with the children a couple of hours ago and we've not seen Mr Pickering. We ain't getting no meal today and probably not never again neither,' Sal said grumpily.

'Not to worry, we've had a few weeks of being spoilt. I don't think any of the other girls get fed on the job and we do get a splendid meal when we get home.'

Spam sandwiches weren't a favourite of Daphne's, but today they tasted spot on. She was looking forward to learning how to drive the Ferguson but as she wasn't in the slightest bit mechanically minded, she wasn't sure she'd be able to master what was required.

After they'd eaten, Joyce clambered onto the tractor with Daphne, balancing precariously on the mudguard – if that's what the metal covering on a tractor wheel was called. She carefully pointed out what each of the levers and pedals were used for.

'You watched me drive it up and down, now it's your turn. It's ever so easy – if I can do it, then you certainly can, as I can't even hammer a nail in straight without hitting my fingers.'

Daphne was determined to master this machine. If Charlie and both Joyce and Sandra could do it, then so could she. It would be something to tell Bob when she saw him again, which she hoped was soon and that he had good news. She wasn't sure if she wanted to risk being his fiancée again, but however much she tried to ignore them, the old feelings had returned.

* * *

Bob knew he should march, ramrod stiff, salute and stand to attention when he entered the admin building but just couldn't find the energy. Good thing the CO at Hawkinge wasn't a stickler for protocol or Bob would be on a charge this morning.

He shambled in, confident his appearance was smart even if his posture was not. A WAAF was waiting for him. Word must have been passed up to the office that he was on his way.

'Corporal Andrews, Wing Commander Bowler would like to speak to you himself.'

Was this a good thing or a bad? He'd expected to be interviewed by a spook, or a junior officer, not the CO. He trudged along behind the girl, unable to summon any enthusiasm, even any fear that he might be in real trouble and wasn't quite sure why he was so demotivated.

Win Co was smiling – not in for a bollocking, then. He managed a salute of some sort, but Win Co laughed.

'No need for that nonsense, young man. Let me shake your hand. You're a bally hero. Not often a member of my ground crew does something heroic.' He strode across with his hand out and reluctantly Bob took it. His arm was pumped so hard he almost toppled over.

Instantly Win Co released his grip and firmly guided Bob to a waiting chair. 'Here, my boy, take a pew. Not feeling up to snuff just yet? Hardly surprising after what you went through yesterday.'

The same dark-haired WAAF placed a tray with tea and cake next to him but for some reason, his arm didn't respond to his command. What the hell was wrong with him?

From a distance, he heard men talking, vaguely recognised the voice of the medic who'd shoved pills down his throat yesterday. With a herculean effort, he managed to focus and snap out of the fug his brain had slipped into.

'I'm sorry, sir, for some reason, I'm not quite awake.'

Both men snapped around and stared at him as if he'd said something extraordinary. The doc spoke first.

'Not awake, you say? How many tablets did you take last night?'

Tablets? 'You gave me some and then the others gave me some.'

'Good god! Silly buggers overdosed your corporal, sir. He needs to sleep it off.'

'Right. Corporal Andrews, I'm giving you a three-day pass starting from whenever you're passed fit for duty by the medics.' The Win Co was speaking as if Bob was deaf or an imbecile, enunciating every word, and Bob nodded to show he understood.

He was half-asleep but had grasped the important fact that he was to get three days' leave. As he tottered, ably held up by a couple of erks, back to his billet he was smiling, knowing that tomorrow or the next day he could see Daphne and give her the good news. He couldn't wait to see his beloved girl again.

20

Joanna had expected the taxi to turn through imposing gates, travel down a long drive and then pull up in front of a magnificent Georgian house or perhaps something older. Instead, they turned directly from the road, through a wrought-iron gate and down a short, gravelled drive to stop in front of a hideous red-brick Victorian house.

'I'd expected something different, Mr Broome, didn't you?'

'I hadn't given it much thought, my lady, I suppose that being called Crawley Hall might have misdirected you. The house might be ugly, but it's certainly large.'

The car rolled to a halt and she allowed Lieutenant Humphrey to open the door for her. She smiled her thanks and he appeared to stand straighter, as if her approval was important to him.

'I expect the grounds are more extensive to the rear of the property, my lady,' he said.

'One would hope so, as there's certainly less than one would expect for a house of this size at the front.' She couldn't help thinking this was an extraordinary conversation to be having, considering the reason they were there.

Joanna moved away from the taxi and heard Mr Broome asking it to wait. The driver obviously refused, as the car drove away, leaving them stranded. She felt a flicker of unease and turned to Mr Broome.

'It's all right, my lady, he's returning to collect us in an hour and a half. It seems an ancient parent lives in a cottage nearby and he's going to take the opportunity to call in and see her.'

'Thank you, let's hope our visit isn't so brief we're obliged to hang about on the pavement waiting.'

'The town isn't far from here, so if we had to, we could walk in and find ourselves something to eat. I'm not a gentleman who likes to miss his meals and it's already long past my normal lunchtime.'

Mr Broome was scarcely older than her, but he was already behaving as if middle-aged. He wasn't married, perhaps he preferred to be a bachelor. She wasn't sufficiently interested in him as a person to make enquiries about this. As long as he fulfilled his position as her legal adviser satisfactorily then he could be a fuddy-duddy if he wanted.

The front door was opened as they approached by a butler dressed in a black tailcoat and dicky bow.

'Good afternoon, my lady, we were expecting only Mr Broome and yourself.'

'I am Lieutenant Humphrey; I was a good friend of Lieutenant Stephen Harcourt and am eager to see him, as I thought him dead.'

The black-clad servant accepted this explanation without a noticeable reaction. 'Then her ladyship will see you all in the drawing room. Refreshments will be served immediately.'

They stepped into a large dark-wood panelled hall from which led several doors. To the right was an ornate, heavily carved wooden staircase. Very little light filtered in through the windows and Joanna thought it a depressing entrance.

The butler stopped outside an open door. To her astonishment, he announced them as if they were arriving for morning calls in the time of Jane Austen.

'Lady Harcourt, Mr Broome and Lieutenant Humphrey to see you, my lady.'

He stepped aside allowing them to enter. At first, the huge, gloomy, over-furnished room appeared to be empty. Certainly, *this* Lady Harcourt wasn't on her feet to greet them. Then a tall, dark-haired, elegant young woman stepped out from behind one of the marble pillars.

'Lady Harcourt, gentlemen, it's so kind of you to come. I am Lady Camilla Harcourt and I welcome you to Crawley Hall.'

Each word was clipped, crystal clear, the diction of someone with a much better pedigree than her own. Joanna had learned to speak as David required her to, but this woman had been born to it. Small wonder she wanted the title to go with her aristocratic demeanour.

'Thank you for allowing us to come.'

Camilla gestured towards a circle of heavy, overstuffed chairs which had been placed around two hexagonal occasional tables. 'If you would care to be seated, I have arranged for a light luncheon to be served, as I doubt that you had time to eat before coming here.'

'That's thoughtful, my lady, but my time is limited and I'd like to see Lord Harcourt before eating. I'm sure that you understand the purpose of my visit is to meet him.'

For a moment, Joanna thought the request was going to be denied, then Camilla smiled thinly. 'Of course, I'll have one of my maids escort you to his rooms immediately. My husband is far too unwell to have more than one visitor at a time.'

Joanna really didn't want to do this on her own and the young lieutenant came to her rescue. 'I'll accompany you, my lady, and then I can slip in after you. If the poor chap's so unwell, you won't want to remain with him long.'

They hurried out of the room. Mr Broome immediately engaged the woman in a conversation about her husband's health and Joanna was grateful for his quick thinking as it gave her and the officer time to reach the stairs.

'How is his lordship today?' Humphrey asked the elderly maid.

'I've not seen him, sir, no one goes in apart from his nurses.'

Joanna supposed this meant that his wife wasn't a visitor either. Alarm bells were ringing loudly in her head and she almost retraced her steps. What would they do if this unfortunate invalid wasn't who this woman said he was?

She reached out and touched the sleeve of her companion. He almost tripped over his feet at her touch. 'I must speak to you before we go into the bedroom.'

He didn't query her request but stopped and bent down on the stairs, as if retying his boots.

'We think this man is an impostor and not your friend, Stephen Harcourt. Please check his neck for his birthmark but don't let the nurses know if you do discover he's not who the family are claiming him to be.'

He nodded, his expression grave. 'Understood, ma'am.' He straightened, said something light about his bootlaces, and they continued smoothly on their way up – not to the main floor but up a second less grand staircase to the second floor.

'Why is Lord Harcourt not on the main floor?' She addressed the back of the black-garbed maid.

'Her ladyship doesn't want him disturbed and it's quieter up here away from their girls. His nurses – there are four of them and they work in twos in shifts – live up here with him.'

'Thank you. That makes perfect sense, as it's what I would do in the same circumstances. Small children can be noisy.'

They reached the upper landing and the maid was breathless from the climb. She paused and pointed to a door on the left. 'He's in there. You'll need to knock and wait. The kiddies live in the nursery wing on the other side of the house, my lady, the little dears can make as much noise as they want over there.'

Joanna heard footsteps approaching the closed door and wanted to follow the maid back down the stairs, but having an armed soldier at her side gave her much-needed courage. She'd noticed the pistol in a leather holster at his hip when he'd jumped into the taxi earlier. He hadn't been wearing it when she'd first met him. The significance of this now dawned on her. Peter must have suggested it.

The door was opened by a tall, burly man in a white coat. He didn't look like a nurse, but then she'd never seen a male nurse.

'Lady Harcourt?'

She nodded but was unable to answer as her tongue seemed to be stuck to the roof of her mouth.

'Who is this? Only one visitor, we were told.'

She found her voice. 'This is Lieutenant Humphrey. He fought alongside Lord Harcourt and thought his best friend was dead. He'll be coming in with me to pay his respects.'

The man beside her metamorphosed from a bashful young man into a formidable and terrifying soldier. He stood, somehow a foot taller, his expression brooking no disagreement. The hand on the grip of his gun was enough to gain them entry.

The nurse blanched and retreated. 'Come in, then. He'll not know you're there and I doubt you'll recognise him, sir. His lordship's very poorly but better here than he was in the infirmary.'

There was that indefinable aroma, the one that she always associated with sickness, with an invalid nearing the end of his life. The large metal hospital bed was positioned so the patient could, if he'd been able to, gaze out of the window at the formal gardens.

The nurse had retreated, leaving them alone in the room. Either this man was indeed Lord Harcourt and the nurses had nothing to fear from the visit or the nurses believed him to be to who the woman downstairs said he was. Either way, this meant they could confirm their suspicions without interruption.

'Stay here, my lady, I'll do what's necessary. Although the lieutenant colonel said nothing about his suspicions, I had my own. No one could have survived that explosion.'

Gratefully she stepped aside and the lieutenant walked forward, softly, respectfully and gently examined the shoulder of the man in the bed. The patient was almost invisible beneath layers of white bandages and appeared unaware of their visit. He moved back immediately, shaking his head.

'I don't know who the hell the poor sod is, but he's not Stephen.'

'It will look suspicious if we leave immediately,' Joanna said. 'Do you think he knows what's going on?'

'Absolutely not. He's better off here than wherever she found him, but I doubt he's going to live for much longer – his pulse is weak, his breathing shallow. It's a good thing I came today.'

There was no need for her to approach the bed and for that she was relieved. She walked to the far end of the room, away from the walls and doors, sure that anyone eavesdropping would hear nothing.

'It's going to be difficult sitting down and eating lunch, knowing what we do.'

'There's a simple solution, my lady. You rush out in tears, and I'll explain that you're overcome by seeing Lord Harcourt so ill, as it reminded you of how your beloved husband must have died at Dunkirk.'

'That's not too far from the truth, Lieutenant. I'm glad you didn't have to remove your weapon from the holster, but I'm impressed that you came prepared. I pray you won't need to use it today.'

'I give you my word we'll all leave here safely. If you play your part, then I'll play mine. Are you ready? I think we've been here long enough to make our visit appear genuine.'

It didn't take much for Joanna to bring tears to her eyes. It wasn't thinking about her departed husband that made her cry, but the death of her dearest friend, Betty, a few weeks ago. She held a lace-edged handkerchief to her eyes, gulped loudly, and then rushed from the room. She fled down the stairs and didn't stop until she was outside.

Conscious that she could be seen from the drawing room, she buried her head in her hands for a few moments and then continued to hurry down the drive, out of the gates to where she could be invisible behind the tall brick wall that encircled the property.

She leaned against it, letting the tears flow, not just for Betty but also for John – the love of her life – who she'd sent away as they could never be together. He was so much younger than her and his background meant he would never be happy in her world. Sometimes love just wasn't enough.

* * *

Daphne thought that driving a tractor wasn't going to be nearly as difficult as she'd feared. There was only the choke, the clutch and a steering wheel to worry about. Joyce patted her on the shoulder and slid down to the ground.

'Right, I'll leave you to it. Don't go too fast and you'll be just fine. I reckon your boss will have us hired out to farms that don't have one of these. I'll go and give the girls a hand at the weeding – can't do that with a machine.'

Joyce had more confidence in Daphne's abilities than she had. The hardest part had been cranking the handle to start the vehicle, so as long as she didn't turn the engine off, she'd be okay.

At first, everything went swimmingly, and she began to think it was all a bit of a lark. Then she was gazing up at a swallow and didn't realise she was approaching the hawthorn hedge and drove straight into it.

She thanked the lord that the engine was still running, but that was the only good thing about the disaster. It took her an hour to extract herself and the tractor and both she and the vehicle were now covered with the debris from the hedge. She glanced over her shoulder at the damage she'd caused. There was now a noticeable hole in what had been an immaculate green border.

Completing the harrowing was paramount, as maybe then Mr Pickering wouldn't be too cross about his hedge. Daphne was halfway down the field when there was a strange gurgling noise, thick black smoke poured out of the engine and the tractor ceased to function.

This wasn't good – this wasn't good at all. Whatever was wrong with this vehicle, it was her fault. Mr Pickering had only had it for a week and now she'd broken it. She slithered down from the seat, attempted to brush the bits of chewed up hedge and foliage from her dungarees and then trudged back to the farm.

The three girls were just arriving at the barn for their midday break. Joyce took one look at her and squealed. The sound was reminiscent of that poor thing that had been slaughtered the other day.

'Blimey, you don't look too clever. What's happened to the trac-tor? You ain't crashed it, have you?' Sal said with a grin. Nothing upset her friend nowadays.

'I drove straight into the hedge and it took me ages to get out. Then halfway down the field there was a lot of smoke and it conked out. I had to abandon it in the middle of the field.'

Joyce had stopped wailing and looked a bit more cheerful. The racket had attracted the unwanted attention of the farmer, who'd been about to go inside for his midday meal. He stomped over, looking none too pleased at being dragged away from his food.

'For god's sake, what's all that racket?' He looked around and took in the situation. 'Where's me bleeding tractor? Have one of you buggered it up already?'

Daphne swallowed and tried to stop her voice from quavering. 'It was me, Mr Pickering, I drove into the hedge and after I finally got it out, it stopped in the middle of the field. I'm so sorry.'

He looked a little less belligerent. 'Did any of you think to put petrol in the tank?'

The three of them shook their heads like little girls in a schoolroom. 'You, whatever your name is, get a can filled and get the blooming tractor back here. I'm going to have my lunch. I expect it to be working when I come out again.'

'It's run out of fuel? What was the black smoke then?' Daphne asked, hardly daring to hope she was to be let off so easily.

'It's your farm, so you two sort it out. Joyce and I are going to have our lunch.' Sandra scowled and stomped off to the back of the barn where the sandwiches and water bottles were being kept safe from scavenging chickens.

Finding a suitable empty can was simple, filling it from the larger one holding a month's supply of petrol was more difficult. Eventually they both ponged of petrol, but the wretched can was full.

'There's no point in taking our bikes, Sal, it'll be as quick to walk. Do you know where the fuel cap is on the tractor, 'cos I certainly don't.'

'I do, that Sandra might be bad-tempered but she was ever so good at learning me all about it. You carry the can and I'll fill up the tank.'

Daphne hoped the problem was just lack of fuel, but she feared it might be something to do with jamming the thing into a thick hedge!

Sal was true to her word and in a jiffy, the tank was full. 'I didn't have to start it. Do you know how to do that as well?'

'I'll give it a go. It's right hard and you have to be smart if you don't want to get your thumb caught.'

Sal wrenched the starting handle around a few times and then the Ferguson coughed back into life.

'Oh, I say, well done, Sal. Now all we have to do is get it back in one piece to the barn.'

'Let's try and get rid of the sticks and that. He'll not like to see his new toy looking so untidy.'

By the time they were both satisfied with the appearance of the tractor and Sal had driven it back with Daphne balancing on the back, lunch break was over. Joyce and Sandra strolled off, looking smug, leaving them to show Mr Pickering that everything was as it should be.

'Right, you two, get the trailer hitched, and you can take an extra delivery down to the village. What has to go is in the dairy.'

Just to be on the safe side, they topped the fuel tank up a second time and then had no trouble attaching the newly acquired trailer. It didn't take long to carefully pack the eggs, milk and box of turnips.

'You drive, Sal, I'll sit in the trailer with the delivery,' Daphne said.

'Right ho, but I ain't too keen on driving this in traffic. Pickering must be mad sending us when he's got two experienced drivers on the farm.'

The trip to the village was progressing well. Sal seemed to have got the hang of this tractor and luckily the road was fairly empty. It was unnerving having vehicles behind them, anxious to get by on the narrow road.

Today they were taking everything they had to Raven's shop. When they pulled up outside, Mr Raven rushed out waving his arms, his slightly grubby white apron flapping around his ample waist.

'No, you can't stop there, it's right in the way and the bus will be coming past in a minute,' he yelled at them.

'All right, no need to shout,' Sal said sharply. She definitely wasn't enjoying this excursion.

'I can't unload this if we take it all the way to the end of the street. What if we unhitched the trailer and pushed it down the side where it's out of the way?' Daphne suggested.

'Crikey, I'd never have thought of that.' Ten minutes later, Sal drove off triumphantly, leaving her to take the small milk churn, trays of eggs and boxes of vegetables through into the yard. They'd agreed that Sal should remain in the grass area just outside the village for fifteen minutes and then come back.

Daphne managed to get the trailer turned so it was facing the correct way to be recoupled when the tractor returned. This little Ferguson was a noisy beast and drowned out everything around it. You could hear it coming a mile away.

Daphne looked up when she heard shouting and her mouth dropped open. She wasn't sure whether she should be laughing or alarmed. By some mischance, Sal had managed to hook the post van to the back of the tractor and was driving merrily along, quite unaware that she was bringing the postman's vehicle along with her.

Sal stopped in front of the general stores and only then did she realise what she'd done. Nobody was hurt, the postman was somewhat out of breath chasing his van, but he saw the funny side and so did everyone else. It would be the talking point of the village for months to come.

21

———————

Bob woke up the following morning clearheaded and eager to begin his three days' unexpected leave. He shouldn't be feeling so happy when three poor sods had died two days ago, but there was no time to mourn their fallen comrades, you just had to accept it, raise a glass and move on.

As he had to obtain a slip from a medic saying he was fit for duty before he could go to the admin office and collect his pass, there was nothing he could do for a couple of hours. He'd been hearing the fighter squadrons arrive over the past hour, as they always did.

Bob spent longer on his ablutions, shaved more carefully, and enjoyed a leisurely shower, as there were no other bods waiting for him to come out. Satisfied he looked smart, he headed for the mess hall for breakfast. This time he was ignored – one was only a hero until the next bloke did something brave.

As he stepped out into the early morning sunlight, he was accosted by a pilot officer – the lowest officer's rank in the RAF – and the man grabbed his hand and shook it. 'At last, Corporal, I've been looking for you. You saved my life the other day. Thank you.'

'Glad I could do it. My three men had died and I didn't want anyone else to do so.'

'Those bastards fly in under the radar when you're not expecting them. It might be some consolation to know that particular kite was shot down in the drink.'

'That's good.' He removed his hand from the fierce grip of the young man and walked away. There wasn't much else either of them could say.

He was lucky that there was someone on duty in the base's small hospital and after a cursory inspection, he was passed fit and given the vital slip. He handed this in at the office and was immediately handed the document allowing him to leave the base for forty-eight hours.

Two days! He thought he had three, but that was still two days more than he'd anticipated. He wasn't going to quibble but get going immediately. He'd already pushed his overnight things into the left-hand pannier behind the pillion. The spare can of petrol, now half-full, was in the right one.

He checked his wristwatch and saw it was just after nine o'clock – he should be at Goodwill House and see his darling Daphne around ten, as it was less than thirty miles from Folkestone to Ramsgate. There was little traffic on the road and he made good time. He loved the rush of the wind in his face, the feeling of speed as he tore down the country roads flat out. His motorbike, an Aerial Red Hunter, could do sixty miles an hour at a push.

Bob rolled into Goodwill House just after ten o'clock. He knew Daphne and the other girls would be working until lunchtime, but he wasn't sure on which farm or where it was situated.

He kicked the bike onto its stand and tipped the spare fuel into the tank. Then he was about to walk to the front door when an imperious voice called out to him from the terrace that ran along the garden side of the magnificent building.

'Are you the same young RAF man who visited before? The one with a motorbike?'

He stopped and looked up but couldn't see who was speaking. He guessed it must be the old Lady Harcourt, as she'd done the same thing last time he'd rolled up unannounced.

'I am certainly a young RAF man, ma'am, and I've certainly been here before. Whether I am the particular person you're referring to I've no idea.' This was a bizarre conversation and he was smiling as he ran up the stone staircase so he could speak to her face to face.

He had pulled off his helmet and goggles by the time he reached the terrace. The old lady was watching for his arrival and returned his smile.

'Good heavens, no, you're not the young man I was thinking of. You're the one that looks like Daphne and came to the party. She's not here, none of them are, but they finish at lunchtime today.'

Miss Harcourt must have overheard her grandma talking to somebody and hurried out to see who it was. 'Corporal Andrews, how nice to see you. I think I heard my grandma telling you Daphne's at work. But what Grandma hasn't told you is that she and Sal are going to visit Charlie, who was shot during an air-raid the other day and is in hospital.'

'Not badly hurt, I hope?' He'd rather liked this young lady when he'd spoken to her, and she'd persuaded Daphne to come down and talk to him.

'No, serious but not life-threatening. A German plane, about to crash, machine-gunned her as it flew over the field where she was working.'

'Disgraceful, don't you think, young man?' Lady Harcourt said. 'Shooting an innocent girl in a field is exactly what one would expect from the Nazis.'

'War is like that, ma'am, I'm afraid. I've heard that several of our boys have been shot and killed whilst parachuting to safety. I expect that our chaps might well do the same thing.'

Miss Harcourt looked distressed and he wished he hadn't mentioned it. 'I intend to pick up Daphne from the farm, miss, she only has twenty-four hours and I want to take her to see her parents, as we didn't get to Chelmsford last time.'

'Would you like me to pack her an overnight case? I'm sure she won't mind me doing it in the circumstances.'

'That would be splendid, thank you, Miss Harcourt.'

The girl smiled – she was going to be stunning when she grew up – a real heartbreaker. 'I'm Liza, nobody calls me Miss Harcourt.'

She dashed off, leaving him with the old lady, but she'd nodded off, so he slipped away to refill his empty petrol can from the stash behind the barn. He'd been told to help himself whenever he was here so didn't need to ask permission.

Joe, the twin brother of Liza, was busy mending a bicycle in the barn and Bob stopped for a moment to speak to him. 'Good morning, Joe, I'm just getting some petrol. I've got a couple of days' leave.'

The youth looked up from his work. 'How did you wangle that?'

Bob's smile slipped. 'Just lucky. Nice to talk to you.' He hurried away before the boy could ask him questions he didn't want to answer. The sight of those three men lying dead on the runway would be forever etched in his mind.

He'd just finished stowing the full can when Liza ran lightly down the steps and handed him a small case. 'I've got her gas mask here. Do you want to take that as well?'

'No, we don't bother on the base, so I haven't got mine. We're only going to her parents' so we're not likely to run foul of an overzealous ARP.'

He now had the address of the farm and it was easy to find, being only a mile or so from Goodwill House. As he rode slowly up the rutted track he had to stop several times to avoid the chickens fussing and clucking in the grass that ran on either side.

He parked his motorbike and looked around for somebody to ask where to find Daphne. He knew she couldn't leave before the designated time, but he wanted to speak to her for a moment, make sure she waited and didn't set out on her bicycle.

There were two small children playing on a patch of grass in front of the farmhouse and they'd seen him arrive. A boy, who looked about four, and a little girl, who looked younger, and they were watching him with interest. As soon as he was on his feet, the boy ran across and his little sister followed.

'I like your bike, mister, can I have a go?'

Bob dropped down to his haunches so he was on the same level as the children. He pulled off his flying helmet and goggles and the child pointed to his head. 'You've got funny-coloured hair like Daphne. She's down the field weeding the turnips.'

'Can you tell me where this field is?'

The child was about to answer when a woman erupted from the farmhouse and looked none too pleased to find her children weren't where they were supposed to be. She stormed across and he got to his feet.

'Your children came to see my motorbike, Mrs Pickering. I'm sorry if that isn't allowed.'

'What are you doing here?' She snapped her fingers at the children and they giggled, joined hands and skipped back to where they should have been, completely unbothered by this show of temper.

'I'm Corporal Robert Andrews. I've come to speak to Daphne, if that's all right.'

'No, it certainly isn't. She's working. Go away and come back at one o'clock.'

No point in arguing and making things worse as Daphne had to

work here. 'I'm sorry to have caused any inconvenience. Would you
be kind enough to tell her that I'll be here to collect her when she
finishes?'

The woman seemed somewhat modified by his politeness. 'Yes,
I'll do that.'

'Thank you,' Bob said and climbed back onto his bike. He was
disappointed not to have been able to see Daphne but she was
working and so it was fair enough.

* * *

He had a couple of hours to kill and Manston was only half a mile
away. He thought he'd visit and see how the repairs were progress-
ing. After all, it was possible he might be transferred back once the
base was operational. Being here would be ideal as then he could
see Daphne when he got a spare hour or so. However much he
wanted to marry her, he was pretty sure she wouldn't want to leave
her job as a land girl.

He cruised to a halt, expecting to be asked to show his ID at the
gate, but the guard just looked up from his newspaper, a fag
hanging from his upper lip, and waved him through. This irritated
Bob. It wouldn't be too difficult for a determined spy to get hold of
an RAF uniform and then he could wander into the base with
impunity.

He shook his head and grinned. There was nothing here to spy
on at the moment and when he'd been stationed here, everybody
was always checked both in and out of the base. No doubt that
would be reinstated when things got back to normal. It wasn't going
to be an active base, but a satellite for Biggin Hill, like Hawkinge
was.

* * *

Joanna thought she would look conspicuous if she remained cowering against the six-foot wall that appeared to encircle Crawley Hall. Therefore, she began to stroll in what she hoped was a non-suspicious manner towards a local hostelry. The road she was walking down was Alton Road and the public house was The Bull – it looked clean and in good order and there were tables and benches set out in a pretty rear garden. It would be perfectly respectable to wait there, but a lady should never go into such a place unaccompanied.

There was a family in the garden with two small children playing with a hoop and a ball. She looked back and was relieved to see both Mr Broome and the lieutenant emerge from the gates of Crawley Hall.

She waved and they saw her. She was now free to go in and hopefully they could all get something to eat. Her stomach was growling, and she feared she was developing a migraine. This happened if she failed to eat at regular intervals.

The young couple looked up as she pushed open the gate. Just in time, she remembered she was supposed to be a grieving widow. These two might well know someone who worked or lived at Crawley Hall. She still had her handkerchief clutched in her fist and dabbed her eyes and gulped as if trying not to cry. The couple looked away as she'd hoped they might. It would be considered impolite to stare at someone who was upset.

She made her way to the table furthest from them and sat with her back to the gate. Easier to pretend to be overcome when her face couldn't be seen. A few minutes later, her companions arrived, a bit puffed and red-faced, by her table.

'My dear Lady Harcourt, how are you feeling? I am so sorry you had to endure such an upset,' Mr Broome said loudly.

She mumbled some nonsense, and the solicitor patted her on the shoulder. The lieutenant almost bowed.

'Would you allow me to fetch you something to eat if food's available here? Also, a stiff drink might restore your composure.'

'Any sort of sandwich, a brandy and a glass of lemonade would be perfect.'

The lieutenant nodded and strode off and Mr Broome sat down a respectable distance from her.

'One wouldn't think such a small place would be able to provide food for passers-by, but let's hope today they can,' Joanna said. 'I'm hungry now and wish I'd eaten breakfast when you did.'

They both avoided any mention of what had happened at Crawley Hall. They could talk when they were in private on the train later.

'They have a ham salad and apple pie and cream. Sounded perfect, so I've ordered three.' The young officer put down a tray and handed her a glass of lemonade and a balloon glass with what smelled like a decent brandy in it.

He and Mr Broome each had a pint of beer. Joanna had never seen the appeal of beer, but men seemed to like it. She'd tried a shandy once and that was barely drinkable – unadulterated beer, either mild or bitter, was revolting.

'Thank you, Lieutenant Humphrey. I'm concerned the taxi will go to the house and, on not finding us there, will drive away and leave us stranded.'

'All sorted, my lady. I gave the frosty butler half a crown and he said he was only too happy to give the cabbie a message. However, it might be wise for me to eat my lunch at the table near the road so I can flag him down when he does turn up.'

Their salads arrived promptly, and the lieutenant took his, and his pint of warm beer, to a position by the gate and left Mr Broome and Joanna to eat alone. She was too hungry to talk and was impressed by the simple but delicious meal the inn had provided.

'You must reimburse Humphrey, Mr Broome, I don't expect him to pay my expenses.'

'He's not doing so, my lady. Lord Harcourt gave him more than enough to cover today.'

For some reason, she wasn't comfortable with Peter paying for today as well as for her dinner tonight. He was becoming rather proprietorial, overprotective, and she didn't think about him in the same way as he seemed to feel about her. She feared no man could ever replace the one she'd had to say goodbye to.

'I left my overnight bag in the cab. I hope it's still on the backseat.'

'The driver was just going to visit his mother, my lady, not to pick up any other fares.'

They lapsed into silence again and concentrated on their luncheon. They'd barely finished the apple crumble when the taxi pulled up outside the public house. As Joanna had had her back to the road, she hadn't been aware the vehicle had been flagged down by the watcher at the gate.

The family was still there, enjoying the warm autumn sunshine, but she averted her eyes and hurried past with her head down, behaving in character. Humphrey had the rear door of the taxi open and she nodded her thanks and got in. Mr Broome had walked around the other side of the car and took his place on the rear seat.

Nobody spoke – she was thinking about what would happen next and no doubt the others were doing the same. As they were crossing the forecourt and heading to the entrance of the station, the London train steamed in.

As one, they increased their pace and the guard stood aside to let them through – presumably he recognised them from their arrival earlier. They jumped into the train just as the guard was waving his flag and blowing his whistle.

Joanna wobbled down the narrow passage until they found an empty compartment. First class was usually less crowded than second or third.

'Goodness me, I can't remember the last time I had to run so fast,' she said as she collapsed into the window seat that faced the way they were travelling. She much preferred to see where she was going.

'I'm hoping that no one else will wish to travel with us, my lady, as we've much to talk about,' her solicitor said solemnly.

'Lieutenant Humphrey, I fear that we might be the last outsiders to see that poor man in the bed,' Joanna said. 'I think that you must make a sworn affidavit stating that he isn't who they say he is.'

'It doesn't matter if he dies, ma'am, as he can still be identified. The birthmark that my friend Stephen had will be recorded on his army record. I don't understand why nobody thought to check.'

'The medical officer who will be visiting on Monday can do that. As you say, it won't matter if it's a cadaver or if the poor fellow's still alive,' Mr Broome replied.

'Mrs Harcourt must know that her deception is about to be uncovered,' Joanna said. 'The more I think about it, the more ridiculous the whole scheme appears. Surely, she must have known that her husband's birthmark is on record? That at any time between when she brought this impostor home and when he's buried, her fraud could be revealed.'

Mr Broome nodded. 'His remains could be exhumed, and the lack of a birthmark would be evident for at least a month or two after his interment. The woman must be unbalanced to have risked so much on so flimsy a plan.'

'I agree.'

'Lord Harcourt is still a young, fit man. It's extremely likely that sometime in the future, he will change his mind about marriage and a family and the line will continue,' Mr Broome said.

Joanna thought this wouldn't happen if what she suspected was, in fact, true. She was unable to have further children after the difficult birth of her daughter, Sarah, and she had a nasty suspicion that Peter wanted to marry her. He had the title and, by marrying her, he would have the estates that went with it. The fact that she had no interest in becoming his wife wouldn't deter him from pursuing her in the hope that she would eventually agree, if that was the case.

Possibly, in a few years' time, when John was just a distant memory, she might reconsider and accept a proposal. Her lips curved and she hid her smile behind her hand. All this was pure speculation on her part, as so far Peter had said nothing and done nothing that indicated his goal was to marry her. She was basing her assumption on the way he looked at her and that was probably rather silly. However, a gentleman would never flirt with a lady like her with anything but honourable intentions.

22

Daphne was glad to finish for the day. Hoeing turnips was hard and even with her new work gloves on, her palms were sore.

'It's time to finish, girls,' she yelled at the others, and they didn't need telling twice. With their hoes over their shoulders, they hurried to collect their discarded bicycles.

'We'll finish this field tomorrow afternoon,' Daphne told them. 'Then it'll be lifting the late potatoes next week and probably the week after.'

Sandra had dumped her hoe on the ground and was getting onto her bicycle, obviously intending to leave it there. Daphne was about to ask her to pick it up, but the girl had something of her own to say.

'Joyce and I will take it in turns to drive the tractor and you two can pick the spuds. We've got more experience on the Ferguson and Mr Pickering wouldn't want you to drive it, Daphne, not after what happened.'

Sal was incensed. 'That ain't right. You ain't in charge here, Sandra, this is our farm and you do what you're told.'

Daphne could sense a row coming and she didn't like

confrontation. 'It's all right, Sal, I don't want to drive the tractor. I thought that I'd harness one of the horses and bring the trailers back when they're full and empty them into the barn. In between, I'll be picking potatoes.'

'That ain't going to work neither, Daphne. I'm taking me turn on the tractor and them two are taking their turn picking them spuds up.'

Sandra had ignored Sal and was already halfway down the field. Joyce shrugged and smiled apologetically. 'She doesn't like to be told what to do. She's always bossing us about. You stick to your guns, Sal – as you said, it's your farm, not ours.'

'What about the hoe? We can't leave it here it might be stolen,' Daphne said.

'It's hard enough cycling with one of the blooming things, I ain't bringing two. Here, I'll put it in the ditch; I don't reckon no one will see it there,' Sal said.

* * *

When the three of them arrived in the farmyard, Sandra, still on her bicycle, was talking to Mrs Pickering. Daphne wondered what this was about, as the farmer's wife had showed no interest in the temporary workers.

Sandra smiled smugly and pedalled off, calling out to Joyce, 'Come on, we want to get back first. There might not be any sandwiches or soup left if we're late.'

Sal scowled. 'I ain't keen on that one. Full of herself, she is, and no mistake. Let's get after them, as they might leave us with nothing.'

Daphne followed her friend at speed and nearly pitched over the handlebars when the front wheel of her bike dropped into a pothole, but she managed to stay upright – just. When they turned onto the road, they picked up the pace and she thought they were gaining on the other two.

Sal was behind her and suddenly yelled, 'Here, Daphne, there's a motorbike coming up behind us. The bleeding idiot's going too fast.'

Then she heard a distinctive growl she thought she recognised. It sounded exactly like the bike Bob rode. The rider tore past, causing her to wobble dangerously. It *was* Bob. He skidded in a semicircle, dropped his precious bike on the Tarmac and his helmet and goggles followed. Daphne all but fell from her bicycle. Her legs seemed to move without her permission and she was running towards him.

He opened his arms and she tumbled into them. He crushed her against his chest. She tilted her face and his mouth covered hers in a kiss of such tenderness, such passion that if he hadn't been holding her, she would have collapsed on the road.

She could scarcely breathe when he raised his head. His eyes blazed down at her. She hadn't needed to ask if he'd got good news – he'd hardly be kissing her if he hadn't.

'Until this moment, I thought I was over you. But I'm obviously not. I love you, Bob, and I can't tell you how happy I am that you're here.'

He lifted her from her feet. 'And I love you, darling girl, and I'm hoping I can persuade you to resume our engagement.'

'I will, of course, I will! But I don't want to get married until the war's over. I've got an important job here to help feed the nation and so have you in the RAF.'

Instead of answering, he kissed her again, his lips hard, demanding, and she was weak with desire by the time they drew apart.

'I understand, sweetheart, but I hope I can persuade you to change your mind. This bloody war might go on for years.'

'If I ever have to move from Goodwill House and you've been posted back to Manston, then I'll consider it. If I have to leave my friends and start again somewhere else, then I might as well marry you.' This was hardly a romantic thing to say after their passionate kiss.

'That'll do me, sweetheart, for now I'm just happy we can be together. I haven't got a ring as I haven't had time to buy one.' His smile said everything. 'I'm hoping you'll come with me to Chelmsford.'

She nodded. 'I've still got the one you gave me last time. I couldn't return it as I didn't know where you were. I left it with my parents. If we're going there now, we can collect it and then we'll be engaged again.'

'I thought you'd probably thrown it in the river – I think that's what I'd have done in your shoes,' Bob said.

'It took you a year to save up to buy it for me. Why would I throw so much money away?'

The rumble of an approaching bus reminded them that they were blocking the road. 'If you pedal ahead of me, we can take your bike back to the farm and go from there.'

'Sal must have gone home. I'm sure she'll tell Lady Harcourt where I've gone.'

He grinned. 'They already know I'm taking you to see your parents.' He picked up his bike, started it with one kick, and then drifted up beside her.

'I'll hold onto the handle behind the pillion, and you can tow me until we get to the lane. Don't scowl, Bob, we used to do it all the time.'

He grinned and nodded. 'Okay, makes sense as we're short of time.'

Luckily, the bus had come from Stodham, and they were travelling in the opposite direction. From the expressions of the passengers who'd seen them, she thought this dangerous mode of travelling might be a topic of conversation at church tomorrow.

A short time later, Daphne was safely sitting behind him, no longer caring that she was unwashed and in dirty dungarees, heading for Chelmsford. She couldn't wait to give her mother the good news.

* * *

Bob pulled up outside a café in Canterbury. A tiny grey-haired lady in a voluminous white apron, smoking a fag, was standing outside the door.

'Take your bike round the back, son, it might get nicked if you leave it there.'

'Right, thanks. Hop off, Daphne, I'll park this and you go in and order for us. Whatever they've got is fine by me.'

She leaned forward and kissed the back of his neck before scrambling off the pillion. He wanted to grab her and kiss her properly. Bob could hardly believe that after losing the love of his life, she was back with him.

He'd stopped at this café before, and the portions were generous and the food good. All fried – but he was happy with that.

There was an outside tap and after removing his helmet and goggles, he rinsed his face and hands and dried them on his handkerchief. He was about to walk to the front of the building when Daphne appeared in the yard.

'The privy's out here. I'm just going to use the facilities and then I'll do the same as you and have a quick wash. I've ordered double everything they've got. Hope that's all right.'

He didn't hang about in the yard but made his way inside through the rear entrance. This involved walking through the kitchen, which was hot and steamy but immaculate. An elderly gent was busy at the stove. He ignored Bob – he was probably used to customers walking through.

There were only two tables occupied of the ten in the café. It was now just after two o'clock and the lunch rush would be over.

There was a table near the front with a large brown teapot, two mismatched cups and saucers, and a small, chipped jug of milk on the oilcloth that covered it. There were also two glasses of water. This was obviously their table.

He downed a glass and had poured out the tea by the time Daphne joined him. She was now dust-free, her glorious russet hair neatly pinned, and her radiant smile was just for him.

'I don't suppose there's a change of clothes in my case, is there?'

'I've no idea. Liza packed it for you.'

She drained her glass before answering. 'That was wonderful, just what I needed. Hopefully, they'll bring us some more. I'm absolutely parched. Obviously, I'll stay with my parents and you'll stay with yours, but I'm not sure where we'll eat. Better to tuck in now just in case our turning up unannounced causes problems for them.'

Two large, overfull plates were plonked down in front of them, followed by another with bread and marge.

'Golly, I doubt I'll be able to finish all this. Still, I do enjoy a good fry-up and bubble and squeak is my absolute favourite.'

In the RAF, blokes always ate first and talked afterwards – not because you thought someone might pinch your food but that you might be called back on duty at any minute.

Bob devoured the lot, and Daphne managed two thirds of hers. 'We need to talk about how we're going to handle this, sweetheart,' he said. 'We can hardly tell your parents the real reason I jilted you, can we?'

Her tea slopped in the saucer. 'Goodness, you're right. If we did that, then Dad would know that we knew about his having a fancy woman.'

'I don't suppose they were very happy when I left, especially as all the arrangements for the wedding had been made.'

'My dad said he would have your guts for garters if he ever got hold of you. Oh dear, I really don't know what to do now,' Daphne said.

'I've been thinking about this ever since I knew we weren't related. It's better he thinks I'm a bad lot than tell him the truth. If you just say that we met by accident, I realised I'd been wrong, and you forgave me and still love me... I don't suppose he'll be pleased, but I'm sure if they know that you're happy, then they'll accept me in the end.'

'As we don't intend to get married for a bit, and when we do, we certainly won't expect my father to pay a second time, then it should be all right. I think it might be best if you go round to your parents' and I go into mine alone. I'll get my ring and then join you.'

* * *

Daphne had never told Bob about the spankings, that she was scared of her father. Both she and her brother had avoided their dad when he came back from the pub, which was often, as his temper was vile and if he saw them, he'd find some reason to beat them.

Bob knew everything about her except this, she was ashamed of being mistreated and had been scared of what Bob might do if he knew. Fortunately, as she'd grown up, she'd been able to stand up to her father and the brutality had stopped.

'Fair enough. If you spend only half an hour at my home and

the rest of the time at yours, hopefully your parents won't complain.'

They had no room for afters but ordered a second pot of tea, as this was probably the only time they'd have to talk, to plan their future. Daphne told him about the two new workers, and he agreed that they needed keeping in their place.

'When's Charlie going to be back at work?'

'Sal's visiting her right now so will be able to tell me tomorrow. Probably another ten days.'

Bob insisted on paying the bill, which was very reasonable considering how much they'd consumed between them. 'We'll be in Chelmsford by teatime, but I certainly don't want anything more to eat today so it won't matter if we miss our evening meal.'

'Mum always has something in the tin, and I'll be happy with cocoa and biscuits before I turn in. We need to leave by ten o'clock tomorrow as I have to go to Goodwill House first and get changed. I also have to pick up my sandwiches for lunch.'

'Might be better if you walk around to my house and I don't actually see your folks this time.'

They arrived outside her home just after six. She removed her case and pecked him on the cheek before rushing in. She went through the side gate and he remained watching until she was out of sight.

His parents were overjoyed that things were back on with Daphne but like him, they doubted her parents would be quite so happy.

* * *

Joanna deliberately put her overnight bag beside her just in case either of the gentlemen had contemplated sitting next to her. Mr

Broome sat in the corner seat on the same side as her and the lieutenant sat opposite him.

'What happens next, Mr Broome?'

'Well, my lady, the police will have to be informed. There is a serious fraud being committed.'

'I don't quite see it that way,' Joanna said. 'There's no financial gain for Mrs Harcourt. If the man she's calling her husband was fit, then obviously it would be a different matter as he could attend the House of Lords and claim expenses and also use his title to gain access to all sorts of business opportunities.' She thought for a minute before continuing. 'My husband was always being invited to sit on various boards because of his title and was given stocks and shares in exchange for the use of his name.'

'The military authorities are also involved. It just isn't on for somebody to impersonate a fallen soldier. Not that this poor fellow has any say in the matter.'

'Exactly the point I was about to make, Lieutenant Humphrey. The man in the bed is far better off being cared for where he is than left to die lonely and uncared for in an institution somewhere. I don't want the police to press charges as long as the woman withdraws her claim. She can say it was a genuine case of mistaken identity...'

'Forgive me, my lady, but she can hardly do that as she'd have been aware the man she was using for this impersonation wasn't Stephen. Also, the fact that his mother and sister were shipped off to America is highly suspicious, don't you think?'

This young man was now making her cross by constantly interrupting. 'Lieutenant Humphrey, I suggest you let me finish a sentence before you jump in with both feet and contradict me.' The young man flushed an unbecoming shade of red and shrunk back in his seat, not meeting her eyes.

'Of course we all know it was deliberate, this was no accident, but I think it would be best for all concerned if we pretended to believe that it was,' Joanna said. 'There are children involved, remember, and it will do no good to have them without their mother as well as their father.'

Mr Broome nodded. 'I tend to agree with you, my lady. Lord Harcourt is the ideal person to visit Mrs Harcourt and explain how things could be arranged to her advantage. It would be unfortunate for the family name to be mentioned in another scandal.'

She bristled at his mention of the fraud committed by David's previous solicitor and his bank. There had been no need to mention this in front of the lieutenant.

'The gossip following the arrest of those involved in defrauding my estate was short lived. The constant bombing of London and other cities, the dreadful loss of life in the air and on the ground, is now the topic of conversation.'

'Then hopefully we can keep this business out of the press. An announcement in *The Times* should be sufficient to settle things.'

'I'm sorry, my lady, but as an officer in the army and a close friend of Stephen Harcourt, I cannot let this travesty of justice go ahead.'

This time, Mr Broome reprimanded the agitated young man. 'You're a lieutenant, you appear to have forgotten that Lord Harcourt is a lieutenant colonel. You will have no say in the matter and unless you want to find yourself on a charge, I suggest you keep your unwelcome comments to yourself.'

Humphrey surged to his feet, glared at both of them and then slammed the sliding door back so hard the glass shook as he left the compartment.

'Oh dear, that didn't go well,' Joanna said. 'If he really wants to make this business public, there's very little we can do about it. I believe the train's stopping. If he disembarks here, he could go to the police before Lord Harcourt is even aware of what's about to happen.'

'Leave it to me, my lady. I'll find him and if he does get off the train, then I'll go with him. I can assure you that no police inspector will take matters further if I'm there to contradict whatever the lieutenant says.'

Mr Broome too exited at speed and when the train steamed out a few minutes later, and neither of the gentlemen had returned, she guessed both of them were now at whatever station they'd just stopped at. As the names of stations and all road signs had been removed some months ago, and she was unfamiliar with this train route, she'd no idea where they were.

On arriving in London, Joanna was obliged to weave her way through a press of businessmen with furled umbrellas and pinstriped suits, each carrying a large briefcase. It would probably have been quicker to travel on the Underground, but this was what was now referred to as the rush hour when businessmen were leaving their offices and heading for the suburbs where they lived.

Joanna went in search of a taxi, rather hoping it might be the antiquated one they'd had that morning, but it was one of the more mundane vehicles. The driver was satisfactorily ancient. All the young drivers would now be enlisted men.

It was a short ride to the Savoy and she had the exact fare, plus a generous tip, in her gloved hand when they pulled up in the forecourt. She could have let the doorman pay and have it added to her bill but preferred not to as David had once told her that he doubted the doorman would hand the tip on to the driver.

There was barely sufficient time to bathe, attend to her hair and make-up, then slip into her simple oyster silk evening gown before she had to hurry downstairs to meet Peter. After a cursory glance in the long mirror, she was satisfied she looked her best.

This gown was cut on the bias, had a V-neck and clung to her figure in all the right places. It was perfect with her fair colouring and she wore only a double strand of perfect pearls. The gown required nothing else.

Peter, resplendent in his best regimentals, was waiting in the foyer to greet her. He moved forward smoothly, obviously intending to make some fulsome compliment, but she forestalled him.

'We need to talk, urgently and privately. I hope we're not too late to stop a disaster.'

23

Daphne could see her mother in the kitchen and paused for a moment, hoping her arrival would be seen. She wasn't sure if she should knock; as this was no longer her home she didn't really have the right to walk in unannounced.

She tapped on the door and opened it simultaneously. 'Mum, I'm sorry to turn up but I managed to get a lift here and so want to see you.'

'Goodness me, you're a sight for sore eyes. You don't have to knock on this door, you daft ha'p'orth. Your dad's gone down the pub for a quick half of bitter. He won't be long.'

'Actually, Mum, I'm glad I can talk to you first.' She took a deep breath and decided there was no point in delaying – the sooner Mum heard the news, the better.

'Sit down, love, I'll make you a nice cup of tea.'

'Bob and I are back together. We met again by chance, he apologised and I forgave him. I've come to get my engagement ring.'

The kettle clattered on the gas stove as her mum dropped it. She spoke with her back turned, which wasn't a good sign. 'Your dad isn't going to be happy about that. He still complains about the money it cost him.'

'There's nothing I can do about that, Mum, but he won't have to pay a second time. We've decided we're not getting married until the end of the war and when we do, we'll pay.'

'That's all very well, Daphne, but it wasn't just the money, it was the humiliation of his only daughter being jilted at the altar.'

'Bob left a week before the wedding – I was nowhere near the altar. If I can forgive him, then so should you and Dad.'

This wasn't going well, and she'd thought that her mum would be on her side. 'I love him, he loves me, and I'm hoping you'll be happy for me. You know I was heartbroken when he left, and he's regretted what he did ever since. We might never have met again, would both have got on with our lives and probably married some-body else, but fate brought us together. I can't tell you how happy I am about that.'

'I don't speak to Mrs Andrews, and you being engaged to him is going to make things difficult for me at the WI and WVS meetings,' her mum said.

Daphne heard the gate bang and her father marched in. Since discovering that he'd been unfaithful, what affection she had for him, which wasn't much, had vanished. He was still her dad and if her mum wanted to be with him, then she had to hide her feelings.

She stayed where she was. He didn't seem bothered by her lack of affection, as his greeting was less than loving.

'Didn't think you land girls got any time off. What are you doing here?'

'Bob brought me on his motorbike. Our engagement is back on and I wanted you to know. He was based at Manston and we bumped into each other and—'

'I'll not have him in this house,' her father said. 'Have you no self-respect, crawling back to him as if you couldn't do better for yourself? He's no good, never was and never will be. I never liked him and don't expect us to come to your wedding or for me to give you away.'

This was too much for her. How dare he speak so harshly when he was hardly in a position to criticise?

'Don't talk about the man I love like that. And more to the point, you've no right to talk to me so disrespectfully. I'm an independent woman, I'll be of age next year and don't need your permission to do anything.'

Her mother attempted to smooth over the situation. 'Ron, don't go on. Everybody makes mistakes and it's our Daphne's decision to take him back.'

'Shut your trap, Mabel, you don't tell me how to behave in my own house.' He shoved her mum, and Daphne was so angry, she blurted out the very thing she'd decided not to say.

'I hardly think that you're in a position to criticise Bob, are you, Dad? What you did to my mum was far worse, as you were married when you were having an affair.'

The words hung in the air. She bitterly regretted having said anything. His affair was none of her business. She had made things difficult for both of them by revealing that the secret was out.

She was focused on her mum and wasn't aware that her dad had charged across the kitchen with his hand raised. She couldn't avoid the blow to her mouth. The shock, the pain, consumed her and she staggered backwards, almost crashing to the floor.

'Get out of my house. Don't you come back here ever again. You're dead to me now.'

Her head was spinning, tears trickled down her cheeks, and she waited in vain for her mother to offer comfort or support. Slowly Daphne straightened.

'I'm going to collect my engagement ring and then I'll go.' She turned to her mother, who was ashen-faced and cowering against the cabinet at the far side of the kitchen. In that moment, she understood how things had been for her mum.

Anything she said would just make things worse. Poor Mum – to be tied to this monster. Daphne wished with all her heart she could offer her mother a home, but until she and Bob were married, this wouldn't be possible.

She wasn't entirely sure if he would attack her again, but he let her walk past. She flew upstairs to her old bedroom, grabbed her engagement ring and one or two other precious mementos, and then left through the front door, not daring to risk a confrontation and another punch.

There was the metallic taste of blood in her mouth where her lip was split. God knows what Bob would do when he saw her.

* * *

Bob was embracing his parents and they were celebrating his good news when the sound of footsteps running down the passageway at the side of the house made him tense. Why was Daphne arriving in such a rush?

He was at the door in two strides. When he saw her face, he knew what had happened. That bastard Taylor had hit his girl and he wasn't going to get away with it.

'No, please don't get involved. Just hold me, no more violence.' Her words were indistinct, but he understood.

Bob took her in his arms and held her while she sobbed against his shoulder, her blood soaking into his shirt. His parents were hovering anxiously by the door but didn't intervene.

'Darling, let's go in so I can have a look at your face. You might need a stitch or two in your lip.'

She didn't argue but continued to clutch the back of his jacket as he guided her gently indoors. His mum pulled out a chair from under the kitchen table so Daphne could sit down and he could deal with her injury.

'Oh, my, what a dreadful thing. Your poor face, we should call the police,' his mum said as she fluttered around, getting in his way. His dad, always the more practical of the two, had gone to fetch the first-aid box and put it on the table next to Daphne.

'Get the kettle on, Gladys love, Bob's going to need warm water.'

Having something to do was enough for his mum to pull herself together. 'There's some in there, and it's already boiled, so all I need to do is put it into a clean basin.'

The blood from Daphne's mouth was dripping onto her shirt and dungarees. Bob pushed down his fury, his determination to deal out the same punishment to the man who'd inflicted this damage on his beloved girl and concentrated on seeing just how bad it was.

'Look at me, sweetheart, let me clean you up.'

She still seemed incapable of speech; maybe that was because her mouth was swelling and talking was difficult. Bob came to a decision. He handed the damp lint to his mother and drew his father aside, where they could talk without being overheard.

'Dad, get down to the police station and fetch Sid. If the police don't deal with this, then I'm going to and could well end up swinging for him.'

'Don't you go near him, not when you're so angry, son. Sid will be doing his rounds and I'll find him, don't you worry.'

Sid Perkins – Constable Sydney Perkins – was the local copper, who lived in the police house with his wife and three children. He was a good bloke, but unless Daphne was in hospital with broken bones, which she wasn't, no prosecution would be brought. Domestic abuse wasn't regarded as a serious criminal offence. He'd go through the motions – but Bob was going to have to deal with this himself.

Daphne still had her eyes closed and he hoped she wasn't aware that he'd swapped places with his mum. He picked up a clean piece of lint, dipped it in the warm boiled water and pressed it against the biggest cut.

Her teeth had gone through her lip when she'd been punched, and the injury was too bad for him to deal with. She needed the local doctor.

'Dad, get Dr Robinson to come. Go there first and say it's urgent. Then go to the police house.'

'I won't be long.'

With pressure applied on the wound, the blood had almost stopped. Daphne still wasn't saying anything or even trying to speak.

'Sweetheart, your teeth went through your upper lip. It's going to need stitches. You might need to go to hospital, but I'm hoping the doctor will be able to do it here. You can't go back to work tomorrow.'

She reached out and squeezed his hand, indicating she understood. There was no point offering her the usual panacea of a hot cup of tea, as she couldn't drink it. It seemed an interminable wait for the doctor. The kitchen clock ticked loudly on the dresser, he stood pressed up against Daphne's shoulder and she leaned against him, her head resting heavily on his thigh.

'I'll go to the front, Bob, then I can let him in. He won't want to come around the back.'

His mother emptied the red-stained water and refilled it before removing her pinny and going to stand guard at the open front door. She didn't have long to wait as he heard the doctor greet her as he arrived.

The doctor was relatively young and had thick-lensed glasses, which probably accounted for him not having volunteered. Bob stood back, letting the doctor see what he had to deal with but keeping his hand firmly pressed against the worst cut.

'I'll just wash my hands and then I'll see if I can sort this out for you. Miss Taylor, I need to examine your injuries. Is that all right?'

Daphne nodded and Bob took her hand. Her fingernails dug into him whilst the doctor deftly stitched the gaping wound.

'There, all done. Brave girl, but much better to have it done now than have to trek to the hospital and hang about waiting to be seen to. I'll write you a sick note – you won't be going back to the farm for a while. You're lucky you haven't lost any teeth.'

Whilst the doctor rinsed his instruments at the sink in the scullery and repacked his bag, the policeman took his place. Sid had arrived during this procedure and had been watching in silence. Now it was his turn to do his duty. He moved a chair so he was sitting at the same level as Daphne.

'I know it's hard for you to talk, but can you tell me what happened?'

She looked up and shook her head. She obviously didn't want Sid involved.

'Sweetheart, either Sid speaks to your father, or I go round there.' There was no need to elaborate, everyone in the room knew he would be the one getting arrested after his visit.

'My father hit me. He hits my mother. She'll be better off without him.'

He could see her cheeks were wet and Bob gently brushed them away with his thumb.

'Was your mum a witness?'

Daphne nodded. Her voice was barely above a whisper, her words indistinct and mumbled. 'She won't say anything unless you can take him away. She's terrified of him.'

'Leave it to me, love, he'll not hurt you nor your mum again.'

* * *

Joanna was disconcerted by Peter's amusement and annoyed at his response to her remark that they needed to talk somewhere privately immediately.

'Might I be allowed to say that you look absolutely stunning, Joanna?'

'No, you may not. I don't want your compliments, I want your undivided attention.'

'Your efficient solicitor, that Mr Broome fellow, got hold of me and explained everything,' Peter said. 'I was able to put young Humphrey straight on a few things and he'll cause no further trouble to our family.'

'Oh! Then I apologise for being so strident. Are you going down to speak to Mrs Harcourt tomorrow?'

'I certainly am and I'm hoping that you'll come with me.'

She shuddered. 'Absolutely not. I never want to set foot in that place again. Even if I did want to go, I couldn't, as I'm spending the morning with Sarah. I've not seen her for weeks.'

A third couple, bejewelled and in full evening dress, tutted loudly as they were obliged to step around them.

'Shall we go to the dining room, Joanna? We can continue our conversation over a decent claret.'

'We do seem to be getting in people's way, so yes, the dining room seems like a sensible option.' He held out his arm and with a smile, she slipped hers through it, feeling rather like a heroine in a romantic novel. 'I think you look very dashing in your best regimentals, although I'm somewhat blinded by the extravagant amount of gold braid and rows of shining medals.'

His laugh attracted attention and none of it was approving. It just wasn't done to laugh out loud somewhere as grand as the Savoy. They were ushered to their table with due ceremony and the maître d' fussed over them as if they were royalty and not just minor aristocrats.

They were both relieved when the meal had been ordered, the wine poured, and they could talk to each other without being hovered over.

'What will you do if this Mrs Harcourt refuses to remove her claim?' Joanna asked.

'She won't.' There was no need for him to elaborate. He wouldn't be a lieutenant colonel in the army at his age if he wasn't formidable and ruthless.

'Then I'll forget about it.' The sound of an orchestra drifted in from the ballroom and she smiled wistfully. 'I do so love to dance.'

'Then, Cinderella shall go to the ball – but after we've dined, and I've had several glasses of wine to fortify myself for the experience.'

'Are you suggesting, my lord, that my gown is only fit for a maid-servant?'

'I'm saying, as you very well know, Joanna, that you look like a woman who should be waltzing in a ballroom. I've already told you that you look stunning, although you rudely dismissed my compliment.'

'Did I? I don't recall such a thing happening. After all, I am Lady Harcourt, and my manners are impeccable.'

He was still laughing and so was she when the beef consommé arrived. The wine was certainly good, the food adequate, but the company was excellent. They abandoned their table, telling the waiter they would be back for coffee and petit fours later.

'I warn you, my dear, that you might come to regret your insistence that we dance. I have very large feet and they have a worrying tendency to step on anything that gets in their way.'

'You are talking nonsense, sir, and I refuse to rise to your teasing. All senior officers are excellent dancers – it's expected of them.

Even David, who would much rather have been outside shooting something than in a ballroom, acquitted himself admirably on the dancefloor.'

'You will recall I refused to dance at the twins' party.'

'That was because you thought yourself too grand to dance.'

His smile was wicked and he didn't deny it. He swept her into his arms and as she'd expected, his performance was superb. Indeed, when they were doing a quickstep, couples moved aside and let them have the centre of the floor to themselves.

When the last note of the music faded, Joanna curtsied, he bowed and there was a round of spontaneous applause.

'Thank you, Peter, I really enjoyed dancing with you. But four dances are sufficient and I would really like my coffee.'

They sat companionably over a silver jug of good coffee, served with cream and delicious petit fours. She sipped the glass of cognac that he'd ordered with appreciation.

'The perfect ending to a perfect evening. Thank you so much. Please let me know what happens tomorrow. I should be home to receive your telephone call sometime in the evening or, if I'm lucky, late afternoon. The trains and taxis are less reliable on a Sunday.'

'I'll do better than that, Joanna. I'll collect you from here and drive you home. Or, to be more accurate, my driver will drive both of us to Goodwill House. I'll be sitting in comfort in the back with you.'

'In which case, you and your driver must stay the night. Since Elizabeth and I have been able to return to our bedrooms, there are two empty rooms on the other side of the house.'

'Thank you, I would like to do that. I'll have to leave at dawn in order to be at my desk on time.' He drained the last of his brandy. 'I'm glad to hear that the repairs are progressing. How many more rooms are still out of action?'

'Just the bedrooms for the twins remain boarded up. The

builder taking care of things has been unable to find any more glass, but the window frames have now been replaced, so they will just need glazing at some point.'

'You do realise that Manston will be back in action as a forward base for Biggin Hill sector by the end of the year?' Peter said.

'I do know that. It will be no more dangerous than it was before if that's what you're implying. Goodwill House has been occupied by the Harcourt family for hundreds of years and it will take more than the Luftwaffe to drive us out.'

'Goodnight, Joanna, I enjoyed this evening.'

'As did I, thank you. Goodnight.'

Peter strode off and Joanna made her way upstairs. He was a charming and attractive man, but he didn't appeal to her. He was too much like David. She didn't need mollycoddling, she was able to take care of herself. Also, she'd said she wouldn't leave Goodwill House, but that was untrue. The Germans wouldn't drive her out, but common sense might well.

24

Daphne had been given a sedative of some sort but told not to take the tablets until she was safely in bed. Although her head was spinning, her whole face hurt, she daren't give in until she was quite sure Bob wasn't going to go round and murder her father.

She pretended to think that an arrest would be made but wasn't stupid and knew her father would just get a talking to from the constable. The longer it took for this decision to be made, the more chance there was that Bob would calm down enough not to risk his own freedom.

'Will you take me up, Bob? I really need to lie down.' Her words sounded strange, not like her at all and just moving her mouth was agony.

'I'll carry you if you want, sweetheart.'

Daphne shook her head and leaned against him so he had to put his arm around her waist. Just moving her feet one in front of the other was far harder than she'd anticipated and without his strength she doubted she'd have got up the flight of stairs and into the spare bedroom safely.

'I'll fetch my mum...'

'No, I want you to help me.'

The longer she kept him with her, the better. Hurting her father would just make matters worse. It wouldn't help Mum and having just got Bob back she had no intention of losing him again.

Vaguely she heard Mrs Andrews come in and between the two of them, they took off her bloodsoaked clothes but left her in her knickers and bra.

'There, love, you get between the sheets and take these tablets. Bob can sit with you until you go to sleep.'

'I might choke, the bleeding might start...'

'I won't leave you alone. You can sleep and I'll stay here and keep you safe.'

She clutched his hand, her eyes imploring. 'Promise. Promise you'll not go round there.'

Bob hesitated and her eyes brimmed. She wasn't deliberately using tears to persuade him, but they did the trick.

'I promise. I don't want to get arrested or go to prison because of that bastard. He's caused enough damage already.'

It was hard getting the pills between her swollen lips, but between them they managed. They went down with a swallow of water; she collapsed back on the pillows. She closed her eyes and waited for the sedative to do its work.

This bed wasn't the usual narrow bed but something a bit wider. The pillows she was propped up on had been pushed against the wall, leaving him just enough room to lie beside her.

She fell asleep in his arms and when she woke twice in the darkness, he was still there, breathing deeply, taking care of her.

* * *

When Daphne awoke the next morning, her heart jumped – Bob wasn't there. Then he spoke from the other side of the room.

'I'm here, darling, I wouldn't break my word to you. I did it once when I left you, but never again.'

Tentatively she raised her hand to her mouth and it wasn't as puffy as it had been and she was able to move her lips a little without the searing pain.

'I'm desperate for the loo. I don't think I can make it down the stairs and out to the garden.' Talking was relatively easy this morning, so she continued, 'I'll need the chamber pot and that's something I don't want you to witness.'

'I'll fetch Mum.'

'No, you won't. Just put it in the middle of the room and let me get on with it. You can empty it, though.'

He chuckled and didn't argue. Her legs were a bit wobbly, but she thought that was because of the aftereffects of the strong sedative she'd taken the night before. She wanted to get up, have a good wash, and go downstairs. How could she do this when she had no clothes?

'Have you finished?' he called cheerfully from the other side of the door.

'I have. You can come in now.'

He pushed open the door and to her delight handed over her freshly washed and ironed dungarees and shirt. The blood had come out and they looked as good as new.

'You read my mind, I'm going to wash and get dressed. Is there water in the jug on the washstand?'

'I brought it up just before you woke, it's still lovely and warm. Are you quite sure you feel well enough to get up?'

'I'm tickety-boo.'

'You're certainly not that but, thank god, you're looking and sounding a hundred times better than you did last night,' Bob said. 'I'll get rid of this and tell my parents you'll be down for breakfast.'

'What's the time?'

'Just after seven.'

'Whilst I'm washing, please telephone Goodwill House and tell them what happened so they can let Mr Pickering know I won't be at work this week.'

He nodded and vanished with the chamber pot. Although talking was easier today, after even this short conversation her mouth was painful, the stitches pulling, she tasted the tang of blood in her mouth.

There was no mirror above the washstand and for that she was grateful. She must look a sight.

As Daphne was washing – very carefully – she had ample time to go over what had happened yesterday. If she'd fallen backwards and hit her head on the stove, then she might well have died. Murdered by her own father. It didn't bear thinking of.

Did her brother know what had happened? Had he always known that their father had been violent towards their mother? She wouldn't be going anywhere today but when Bob had to return to Folkestone first thing tomorrow, she'd go back too.

Dr Willoughby would be able to take out the stitches and tell her when she was fit to go back to work. Charlie might well be out of hospital and they could spend time together, get to know each other better.

'Are you ready, darling? I'm growing roots propped up here outside the door,' Bob said.

'Come in, we need to talk before we go down. And I want your honest opinion about just how bad I look.'

The door opened and he smiled and took her in his arms. They couldn't kiss, but having him hold her close, feeling his heart beating next to hers, was all she wanted at the moment.

'I love you so much, my darling, and I want to marry you as soon as I don't need that man's permission,' Daphne said.

He kissed the top of her head. 'Then next May it is.' He stepped away and gestured that they sit together on the bed for a moment.

'Your brother came round last night. He's on leave. He'd no idea what had been going on and he's taken your mum back to live with them. He's coming back later today and will bring her with him.'

'That's the best news there could be in the circumstances. I'm surprised she was allowed to leave in one piece.'

'Sid went to fetch your brother and remained there whilst your mother packed her things. There was nothing your father could do about it,' Bob said.

'Mum can now enjoy her grandchildren without fear of being hurt. It was almost worth the injury for things to work out like that for her.'

He smoothed her hair from her forehead. 'If you hadn't made me promise, I'd have gone round there and probably killed him. Thank you for saving my life.'

'You know, I think during this year we've grown up. Being apart has made us really appreciate just how much we love each other. We're so lucky. Not many couples are best friends before they get married.'

He groaned and pulled her close. 'Don't keep talking about marriage. I want to make love to you; I want to have you naked in my arms and show you just how much you mean to me. Waiting until next May is going to kill me.'

Gently Daphne pushed him away. 'I want to wear white at my wedding, so you'll just have to take a lot of cold showers until then.'

It didn't matter how long they had to wait, they'd found each other again and had the rest of their lives ahead of them.

* * *

Joanna was meeting her daughter, Sarah, for breakfast and therefore was up, bathed and dressed in good time. Spending the evening with Peter had been most enjoyable, but she needed to make it clear to him that she wasn't interested in him in a romantic way.

Although he'd behaved like the perfect gentleman, sometimes she'd detected a definite gleam in his eyes. There would be ample time on the drive home to explain how she felt. If she couldn't be with John, then she would remain single.

Being in love with someone so unsuitable, someone much younger than herself, wasn't something she'd anticipated so soon after the death of her husband at Dunkirk. Good heavens – if anyone ever discovered her appallingly wanton behaviour a few months after she was made a widow, she would be the scandal of the neighbourhood. The fact that she and David had slept in separate bedrooms, had barely spoken in the last few years he'd been with her, had meant he was a stranger to her when he died, and she certainly hadn't loved him.

Peter was exactly the sort of man everyone would expect her to marry – not now, obviously, but next year, perhaps. By doing so, she would unite the family and there would be another Lord Harcourt to match her own title. The fact that she couldn't give him an heir meant she wasn't eligible, even if she did want to be his wife.

She reached the plush foyer and Sarah was already there. 'Mummy, I'm so pleased to see you. It's been a wretched week and I've had the worst possible news.'

Joanna opened her arms and her beloved girl hugged her, barely keeping back her sobs. 'Shall we go upstairs where we can talk? I can have breakfast sent up so we don't have to go into the dining room at all.'

'Yes, if you don't mind.'

She prayed the bad news wasn't that Angus had been severely

injured or was missing, presumed dead. Sarah's future husband was a squadron leader in the frontline of the relentless action in the air.

The suite had comfortable sofas, as well as an area for dining. Sarah slumped into the nearest chair and Joanna picked up the in-house telephone and ordered breakfast for two.

'Now, my love, tell me what's wrong.'

'Angus wants us to get married now, not wait until I'm qualified. I've told him no and he said he'll end the engagement if I don't agree, as he sees little point in us being apart for so long.'

'You're barely eighteen – I agreed to your engagement on the understanding that you waited until you were of age. Angus knows that as I made it very clear to him at the time.'

'He does know that but says we can get married anyway as the authorities are far too busy to bother about such things,' Sarah said.

'Where is he stationed now? He must be completely exhausted and on duty constantly.'

'The squadrons work on rotation – his has gone to Somerset for three weeks, where they'll just have routine patrols. He wants his answer when he comes back.'

'Do you love him?'

'How can you ask that, Mummy? You know I do.'

Joanna thought for a minute before answering. She'd changed so much in the last year and now wanted her daughter to be independent also. 'Then I can't see the problem. There's no need for anyone to know at the Royal Free. Are you sleeping together?'

'Mummy! Of course we're not.'

'Then you have your answer. He's a man, he wants to make love to you, and if you won't sleep with him until you're married, then he's trying to move things on.' She smiled and patted her daughter's hand. 'He's a resourceful young man, he'll make sure you don't get pregnant, so sleep with him.'

Sarah looked at her, wide-eyed. 'Golly, I never thought to hear you say such a thing. Are you sure we could be together without risk?'

'Absolutely. I can't believe you don't know this yourself, my love, after all, you're training to be a doctor.'

'I know, sometimes I'm not rational when it comes to my personal life. With the generous allowance that I'm now getting from you, I've already been able to rent a little flat not too far away from the hospital. He could stay there overnight and nobody would be any the wiser.'

There was a knock on the door and Sarah rushed over to let in a waiter with a large trolley. The two of them cleared everything set out on the table and spent the remainder of the morning talking about the twins, Peter and the harrowing experiences Sarah was having dealing with the air-raid victims in the East End.

'Thank you so much, Mummy, I knew you'd come up with a solution, but I must say I didn't expect you to suggest we slept together.'

This was the perfect opportunity to tell her daughter about John, but this must always remain a secret.

'I have to go, I'm on duty in an hour and sometimes even the Underground doesn't run smoothly. Goodbye, darling Mummy, kiss Grandmama and the twins for me.' Sarah embraced her and then, smiling happily, she rushed off to continue her studies and no doubt make plans to welcome her fiancé into her bed.

Joanna's thoughts turned unwillingly to the man she'd lost and, with all her heart, she wished it could have been different.

* * *

Joanna was waiting for Peter when he arrived, so there was no need for him to come into the hotel. This time, the car he was in wasn't camouflaged but a large black vehicle – not a Bentley but something equally smart.

She settled onto the comfortable rear seat and pushed down the armrest. He stretched out his legs, leaned back and then told her about his morning visit.

'You can forget about those other Harcourts. The unfortunate patient passed away whilst I was there to make things somewhat simpler. How did your time with Sarah go?'

'Wonderful. I find it hard to believe that someone as young as her is doing such a responsible job,' Joanna said.

'A lot of the boys in blue fighting so hard to protect our skies are not much older than your daughter.'

There was a sliding glass door between themselves and the smart ATS driver so they could talk freely without fear of anything being overheard.

'Her fiancé wanted them to get married immediately and she isn't ready to do that. I told her what he really wanted was to sleep with her and if she were prepared to do that, then they could carry on as before and get married when she was qualified.'

He raised an eyebrow and smiled. 'How very modern of you, Joanna. I don't believe there are many women in your position who would have made such a suggestion.'

'I wouldn't have done a few months ago. There's something you don't know about me and I think if we're going to be friends, then I need to tell you.'

When she'd finished explaining about her brief but passionate and loving affair with John, and that she was still in love with him, Peter surprised her by his reaction.

'Thank you for telling me, as it explains a lot. I do find you very attractive, Joanna, but I too have secrets. I'm not a bachelor but a widower. I was blissfully married to Estelle when I was just out of Sandhurst. We were delighted when after a year she became pregnant. She died in childbirth and Caroline, my tiny daughter, survived her by only a few days. My world fell apart, I almost ended up in an asylum and vowed then never to put myself in such a position again.'

'How incredibly sad. I'm sure your wife wouldn't want you to live alone because she's gone.'

He stared at her as if she was speaking in riddles. 'Good god, Joanna, I'm not still grieving her loss. I'm protecting myself. Being in love is a wretched business, exposes you to the most awful pain. I've concentrated on my career and have been successful and have absolutely no intention of falling in love with anyone else.' He was looking out of the window and couldn't see her look of dismay at his admission. He wasn't the man she'd thought him to be, to not want to take the risk a second time.

'I would like to sleep with you, I find you attractive, but hesitated to make my feelings clear as marriage isn't an option,' Peter said. 'Obviously, you're not the person I thought you were and I'm hoping I can persuade you to become my mistress.'

Joanna leaned forward and slid the glass divider open. 'Stop the car.'

She didn't look at the man beside her; she was too angry. The car pulled smoothly into the kerb and without looking at him, or saying another word, she picked up her small case and jumped out. She slammed the door after her and told the driver she could return to London.

Peter made no move to follow her and for that she was grateful. What had possessed her to reveal her secret to him? She thought he could be a part of their family, a good friend, and now she never wanted to see or speak to him again.

He had obviously been as shocked by her admission as she'd

been by his. They'd both behaved badly, but she didn't regret her actions. She was beholden to no man, would be no man's mistress, and it was a relief to have one unnecessary complication removed from her life.

In future, she would concentrate on her family, her duty and never put herself in such a hideous position again.

ACKNOWLEDGMENTS

I would like to thank my brother, Tony, for being happy to listen, and for putting me right when my ideas aren't credible. I'd also like to thank Jean Fullerton, who always gives me good advice and especially with this book.

Finally, as always, thanks to the wonderful team at Boldwood who work so hard to make my books as good as they can be and are always supportive and encouraging.

BIBLIOGRAPHY

Chronicle of the Second World War edited by Jacques Legrand and Derrik Mercer

A to Z Atlas and Guide to London, 1939 edition

Oxford Dictionary of Slang by John Ayto

Wartime Britain by Juliet Gardiner

How We Lived Then by Norman Longmate

The Wartime Scrapbook by Robert Opie

Land Girls at the Old Rectory by Irene Grimwood

Ramsgate August 1940 by D. T. Richards

The Land Girl Manual 1941 by W. E. Shewell-Cooper

Land Girls and their Impact by Ann Kramer

Land Girl by Anne Hall

The Women's Land Army by Bob Powell and Nigel Westcott

A Detailed History of RAF Manston by Joe Bamford and John Williams, with Peter Gallagher Fonthill

Old Ordnance Survey Map, Ramsgate 1905, The Godfrey Editions

Old Ordnance Survey Map, Chelmsford 1919

Old Ordnance Survey Map, Wivenhoe 1896

Old Ordnance Survey Map, Romford 1915

BBC Archives: World War II

Chelmsford by Joseph Marriage

They Fought in the Fields by Nicola Tyrer

I Join the Fray by Ronald Alston

Groundcrew Boys by Peter Heard

MORE FROM FENELLA J. MILLER

We hope you enjoyed reading *A Wartime Reunion at Goodwill House*. If you did, please leave a review.

If you'd like to gift a copy, this book is also available as an ebook, large print, hardback, digital audio download and audiobook CD.

Sign up to Fenella J. Miller's mailing list for news, competitions and updates on future books.

https://bit.ly/FenellaMillerNews

Why not explore the rest of Fenella J. Miller's wonderful Goodwill House series...

ABOUT THE AUTHOR

Fenella J. Miller is the bestselling writer of historical sagas. She also has a passion for Regency romantic adventures and has published over fifty to great acclaim. Her father was a Yorkshireman and her mother the daughter of a Rajah. She lives in a small village in Essex with her British Shorthair cat.

Follow Fenella on social media:

 twitter.com/fenellawriter
facebook.com/fenella.miller

Sixpence Stories

Introducing Sixpence Stories!

Discover page-turning historical novels from your favourite authors, meet new friends and be transported back in time.

Join our book club Facebook group

https://bit.ly/SixpenceGroup

Sign up to our newsletter

https://bit.ly/SixpenceNews

Boldwood

Boldwood Books is an award-winning fiction publishing company seeking out the best stories from around the world.

Find out more at www.boldwoodbooks.com

Join our reader community for brilliant books, competitions and offers!

Follow us
@BoldwoodBooks
@BookandTonic

Sign up to our weekly deals newsletter

https://bit.ly/BoldwoodBNewsletter

Printed in Great Britain
by Amazon